Readers love
SCOTTY CADE

Only Forever

"This is a ROMANTIC heartwarming tale, a curl up in a chair with a good book kind of story, and I highly recommend it."

—The Novel Approach

"I really enjoyed it and I'm glad I went in blind…"

—Jessie G Books

A Lethal Mistake

"Scotty Cade blew me away with this book."

—Gay Book Reviews

Losing Faith

"I recommend it to anyone who enjoys a romance that begins in the dark days of grief and doubt and ends with an HEA that is so satisfying you feel it in your heart."

—Happy Ever After, *USA Today*

"…this book is phenomenal in the amount of feeling and emotion and love and pain that come across."

—*Divine Magazine*

By Scotty Cade

Acting Out
Forever for Now
From a Jack to a King
Knobs
Losing Faith
The Mystery of Ruby Lode
Only Forever
Someone to Kiss
Sunrise Over Savannah • Chasing the Horizon
An Unconventional Courtship • An Unconventional Union

BISSONET & CRUZ INVESTIGATIONS
The Royal Street Heist
Veiled Loyalties
A Lethal Mistake

FINAL ENCORE
Before the Final Encore
Final Encore
After the Final Encore

LOVE SERIES
Wings of Love
Treasure of Love
Bounty of Love
With Z.B. Marshall: Foundation of Love

Published by Dreamspinner Press
www.dreamspinnerpress.com

FROM A
JACK TO A
KING

SCOTTY CADE

Published by

DREAMSPINNER PRESS

5032 Capital Circle SW, Suite 2, PMB# 279, Tallahassee, FL 32305-7886 USA
www.dreamspinnerpress.com

From a Jack to a King
© 2018 Scotty Cade.

Cover Art
© 2018 Paul Richmond.
http://www.paulrichmondstudio.com
Cover content is for illustrative purposes only and any person depicted on the cover is a model.

Trade Paperback ISBN: 978-1-64108-123-8
Digital ISBN: 978-1-64080-114-1
Library of Congress Control Number: 2017911512
Trade Paperback published July 2018
v. 1.0

Printed in the United States of America
∞
This paper meets the requirements of
ANSI/NISO Z39.48-1992 (Permanence of Paper).

To my husband, Kell. Without your love, encouragement, support, and patience, I would not be able to do this. My love runs deeper than any ocean, and each day I count my blessings that you chose me with whom to spend the rest of your life. I love you.

I would be totally remiss in my social duties if I didn't properly thank Kimberly "Kimmers" Sewald for introducing me to Annie Maus, who helped me navigate the very sensitive topic of sexual addiction. Thank you both for the help and support. I hope I got it right.

Also, I'd like to thank Ned Miller for recording the original version of "From a Jack to a King," which inspired this novel. It was one of my grandmother's favorite songs, and I remember her singing it to me many times when I was a kid. The song was first recorded in 1957, but was unsuccessful until Ned persuaded his label to rerelease it five years later. Upon rerelease, the song became a crossover hit, charting in the top ten on the *Billboard* US country, pop, and adult contemporary charts. Thank you, Ned Miller, for being my inspiration.

FOREWORD

FROM A Jack to a King is a light contemporary romance that touches briefly on two very serious topics I would never take lightly. One is the effects of bullying on children and how it affects us as adults. Kell and I were both bullied as teenagers, so my research consisted of twenty years of conversations between us, comparing our experiences and how we dealt and still deal with the aftereffects today. Both of us have obvious scars that run deep and the raw emotions that accompany those scars. Bullying is an epidemic, and although a lot of attention has been brought to the forefront in recent years, not nearly enough, in our opinion, is being done to end it.

Secondly, one of the main characters in this novel is a recovering sex addict. That's where the bulk of my research took place. I read everything I could find on the internet, communicated with a specialist in the field, and did the best I could to accurately portray the effect of the addiction while in recovery, Sex Addicts Anonymous (SAA), their 12-Step program, and the recovery process.

But please recognize I just skim the surface on both topics, and if I got anything wrong, I apologize from the bottom of my heart. It was not intentional, and I have the utmost respect for anyone dealing with the effects of bullying or sexual addiction.

One last thing. After reading this book, if you recognize any of the behavioral signs of a sexual addiction in yourself or someone for whom you care, help is always available. I've included contact information for Sex Addicts Anonymous below.

USA/Canada: 1-800-477-8191, Elsewhere: +1-713-869-4902
Postal mail: ISO of SAA, PO Box 70949, Houston, TX 77270 USA
Email: info@saa-recovery.org
https://saa-recovery.org/

PROLOGUE

SWEAT POURED off King Slater's body as he pounded the tight ass of the guy lying on the hood of a black Jaguar. The stranger was moaning loudly, his eyes closed, his head thrown back, and his arms spread across the front of the car almost as if he were being crucified. Listening to the odd sounds, King smiled inwardly. The poor guy sounded more like a wounded animal than a man enjoying the exceptional fuck being bestowed upon him.

King sighed. He'd been doing this a long time, and usually at about this point in any scene, he'd start to lose interest. This shoot was no exception, but like the professional he was, he knew he had to make it look good for the cameras. He repositioned his knees, pressing them against the bumper for more leverage and opened his mouth to speak, but stopped short. What was his costar's name again? Jim? Jared? *What the fuck, King? Think!* He was about to come up with something generic to say when the guy's name finally popped into his head. *Josh? Yeah, Josh. That's it.*

In a deep, sultry, and velvety-smooth voice, King said, "That's it. Take it, Josh. Take my big cock and take it deep."

"Yeah," Josh moaned. "Give it to me hard."

King gripped Josh's ankles and spread his costar's legs wide to give the camera a good clear shot of King's cock as he rammed it into Josh's ass. Crucifixion or no crucifixion, King had to admit his costar was taking each thrust like a champ.

In an attempt to fend off boredom and not think about the sun baking his skin, King focused on Josh's Adam's apple as it moved up and down with each swallow. When that could no longer hold his attention, he counted the drops of sweat that slid down his nose and onto Josh's torso. *A few more minutes and you're done, King. Just a few more minutes.*

King had done the drill hundreds of times, and there was nothing romantic or heartfelt about it. The trick to his success was to make the camera think there was. To see how "into it" he was. Of course, it was nothing more than a fuck with a stranger on the hood of a car, but he drew from his years of acting in high school and college. From the sound of his voice to his facial expressions—and especially his body language—he had all the markers down to a tee. Right on cue, he summoned his orgasm, as if calling to an old friend. In preparation, he rolled his head back in faked ecstasy.

Although the car was positioned in the shade of a twelve-foot cactus, that did little to stifle the afternoon heat. By now both men were panting uncontrollably. Josh pumped his own dick enthusiastically as King slammed into him, releasing an even louder moan as he blew his load all over his abdomen.

If this kid is gonna make it in porn, he's got to work on those sounds.

King pulled out, ripped off the condom, stroked his erection a couple of times, and emptied his release to mix with Josh's. When he was totally spent and running on autopilot, King collapsed on top of Josh and kissed him passionately for the camera.

"Cut! Great job, gentlemen."

King broke the kiss, stood, and stretched his back, the remnants of his orgasm still gripping him. He definitely felt like a prime candidate for dehydration, heatstroke—or both.

"Are all of your orgasms this intense?" Josh asked, looking up at King with puppy-dog eyes.

"Pretty much," King said, still trembling a little.

"I mean—I noticed it in your videos online," Josh gushed, "but to see it up close…. Man, I wish mine lasted that long."

King smiled, wiped the sweat from his brow with the back of his hand and looked around. "Whose idea was it to shoot at two o'clock in the afternoon in the fucking Nevada desert?" he asked teasingly, still panting.

"Sorry, man," the director said. "It was the only time we could get the crew together."

King and his costar accepted the bottles of cold water and damp towels the assistant handed them. Each downed the water and then wiped their faces, necks, and the combined semen off their abdomens.

King tossed his soiled towel to the assistant and offered his hand to the guy he'd just fucked on camera while acting as a guest star for Falcon Studios.

Josh accepted King's hand, and King pulled him to a sitting position and then off the car. Josh's ass squeaked, bounced, and skidded off the scorching hood. "Ouch!" he said, hopping from foot to foot when his feet hit the burning sand. "Damn, that's hot."

King opened his arms. "Here, let me help."

"Thanks, man. At least you got to wear boots."

King look down at his feet. "Yeah. Lucky me." King, with his six-foot-four-inch frame, scooped Josh up easily and carried him all the way to the production van, where their clothes awaited them. "Better?"

"Much," Josh said. "Thanks again."

King smiled. "Good job back there, by the way."

Josh looked up at him with that same puppy-dog expression. "Thank you. It was an honor to work with such a legend."

King frowned. "Hey! *Legend* makes me sound really old. And dead!"

"Well, you're a legend to me," Josh said. "And trust me, you're not old... or dead. How did you last so long? I thought you'd never come."

King smiled. "Secrets of the trade, my young friend." King didn't tell the guy it was boredom or, at the very least, lack of interest keeping him from coming. *He'll figure that out soon enough on his own.* "How many of these shoots have you done, anyway?"

"Counting this one?"

King nodded.

"Two."

"Two?" King looked at the director.

The director smiled. "Hey! He got the highest ever ratings for a first-timer, so give the kid a break. Everyone's gotta start somewhere."

King shook his head. He had to admit the guy was damn hot and built like a brick shithouse, but it was really hard to get into sex with someone when the director was orchestrating your every move. But he *was* getting paid handsomely for the shoot, and besides, they paid all his expenses to and from Las Vegas. So if they wanted him to fuck the tight ass of a hot twentysomething newbie, he'd do it with no complaints.

His costar wiggled into his shorts and flinched. "Man, I don't think I'll be able to walk right for a week."

"I hope it was worth it," King said.

"Fuck yeah. So worth it. In fact, if you're ever back in town and just want to... ah, you know, have some fun, look me up."

King knew the chances of that happening were zilch, but he was polite just the same. "I'll do that." He put his underwear on and was about to reach for his jeans when his cell phone chirped. He dug his personal phone out of his jeans pocket, glanced at it, and slipped it back in. With anticipation, he fished out his other phone, the one he used for his escort service.

Earlier in the day, he'd tweeted and posted on social media that he'd be in Las Vegas for a few days doing a shoot if anyone was interested in his company.

"Sorry. Gotta take this." He walked away from the production van and answered the call.

"King Slater."

"Hi. Um. My name is Paul, and I was wondering if you were free tonight."

King chuckled. "I might be available. But I'm certainly not free."

"Oh right. Not what I meant. Sorry, I'm a little nervous," Paul said.

"In fact," King added, "not only am I not free, I'm five hundred an hour. So if you have that kind of money and you're interested in a little fun, there's no need to be nervous."

"Uh… yeah," the caller said. "I saw that on your profile. And don't worry. I have the money."

"I don't worry," King said. "You pay upfront by giving me your credit card before we even meet."

"Will you accept cash?" the guy asked.

"When we meet, I can," King explained. "But in case you don't really have it, I put a hold on a credit card and then release it if you use cash."

"Okay. I can do that."

"So. Are we on?"

"Yeah."

"Okay. Hold on while I open my credit card app," King said.

"I'm ready when you are."

Paul gave him all his payment information, and King typed it into his phone.

"Okay. So that's two hours at five hundred an hour. Where do I meet you?"

"At my hotel?"

"Sure. Which one?"

"MGM Grand. I haven't checked in yet, but I'll text you the room number as soon as I do. Say midnight?"

"Midnight it is," King said. "Hey, are you into anything weird I should know about?"

"Na," Paul said. "Just the usual."

"Bottom or top?" King asked nonchalantly. "By the way," he added, "I charge more to bottom."

Seconds passed with silence on the other end of the phone. King was about to repeat the question when Paul finally spoke. "I'll bottom."

"Perfect. Just the way I like it. I'll see you at midnight."

CHAPTER ONE

BAY WHITMAN stood in the foyer of his suite at the MGM Grand Las Vegas Hotel & Casino and gazed into the gold-framed mirror. With shaky hands, he adjusted his bow tie one last time and slipped on his perfectly tailored midnight-blue Armani tuxedo jacket. He pulled his french cuffs down so exactly one-half inch of white was showing at the end of each of his dark sleeves, exposing just a hint of his black-onyx-and-diamond-encrusted cufflinks.

Adrenaline surged, same as before every big poker game, and he loved it. Gambling was like cocaine to him, and right now the blood was pumping through his veins as fast, steady, and powerful as the water flowed over Niagara Falls. In the early years, when he didn't have a lot of disposable income, the quarter slots were what gave him goose bumps, but even though the game had changed and the stakes are much higher, the thrill was equally intense. Gambling was the only thing that made him feel alive. And like an addict, he desperately craved the high he got when he stared down his opponent and bluffed his way to a winning hand.

Bay stepped back from the mirror, took a nervous breath, held it, and closed his eyes. He focused on the backs of his eyelids until his lungs were about to burst. He exhaled, hissing through slightly parted lips. This was something he did every time he was about to go out in public. A ritual, so to speak, to help him navigate the life he'd unexpectedly created for himself. *Can't bluff with a sweaty brow and shaky hands, my boy. You need to be steady and sure. Always!*

When Bay opened his eyes, he was finally beginning to see the signs of his calm, confident, and collected alter ego. "Not too shabby for a nerd."

He chuckled. *Nerd?* That was only partly true. Yes, he was undoubtedly a nerd, but he was also a *New York Times* best-selling mystery writer with a large backlist of successful crime novels under his belt.

Surrounding his latest release, Bay had been scheduled for several personal appearances and book signings in Las Vegas, so he'd decided to jump on a plane a day early to treat himself to a little fun in his favorite stomping ground.

This little excursion wasn't without merit. It was a *pat on the back* for not only making, but beating, a very important deadline. Yesterday afternoon, one day ahead of schedule, he'd typed *The End* on the second of a three-book deal with his publisher featuring his beloved main character—playboy private eye Jack Robbins. He'd learned quickly how difficult it was to manage the demands of a promotional tour while his head was stuck in a work in progress, so he'd always done his best to set his deadline a little before a release date, which afforded him a clear head for the influx of press attention that accompanied each new book. The three novels were already contracted to be made into a trilogy of movies, and the studio was touting Jack Robbins as a cross between Jason Bourne and the American version of James Bond. *No pressure there!*

A shiver ran up Bay's spine as he contemplated what was at stake. The big screen. *Jack Robbins is going to hit the big screen.* A medium totally unfamiliar to Bay, one where he wouldn't be able to hide. As soon as the *you're not good enough*s tried to creep into his consciousness, he pushed them, along with all the other feelings of inadequacy, from his mind and focused his attention elsewhere. In particular, on the exceptionally high-stakes game he was about to partake in. One with some pretty big hitters. Bay knew he needed to be on *his* game.

He looked in the mirror one last time and focused on his eyes. He sighed with relief when he saw no signs of the very successful but equally nerdy writer who was plagued by almost crippling insecurities and self-doubt every day of his life.

In his mind, all he saw was Jack Robbins. The personality his adoring fans were accustomed to and his opponents at the poker table were intimidated by. *I'm ready.*

He looked at his watch. Four forty-five. *Better get going. The game starts at five, and I don't wanna be late.*

Bay left his suite and strolled down the hall to the elevator. By the time the doors opened, Bay Whitman had completed his mental transition from the shy geek to the debonair playboy. He'd become sophisticated, worldly, charming, and perfectly imperfect in every sense. A man's man, with the combined swagger of Tom Cruise, James Bond, and George Clooney, all rolled into one. Bay Whitman, for all intents and purposes, was now Jack Robbins.

Of course Bay wasn't delusional. For starters, he looked nothing like his main character. Jack was extraordinarily handsome. Six-four, an extremely muscular two hundred and forty-five pounds, with hazel eyes—the green almost emerald—a neat, close-trimmed beard, and medium brown hair streaked with shades of blond.

But in public, Bay borrowed Jack's larger-than-life personality. And why not? He'd created the character, and he could hide behind him if he wanted to. It was the only way he could survive the world outside the confines of his New York apartment.

The elevator doors opened, and Bay stepped inside. He flashed a broad smile at the occupants, with a barely perceptible lingering glance at an attractive woman who appeared to be alone, and when he turned to face the front, he studied their expressions in the mirrored sheen of the elevator doors. One man elbowed an older woman standing next to him, probably his mother, and another quietly whispered to a companion as they recognized the famous author. This wasn't ego on Bay's part. In fact, he absolutely hated it when people recognized him. He was simply amazed that people knew who he was. Shy, nerdy Bay Whitman.

His discomfort grew as others in the elevator also started to figure out he was a celebrity, finally connecting the face in the reflective walls to the headshot on his author bio. He could feel their eyes on him and their delight at seeing him—or the man they thought he was.

As the elevator started its descent, Bay compared himself to the persona he'd temporarily adopted. If these people knew the truth, would they admire the shy, insecure, and antisocial introvert Bay Whitman really was? The recluse who was more comfortable alone in a dimly lit office writing his mystery novels than jet-setting the world doing press interviews and television shows, and being the center of attention at endless book signings.

Bay had created the handsome, confident, strong Jack Robbins as the man he wanted to be, wished he could be. It was an outlet for him. A way to be... well, *more than he was*. But when Bay's first Jack Robbins novel unexpectedly hit it big, he was suddenly thrust into the public eye. Jack's character became a necessity for Bay's survival. The only way to handle his newfound stardom and cope with his shyness. A mask, so to speak, or... almost a second skin. He'd convinced himself it was no different from a clown or a drag queen hiding behind a costume or a face full of makeup.

Bay looked at his own reflection in the mirrored doors. He'd been called handsome on more than one occasion, but he couldn't see it. All he ever saw was the tall, skinny, and extremely awkward introvert. The nerd with the big ears, horn-rimmed glasses, and unruly hair who was chased home from school every day by bullies. The kid who escaped his reality by reading about Sherlock Holmes and Lew Archer or sitting in front of the television watching reruns of *Ironside* and *Perry Mason* on TV Land.

But tonight, strangely enough, Bay had a rare surge of confidence and allowed himself to see, if just for a moment, what he was told the rest of the world saw. He studied his tall, lean frame, a bit shy of six feet, his muscular build, and the crystal blue eyes enhanced by tinted contact lenses. The halogen lights reflected off the hint of silver at his temples and caught his attention. The effect created a dramatic contrast against his jet-black hair, expertly coiffed courtesy of LeDoux Kesling, the wildly popular hairdresser to the stars. All that combined with his spray tan and gorgeous designer tuxedo, worn at the insistence of his stylist, made quite the impression. Even *if* it was only a façade.

The elevator slowed to a stop, and Bay took another deep breath and exhaled. When he heard the ding and the doors opened, Bay Whitman was on.

He marched across the casino and tried not to pay any attention to the heads turning. He didn't have a vain bone in his body, and all this attention made him terribly uncomfortable. It was all so unbelievable. But deep down he knew none of this was for him. It was all for the man they thought he was. He'd been told his stature commanded respect and his confidence was something most men admired and most women swooned over. The swagger in his walk was unmistakable. But still, it wasn't him. None of this was him.

Bay walked up to the velvet rope, showed his identification to the security guard, and was escorted to a private room where three men and a croupier were waiting. Bay's heart raced as he walked through the door. The first thing he saw was an extremely handsome gentleman walking up to greet him.

"Good evening, Mr. Whitman," the man said. "Welcome to the MGM Grand. I'm Marco Tonucci, and I'll be your croupier this evening. Glad you could join us."

Bay winked and smiled warmly. "I wouldn't miss it. Thank you."

Bay recognized Rich Devlin and Zeke Cambridge, the Academy Award–winning actors from the famous Hawkins Boys action-movie franchise, who happened to be best friends in real life and were currently filming their next movie in Vegas. The two men were chatting away at the bar, but the third gentleman was on his cell phone with his back to Bay. When Zeke and Rich saw him, they stopped talking, flashed broad smiles, and walked in his direction.

Zeke was the first to reach Bay and held out his hand. "I'm Zeke Cambridge. I love your work, Bay. Jack Robbins is *the man*."

Bay accepted the outreached hand and returned the smile. "Thank you for the kind words. I'm a big fan of yours as well."

Rich stuck out his hand also. "What am I, chopped liver? And what's this I hear about a Jack Robbins movie in the works? If that happens, I think you might give us a run for our money."

"I seriously doubt that," Bay said with a chuckle as he accepted Rich's hand and shook it firmly. "And for the record, I love your work too."

Rich slapped him on the back.

When the third man ended his call and walked over, Bay thought he recognized him.

"I'm Paul Gilman," he said, smiling.

Bay perked up, realizing he was right. "*The* professional poker player extraordinaire?"

Paul chuckled. "In the flesh."

"You're a legend in these parts," Bay teased.

"I don't know about that," Paul replied. "But I'm a huge fan of *yours*. I like Jack, but I love your early stuff even more."

Bay had written and self-published a half-dozen or so crime dramas before he made it big with Jack Robbins. And of course those had been rereleased between the Robbins novels and had become wildly popular as well.

"Thank you," Bay said. "It's good to know someone likes the oldies."

Before Paul could respond, Zeke stepped back and looked at Bay. "Nice tux, by the way."

Bay smoothed the front. "This old thing?"

Zeke smiled. "Hey! Someone get this man a drink so we can get this party started."

Bay looked over his shoulder. "Flanagan on the rocks, please,"

"Hugo Boss?" Zeke asked, still admiring Bay's tuxedo.

"Armani," Bay corrected.

"Great taste in clothes and scotch," Rich added. "A man after my own heart."

"Shall we?" the croupier asked, gesturing to the table.

Looking at the other three men, Bay nodded. "I'm game."

Bay took a seat to the far left at the table with Rich next to him, Zeke, and then Paul to the far right.

The waitress placed Bay's drink in front of him, smiled, winked, and then quickly disappeared.

"What's your pleasure?" the croupier asked.

Rich rubbed his hands together. "How about a little Texas Hold'em?"

"I'm in," Zeke said.

"Me too," Bay added.

Paul simply nodded.

"Here we go, gentlemen."

The croupier spread the deck across the table and each man picked a random card and flipped it over. Rich had the high card, so the croupier slid the dealer button to him. "Mr. Devlin will act as our dealer for the first hand. And Mr. Whitman will have the small blind and Mr. Gilman the large."

The croupier scooped up the cards, discarded them, and pulled another deck from the dealing shoe. "Gentlemen, we've already established that small blind will be twenty-five hundred dollars and large blind five thousand. Good luck."

The croupier dealt the preflop, which gave each of the players a round of cards and then another. Bay held his hands over his hole cards and lifted his eyes slightly. He glanced around the table as Rich, Zeke, and Paul looked at their cards. None of them showed any detectible emotion, so he lifted the corner of his first card and took a peek. *Not too shabby!* An ace of spades.

Bay looked at his second card and smiled inwardly. *Yes!* A ten of spades. He eyed the other players again, and everyone still had the same blank expression. Hence the term *poker face*. The croupier gazed at Bay but didn't speak. Since he was sitting to the left of the person with the dealer button, it was up to him to call, raise, or fold for the first bet.

"I'll raise," he said, which meant he was in for twice the big blind, or ten thousand dollars. He slid the appropriate number of chips to the center of the table and sat back.

"Damn, Bay," Rich said. "Right outta the gate?"

Bay simply smiled confidently.

The next move was up to Paul. He looked at his cards again. "I'll call." He slid the same number of chips to the croupier and turned to Zeke.

Zeke glanced around the table. "I'll call," which meant he, too, was in for ten grand.

"Mr. Devlin?" the croupier asked.

Rich smirked. "I'll call."

The pot was now worth forty grand, Bay's heart was fluttering wildly with excitement, and he could almost feel the hairs on his arms standing at attention.

Bay watched as the croupier started the flop by dealing the burn card, which is the top card in the deck and gets placed facedown on the table. He then dealt three cards faceup in front of him. The first was the nine of spades, then the ace of hearts, and finally the six of spades. It was now up to each of the players to make the best hand they could with the two cards they were already dealt and the three cards in the flop. It was time for the second round of betting.

With practiced ease, Bay kept his expression emotionless. He had a good chance of ending up with a flush, since he was already holding two spades and there were two more spades in the flop.

The croupier looked at Bay. Since all four players were still in the game and he was sitting to the left of the dealer, it was again up to him to raise, check, or fold. "I'll raise again," Bay said confidently.

Rich giggled nervously while Zeke and Paul eyed Bay without expression, apparently seeking a chink in his armor. Bay slid the chips to the center of the table and sat back in his chair again.

The croupier turned to Paul. "It's to you, Mr. Gilman."

Paul looked at his cards again and studied the flop. "I'll call."

Bay smiled as Paul slid his chips to the croupier.

"Mr. Cambridge?" the croupier said.

Zeke pushed a stack of chips across the table. "I'll call as well."

Before the croupier could ask, Rich slapped the table. "I'll fold. I've got shit."

Next was the turn. The croupier dealt a burn card facedown again and one more card faceup next to the other three.

Damn! Deuce of hearts.

But Bay was feeling confident. And he had a good run going, so it was time to apply his bluffing skills. "I'll raise."

"Oh man," Rich said. "I'm glad I got out when I did."

Paul and Zeke eyed Bay again, but neither said anything.

Bay slid another $10,000 in chips across the table.

"I'll call," Paul said, sliding his chips over.

"Me too," Zeke said, following Paul's lead.

Bay grinned to himself. *Yes. Come on, Lady Luck.*

It was time for the last card, or the river as it's called. The croupier once again dealt the burn facedown and one last card faceup next to the other four.

Seven of spades. *Hallelujah!*

"I'll raise," Bay said, sliding ten grand more in chips over to the croupier.

"I'll call," Paul said, pushing over the equivalent in chips.

"Fuck," Zeke said. "I'm out."

Bay peeled back the corner of his first card, locked eyes with Paul, and then slowly flipped it over. This was where it always got interesting. As Paul looked back and forth between Bay's card and the flop, his expression or lack thereof wasn't what held Bay's attention. What was happening behind Paul's eyes told the real story—and tonight Paul did not disappoint. As soon as Paul saw Bay's card and realized the possibilities of his hand, Bay picked up a little something in Paul's eyes. And that simple *little something* caused goose bumps to form on Bay's arms and made his heart rate steadily increase.

Bay smiled confidently as he flipped over the second card, eyes still locked on to Paul's. He almost came in his shorts when he recognized exactly when Paul knew his goose was cooked.

"A flush," Bay said.

Paul smiled weakly. "Nice hand." He slid his cards to the croupier without even flipping them over.

A player who conceded a game wasn't required to reveal his cards, but Bay would have liked to have seen the hand he'd beaten. He'd bet his life Paul had three of a kind or even a flush, but Bay's flush was ace high, so that would have sealed the deal. Either way it didn't really matter. Bay was up $40,000.

"Damn that was intense," Zeke said.

"No shit," Rich agreed.

The croupier stacked the chips, pushed them across the table, and deposited them in front of Bay.

Bay took a five-hundred-dollar chip off the top and tossed it over to the croupier. "Thank you."

The croupier nodded, smiled, and dealt the next hand.

IT WAS just before eleven and they'd been at it for almost six hours. Rich and Zeke had excused themselves a little while ago, and Bay and Paul had agreed to one more hand. The night had been mostly in Bay's favor, and he had over a half-million dollars in chips in front of him. On the other hand, the night hadn't been as kind to Paul. From Bay's best calculations, the poor guy was in the red almost as much as Bay was in the black, and he was down to four one-thousand-dollar chips.

Bay and Paul were at the river stage of the last hand. There was $80,000 in the pot, and Bay knew Paul must have an impressive hand since he continued to bet when his funds were so depleted. But Bay had an impressive hand as well. Very impressive.

Bay locked eyes with Paul as the croupier removed the burn and prepared to flip the river card faceup and add it to the flop. Already on the table were a six of clubs, seven of spades, ten of clubs, and three of hearts. Bay saw the makings of a straight and figured that's what Paul was working up to. The croupier flipped the card and laid it on the table. Three of clubs. Bay saw a definite twinkle in Paul's eye and figured he had the straight.

This time it was up to Paul to raise, call, or fold. Bay felt certain there would be no folding since Paul had come this far, but in order to raise, he needed $5,000. He had only $4,000 on the table, and unless he had chips in his pocket, all he could do was call.

"I'll raise," Paul said.

The croupier looked at Paul. "Excuse me, Mr. Gilman, but you need $5,000 to raise."

Paul slid the four chips to the center of the table and looked at Bay. "I have an escort worth a grand scheduled to join me at the hotel in an hour. Will you take that as collateral for the final thousand?"

Bay thought for a second. He had no use for an escort. He was pretty inexperienced in that department, but what the hell? He was in Las Vegas—and what happens in Vegas, stays in Vegas. Right? Besides, he couldn't remember the last time he'd had sex. He'd had offers, of course, but he'd turned them down all but a couple of times, never knowing if they were made because of his celebrity or, even worse, his Jack Robbins persona. An encounter with an escort should be pretty cut-and-dried. *Wham, bam, thank you, ma'am.*

"Sure," Bay said before he could stop himself.

Since Paul was out of chips, Bay had no reason to raise again, so he called.

Paul flipped over his two cards. One was a nine of clubs and the other was an eight of spades. "Straight," he said, smiling.

Bay smiled back and flipped his cards over. "Four threes."

The blood drained out of Paul's face, and he hung his head briefly. When he raised it again, he was smiling. "Definitely not my night," he said, standing. "But hey. You win some. You lose some."

He offered his hand to Bay. Bay accepted it and the two men shook. "It was a pleasure, Paul. I hope we get to do it again."

"Likewise," Paul said. "Oh! I almost forgot. What is your room number?"

"It's 3001," Bay said. "Why?"

"Because your escort will be there at midnight."

Bay was about to protest when he changed his mind. He was still undecided, but he simply said, "Thanks."

Paul turned and walked out of the game room without another word.

"Can you verify your winnings with me, Mr. Whitman, before I call the cashier to cut you a check? Or would you prefer a wire transfer?" the croupier asked.

"Certainly. And a check will be fine."

BAY HAD just returned to his suite and put his rather large check in the safe when he heard a knock at his door. He walked through the foyer and then stopped dead in his tracks. *Shit! The escort.* He nervously smoothed the front of his jacket, then opened the door. When he saw the person standing on the other side, his mouth fell open and stayed there. He blinked twice to make sure he wasn't imagining things. He wasn't, and he could neither move nor speak.

CHAPTER TWO

WHAT THE fuck? Jack? Jack Robbins? The man on the other side of the door was the spitting image of the character Bay had created. He was leaning against the wall across the hall from Bay's door in a fashionable dark suit, arms folded across his chest, feet crossed at the ankles, flashing a million-dollar smile. *This must be some sort of joke. Jack's not real.*

Bay studied the guy in disbelief. He was extremely handsome, of course. And given the way Bay had to look up to meet the man's eyes, he was definitely the same height as Jack. Not to mention possessing the same hair, same eyes, same neat beard, and the same muscular build Bay had written about. And that smile? It was definitely the sly, sexy smile Bay had created for Jack when he was trying to seduce a new conquest. *This man is Jack Robbins. Wait! A new conquest. Am I the conquest?*

Bay's visitor cleared his throat, which brought Bay back to reality somewhat. He couldn't stop staring, but he attempted to speak. "How… can I help you?"

"Damn, you're hot. Please tell me your name is Paul?"

Paul? "Ah. No. Sorry," Bay said.

The man's smile faded. "Shit."

The stranger checked his cell phone, looked at the number on the door, and shook his head with a disgusted expression. "My apologies, man. Must have gotten stood up."

Bay was about to close the door when it hit him. *Paul. Paul Gilman. The escort. Oh shit!*

"Wait!" he called out. "Did you have an appointment with Paul at midnight?"

The guy stopped and looked back quizzically. "As a matter of fact, I did. And if you're not Paul… how did you know that?"

Still in shock from seeing Jack Robbins living and breathing, Bay nervously beckoned the guy back. "Because I won you in a poker game."

One corner of the man's mouth curled up into a little smile, and his eyes twinkled with mischief. He took a few steps back and resumed his position leaning against the wall. "Now did you? That's funny. I didn't realize I was transferrable."

"Oh jeez." Bay realized what he'd just said. "I'm so sorry, I'm talking about you like you're a piece of meat or something."

The guy laughed, and his entire face lit up. "Hell, I'm not offended. I've been referred to as a piece of meat on more than one occasion."

Bay suddenly wished he was back in the safety of his New York apartment writing about Jack instead of standing in the hall of a Las Vegas hotel talking to his likeness.

"So with whom do I have the pleasure of spending my next two hours? If I may ask?"

"Oh sorry. I'm Bay." Bay stuck out his hand.

"Bay?"

Bay nodded.

"Odd, but nice."

"Thanks. It's a family name," Bay said. "Look, you don't have to stay. The guy thought he had a winning hand, but I raised and he was out of money, so he offered you up to even the pot."

Instead of accepting Bay's hand, the guy folded his arms over his chest again, smiled, and looked Bay up and down. "And his loss is definitely my gain."

Bay smiled weakly and warmth crawled up his face. "Yeah. No… I mean—" He realized the man was flirting with him, as Jack did with so many of his conquests. *This is uncanny!*

Bay withdrew his hand, and the man took a step toward him. "I'm King Slater."

He was so close now, Bay could smell his spicy cologne. "Nice to meet you, King." They locked eyes, and King seemed to be waiting for some sort of recognition. But his name didn't ring a bell.

King appeared amused by Bay's nervousness and discomfort. "I'll show myself in," he said, still smiling seductively at Bay.

Bay watched in amazement as King walked right past him. He even had Jack's swagger down to a T.

After quickly looking down the hall in both directions before closing the door, Bay followed King into the living room. King suddenly stopped, and Bay almost ran into his back. When King turned around, still grinning, he looked into Bay's eyes, cupped the back of Bay's neck, and pulled him close to press his lips against Bay's in a slow, tender kiss.

A slew of reactions flooded Bay's head. *Stop him* came first. Then before Bay could move, King deepened the kiss. His lips were moist and warm, and Bay's nether regions tingled. He froze, mentally and physically. *What the hell?* He had never been kissed by a man. Not that he was against it; it had just never happened. Sex had never been a real part of his life. He'd always figured no one would want him, so why bother? Since his fame had blossomed, the couple of encounters he'd had were with women, and on both occasions they'd slept with Jack Robbins, not Bay Whitman. He imagined that neither he nor his partner could have gotten through *that* experience.

When the kiss ended and King stepped back, looking quite pleased with himself, Bay was speechless. He instinctively touched his lips and recalled the pressure that had been there.

King smiled again. "Don't be embarrassed, I have that effect on guys all the time."

Jesus, Bay! Think! What would Jack do? But that was easier said than done when Jack was standing right in front of him. Live *and* in the flesh.

Bay lowered his hand, shoved it in his pants pocket, and tried to strike a casual pose.

King folded one arm over his chest, brought his finger up to his chin, and eyed Bay curiously. "Bay, you are one hot man. Are you sure I have the right room? Most of my clients are older, out of shape, and relatively unattractive."

"I'm sorry, King. I'm…." The words left his lips before he could stop them.

"Straight?" King finished the sentence. "A lot of my clients are"— King made air quotes—"straight."

King took a step closer to Bay and was again near enough that Bay could smell his cologne. He gripped Bay's asscheeks and squeezed, then tilted his head, leaned in, and gently bit Bay's neck.

A chill ran down Bay's spine as King nibbled on his skin, his lips warm and firm. He knew he should stop King, but the physical attention was wonderful.

Finally, Bay brought both hands up, laid them on King's chest, and pushed gently. "Seriously."

"Seriously what?" King asked breathlessly, looking a little shocked.

"Seriously, I'm straight," Bay said again.

"Seriously?" King asked, taking a step back and looking confused.

Okay, granted, Bay had never identified as straight or gay. But with the events of the last few minutes and the way King's touch affected him, he might at the very least be bisexual. He'd have to think about that possibility later. His past sexual encounters, few as they were, had been with women. They had been satisfying, but now a man was standing in front of him, kissing him and nibbling on his neck, and damn if it didn't feel really good.

"Just my fucking luck," King said, brushing his hands together like he was done with the charade. "I finally get a gorgeous client, and he doesn't want me."

"You think I'm gorgeous?" Bay asked, hearing the surprise in his own voice.

"Have you looked in the mirror?" King asked. "*You* are one handsome motherfucker."

Bay knew he should let King be on his way, but he was intrigued. Suddenly he wanted to know more about him. Jack Robbins was a character of his imagination, and Bay could only take him so far. If Bay were able to spend some time with a real Jack Robbins, in the form of an escort named King Slater, the possibilities were endless. Hell, he could take the character to a whole new level.

"Look," Bay said before he could think better of it, "don't go. I have you for two hours, right?"

King eyed him suspiciously. "Yes… technically."

"Then I want my money's worth."

"Now you're talking." King wiggled his eyebrows.

"Wait," Bay said. "Not for sex."

The disappointment on King's face was obvious. "For what, then?" he asked. "A card game?"

"Maybe."

King flashed a gorgeous Jack Robbins smile. "Only if it's strip poker."

"Deal," Bay said, pretty certain he could bluff his way through a poker game with a gay escort.

"One article of clothing per bet," King said, "or its no deal."

Bay smiled. "I think I'm gonna need more scotch for this."

"I've gotta pee."

Bay pointed to the bathroom as he walked over to the phone and ordered a bottle of Flanagan from room service.

An hour later, King had literally lost his shirt. Along with his suit coat, his tie, his cufflinks, and his undershirt. Bay still had everything intact except his tuxedo jacket, which he bluffed into losing because he was getting warm.

"I'll match your shoe, and I'll raise you a shoe," King said.

"I'll call." Bay laid out four deuces.

"Damn," King said, tossing his cards on the table. He untied and slipped off his left shoe and then his right and added them to the pile of his discarded clothing. "Those are eight-hundred-dollar shoes."

"Have you had enough yet?" Bay asked.

"You're fucking kidding me, right?" King looked down at his socked feet and started counting. "I've got two socks, my slacks, and my underwear. That gives me four more bets before I'm out of clothes."

Bay had to admit King was an exceptionally good-looking man, and he was having trouble keeping his eyes on his cards. It was quite a shock to find himself attracted to another guy, but he would deal with that later. For now, he was enjoying King's six-pack, his chiseled, well-defined chest, and his massive arms. Each time King removed another article of clothing, Bay studied him, hoping to remember every detail of the man's body so he could add another dimension to Jack. He was especially intrigued by the tattoos on King's arms and chest. *I think Jack needs to get some tattoos very soon.*

"Did those hurt?" Bay asked while he shuffled the cards.

King followed his gaze. "The tats?"

Bay nodded.

"A little. Especially the tribal band. The skin is really sensitive on the underside of your arm."

"Do you have more?" Bay asked hesitantly.

King flashed another smile. "A gentleman never tells. I guess you'll just have to wait and see for yourself." He looked at his cards and threw three down on the table. "I'll take three."

Bay dealt him three more cards and then himself two. "Dealer takes two."

King looked at his cards. "I'll bet a sock."

Bay fanned his cards out in his hand and studied them. "And I'll match that sock and raise you another sock," he said, locking eyes with King.

"I'll call." King smiled broadly and laid out three queens.

"That's good," Bay said. "But not good enough."

He laid a ten-high straight on the table.

King peeled off both socks and added them to the pile. "Easy come, easy go." He downed a shot of scotch and slapped the table. "Okay, Bay. Looks like I've got at least one more round to redeem myself. Let's play cards."

Ten minutes later, King was standing in front of Bay as naked as the day he was born. His arms were folded across his chest and he seemed to be waiting for Bay to make the next move.

And he did have more tattoos. One surrounding his belly button, one on his thigh, one on each calf, and a tramp stamp on his lower back, right above the crack of his ass.

"Now what?" Bay asked, looking up from his seated position and struggling not to stare at King's impressive endowment.

"I've got one more thing to bet," King said.

"Really?" Bay scanned King's naked body and motioned with his finger for him to turn around. When King did and there wasn't a stitch of clothing left on him, Bay spoke. "I can't imagine what."

"You forget I'm an escort," King said, wiggling his eyebrows again. "I have talents."

Bay chuckled when he realized King's response was something he could clearly hear Jack saying if he were in the same situation.

"Touché," Bay said. "But I'd save those talents for someone who would enjoy them more than me."

King's smile faded. "Fuck you, Bay. I'm outta here." He reached down and started sorting through his clothes.

"What are you gonna wear home?" Bay asked.

"What? My clothes—oh, I see your point. Oh fuck it. I've left better places then this naked."

He dug in his pockets, retrieved his wallet, keys, and two cell phones, stood, squared his shoulders, and headed for the door. "Good night."

Bay jumped up and beat him there. "Wait! I was only teasing you. Besides, your clothes would be way too big for me. Get dressed."

King seemed to deflate just a little, and Bay saw another side to the cocky escort. *Yet another dimension.*

Now King seemed uncomfortable being naked as he sorted through his clothes and slipped on his underwear and pants. He put on his shirt, wrapped his tie around his neck, and sat on the couch with his shoes and socks at his feet. Sighing, he rested his head in his hands.

King eventually looked up at Bay with weary eyes and ran his hand through his hair. "Do I gross you out that much?"

"Of course not," Bay said. "You're a very attractive guy." He hadn't meant to hurt King's feelings. He walked over and sat down next to King. "There's a lot going on here you don't know about."

King met his eyes. "Then enlighten me."

"What are your rates again?" Bay asked.

"Five hundred an hour."

"I think I would be out of money before I got halfway through my story."

King didn't respond, but he quietly slipped on his socks and shoes, stood, and walked across the room with Bay right behind him. When he reached the door, he stopped and turned. "It's been fun. I mean... until the rejection part."

Bay laid a hand on King's arm. "Please don't take offense. As I said, you're an incredibly good-looking guy. I'm just... well, to be honest, a great big mess."

"You don't seem like a big mess to me," King said.

"Yeah, well. Sometimes things aren't what they seem."

King stared down at the hand resting on his arm, and Bay quickly removed it.

"Good night, then," King said, opening the door. He handed Bay a card. "In case you change your mind."

King turned to leave.

"Wait," Bay said, following him into the hall but unsure why.

King stopped and looked back.

"Are you available tomorrow night?" Bay asked. "Same time? Same place?"

"Sure," King said. "I'll sit around and play strip poker with a straight man for five hundred an hour any day. No problem. Good night, Bay."

Bay watched King until he turned the corner of the hallway. He stepped back inside, closed the door, and leaned against it as the events of this bizarre night ran through his head. The fact he'd won an escort at all was peculiar in itself. But to have the escort be a gay man who looked just like Jack Robbins... well, that took the cake. And if he were being completely honest, he was certainly intrigued and, oddly enough, attracted to King.

Bay shook the thoughts from his head and walked into the living room. He cleared the scotch bottle and the two shot glasses and put them on the bar. Then he went back to the table for the cards. King's last hand was facedown on the table, and curiosity got the best of Bay. He turned over the cards one by one. "Son of a bitch."

King had folded his last hand with an ace-high straight to Bay's three of a kind. *King wanted to get completely naked in front of me. He really did like me.*

CHAPTER THREE

KING COULD feel Bay's eyes on his back as he sauntered down the hall, pissed off and pouring on the famous Slater swagger. He finally exhaled and relaxed when he turned the corner and stepped into the elevator bank. He pressed the Call button, and while he waited for an elevator door to open, he had half a mind to go back to Bay's room and give the man a piece of his mind. But for some reason he was nervous around Bay. And right now, angry at him. Besides, what good would it do? Why risk losing the grand from tomorrow night's gig? What was he pissed about anyway? A grand for two hours of strip poker? And that had been at *his* suggestion. *Hell. In my early days, I did a lot more than that for a lot less money.*

King's mood eased. He realized he should probably be thanking Bay. After all, it could have been a lot worse. Bay could have been a fat, balding guy who was itching to get fucked by a porn star. Or the proverbial closeted straight guy on a business trip who had a wife and kids back home. Or even worse, a repeat of his last gig. An overweight, closeted, well-known Las Vegas celebrity in a bra and black hose who wanted to beat off while he licked and worshiped King's sock-clad feet.

King had seen it all—hell, he'd done it all. But this had been nothing but poker. Easy money. However, he didn't miss the irony in the situation. Bay was gorgeous, well-spoken, and seemed to be intelligent. He was incredibly fit and had great taste in clothes. That tux fit him like a second skin, and just his luck, all the man wanted to do was play cards. Life could be a bitch sometimes.

The elevator dinged and brought King out of his head. The doors opened, and he stepped into the empty elevator and pressed the button for the ground floor. When the doors slid open again, he was in the lobby. Judging by the number of people milling about, one would have thought it was six o'clock in the evening instead of two thirty in the morning.

As he strolled to the parking garage, it dawned on him he was no longer angry at Bay. Yeah, he was pissed off at first, but he acknowledged that his ego—along with his feelings—had been hurt. This was the first time he'd been rejected since he'd made it big in the porn industry, and it had set off feelings of inadequacy he thought were long ago put to bed. Sure, he'd had a few guys who only wanted to talk or wanted to get to know a porn star, but those were few and far between. He'd never actually been rejected before. And he hated to admit it, but it stung. Probably because he really liked Bay. He'd been attracted to him, which was odd enough in itself. *Be grateful, King. A guy like Bay could really fuck with your recovery.*

But Bay hadn't wanted him, and it had bloody well taken him by surprise. *Could I be losing my touch?*

King did the math. It had been over three years since he'd even looked at another guy as anything other than an ass to lick, a hole to fuck, or a dick to suck. And all for either the sake of the camera or for his escort business—a means to make a living. When sex was a person's line of work, things in the romance department could get skewed. Add King's recovery to the mix, and the result might be a big old clusterfuck.

As popular as King was right now, he had to admit that the simple fact that Bay didn't find him the least bit attractive had bruised his ego. *Nothing like rejection to bring you down off your high horse.* But in all fairness, Bay had said he was straight. *Maybe that's why he didn't recognize me or my name.* King's usually spot-on gaydar hadn't gone off, so maybe Bay *was* straight, but he also threw off some very strong vibes in the other direction. *Maybe he just* thinks *he's straight.*

As he exited the parking garage and pulled onto the Las Vegas Strip, King recalled the way Bay had studied him intensely as King removed each item of clothing. Almost like he was trying to commit what he was seeing to memory. Straight guys didn't do that, right? King smiled to himself. Was he committing it to memory for later use? *Maybe. Or maybe he's just coming to terms with his sexuality and needs a push in the right direction.*

So maybe King hadn't lost his touch after all. He knew he was probably blowing smoke up his own ass, but it did make him feel a little better and more optimistic about their next encounter. He was definitely intrigued, and he had one more chance to crack the coconut, so to speak. He smiled. Tomorrow night, he was going to do his best to seduce Bay Whitman.

King stopped for a red light at Sahara Avenue. Significantly cheered, he looked up and saw a billboard advertising a gay bar called Badlands Saloon with an arrow pointing right. The tagline read, "Drink, dance, and be a fairy! Two-step with hot cowboys to the latest country tunes."

Below the text were two handsome men in Stetsons, arm in arm, smiling broadly. The thought of hot cowboys sent chills down his spine. He'd always been a sucker for a cowboy. And he loved to two-step. But when the light turned green, King clenched the steering wheel tightly with both hands, hit the gas, and drove right through the intersection without turning. *It's a trigger, King. Remember the program. Stay away from triggers.*

When he pulled into the parking lot of Caesar's Palace, he took the elevator to his room, locked the door behind him, and sighed with relief. He'd dodged another bullet in his recovery, and he was feeling pretty damn proud of himself.

King undressed and threw his clothes on the chair next to his bed. His room was no suite like Bay's, but it was nice enough. Nice enough for a shy, tall, and lanky kid from Ohio with a bad haircut and no friends who'd finally come into his own and sort of fallen into the porn industry.

You've got an early call in the morning and another one in the afternoon, so you better get some sleep. Don't wanna look like you've aged ten years in one night.

King closed his eyes and saw Bay's handsome face staring back at him. He smiled.

Tomorrow night, my friend. Just wait until tomorrow night.

BAY CRAWLED into bed, lay on his back, and pulled the covers up to his neck. As usual, his confidence had fallen to the floor with his Armani tuxedo, and it was plain old Bay Whitman in this dark hotel room in the big city of Las Vegas. But tonight his mind raced with excitement along with his usual fears, doubts, and insecurities. He'd asked King Slater back here again tomorrow night. But why?

As he thought about it rationally, he realized he had multiple reasons. For starters, Bay knew a lot of writers who based characters off living people, but he'd created Jack purely from his imagination. Jack was the person he wished he could be. But since Bay could only imagine what being Jack felt like, that made him sort of one-dimensional in Bay's mind. Which meant he could only take Jack so far. But if everything went well tomorrow night, he was going to be able to develop another dimension of his character by simply spending time with King, getting to know him better, and picking his brain. If he was lucky, he would get a shitload of opinions other than his own to write about. Opinions he could morph into a new-and-improved Jack Robbins. A male escort King might be, but Bay could tell he wasn't a stupid man. And Bay was looking forward to seeing what was behind the escort. What made him tick.

On the flip side of the coin, he genuinely liked King. And he was mesmerized by the fact King seemed to like *him*.

King exuded a great deal of confidence, and that in itself was attractive to Bay. He was handsome, witty, charming—everything Bay wasn't. All qualities Bay had written into his character. But if Bay were being honest, he had to admit the man was also sexy as hell. Bay clenched the covers at his neck a little tighter. Being attracted to another man was something he hadn't expected, and it was a bit unnerving. He needed time to work through it, so he decided that for now, he would stick with getting to know King Slater. Aka Jack Robbins.

But as Bay lay there, the nagging question of the attraction crept back into his mind. He'd definitely felt *something* when King kissed him, when he'd gripped Bay's ass and nipped at his neck. He certainly hadn't tried to stop King. But what had he felt? Could it have been the thrill of meeting his alter ego in person? The fact that the man who personified Bay's creation *liked* Bay, had flirted with him and come on to him?

Again, there was no easy answer. Did being attracted to King make him gay—or at the very least bisexual? The thought didn't repulse him. He'd simply never thought about it. Sex was something he'd *had* a couple of times, not something he identified as an essential aspect of who he *was*.

Bay rolled over, pulled the covers over his head, and squeezed his eyes shut in an attempt to quiet his brain. But after a few minutes of fighting his thoughts, he realized it was not going to happen. Huffing, he pulled the covers back and got to his feet. He walked through the darkness of his room and pulled the draperies back. The lights of the Las Vegas Strip were alive and dancing proudly against the dark backdrop of the predawn sky.

Another image of King popped into his mind, and instead of trying to block it out, he embraced it. King was smiling at him, and his grin was big and genuine. It dawned on him that spending time with his new acquaintance was probably going to come at a cost. And he didn't mean the five hundred dollars an hour King charged for his company. That was research, and so very worth it. But what if the only way to keep

King coming back was to sleep with him? Did he want to do that? What if King put two and two together and realized Bay was using him as inspiration for his character? That could get ugly.

The sun was just peeking above the horizon when Bay finally climbed back into bed. He had no more answers now than he'd had hours ago, but he was too exhausted to fight sleep. It came almost at once.

Bay was running as fast as he could, looking back over his shoulder every now and then to count the number of boys chasing him. There were at least four, maybe five, and they looked like they were ready for trouble. He ran so fast, his heart pumped pure adrenaline through his veins, but his lungs were close to betraying him. The faster he ran, the slower his pace became. One last turn and he found himself cornered at a dead end between the gym and the math building. He tried to open the gate, but it was locked. In a last-ditch attempt to escape, he tried to scale the twelve-foot-high fence.

Bay raised his leg as high as he could and put the toe of his sneaker in the link. He hoisted himself up and did the same with his other toe. Another, and then another. He could see the top, He could almost reach it. I'm gonna make it. *Then just like that, hands at his ankles yanked him back to the ground.*

"Where you going, Bayberry?" one of the boys screamed as Bay took a foot to his rib cage.

"Ha-ha! I think we should call him Bayfairy," another boy yelled. "'Cause he's a big ole fruit."

By the time the bullies were finished with him, Bay had a black eye, busted lip, and likely several bruised ribs. This was the third time this week. One kid had said it was because he was a sissy and wasn't into sports or girls. Another boy had teased him about having to have free lunch and wear hand-me-downs from Goodwill. But none of the reasons mattered. The torture at school, albeit more physical, was nothing compared to the torture at home. When he'd gotten home and limped into the house, his mom and dad were so busy fighting they hadn't even noticed him—the bruises and the bloody lips.

Bay huddled in his bed, alone and so insignificant it was difficult to breathe. He pulled the covers up around his neck and prayed to anyone who would listen to please let him go to sleep and never wake up again.

Bay opened his eyes and wiped away the tears lingering on his cheeks. He stared up at the ceiling, unable to move, and waited for his heart to calm. These nightmares came a couple of times a month, and all he could do was hunker down and weather the storm until he was able to process the fear and sense of inconsequentiality that infused every fiber of his being. *One day at a time, Bay. One day at a time.*

CHAPTER FOUR

DESPITE THE fact that Bay had lost a little over ten grand at the poker table, he still had a bounce in his step and a smile on his face as he walked across the casino lobby toward the elevators. After all, it was a mere pittance compared to what he'd won the night before. He pressed the Call button and tapped his foot while he waited anxiously for a ding to signal the arrival of an elevator.

Even though he'd lost money tonight, the game had been as much fun as the previous night's, but with an added twist. The night started out innocently enough. Rich and Zeke were in rare form and quite animated, clowning around and teasing each other unmercifully. By the time the fourth player arrived, Bay was nearly in stitches. When the door opened, three big, stocky bodyguards preceded none other than the crown prince of Najirah, who was somewhat flamboyant and handsome as hell. They all shared a drink before game time, and the prince turned out to be not only good-looking, but delightful, witty, and charming, albeit a little nervous. In an attempt to ease the prince's anxieties, Bay chatted him up a bit by asking about his homeland, complimenting him on his extremely well-tailored tuxedo, and generally taking an interest in him, while Rich and Zeke continued their antics. And that was when things started to get interesting.

When they took their seats to begin the game, the prince sat next to Bay. He raised his hand, and one of his bodyguards brought over a bottle of Boërl & Kroff Brut Champagne and four flutes. Bay had researched this champagne for one of his novels, and although he'd never tasted it, he knew it was just south of twenty-five hundred dollars a bottle. As soon as that bottle was poured, they toasted, and another bottle was delivered to the table, which by the second hand of cards, the prince had consumed by himself.

At that point, the prince started occasionally brushing his knee against Bay's, which Bay wrote off as coincidence at first. But after they'd consumed the next bottle of champagne, the occasional grazes elevated into the prince rubbing his shoeless foot up and down Bay's calf. And if that wasn't enough, as the night wore on, the prince became very *handsy*.

Between each round of cards dealt, the prince batted his eyelashes and smiled seductively at Bay as his hand found Bay's knee under the table and squeezed and kneaded as if it were a ball of dough.

In all the years before, no man had ever come on to Bay. And now in the last twenty-four hours not one but two had done so. Bay chuckled. *One kiss from a man and I guess I'm fair game.*

After the last round was won, Bay didn't waste any time heading back up to his room. He waited at the elevators with anticipation, and at last the bell dinged and the doors opened. Bay stepped into the empty mirrored car and studied his reflection. He straightened his slim black bow tie and brushed a particle of lint off his left shoulder. Tonight he was wearing a black three-piece Dolce & Gabbana tuxedo, yet another purchase by his stylist, with an ivory pleated shirt. Satisfied he looked his best, Bay turned around, crossed his hands in front of him, and instinctively looked up to watch the digital readout as the elevator car rose floor by floor. His mind once again drifted back to his night. Yeah, it had been fun. The prince had eventually caught on to the fact that Bay wasn't returning his advances and gave up. But if the truth be told, even with all that entertainment, Bay hadn't been on his game—and he had a hunch why.

When the doors opened, Bay stepped out of the elevator and rounded the corner. He stopped dead in his tracks. That hunch became a sure thing.

King Slater was waiting outside Bay's hotel room, leaning with one shoulder against the wall, his arms folded across his chest, and his feet crossed at the ankles, much like he had the previous night. *That's gotta be his signature pose.*

King was wearing a handsome white dinner jacket, tuxedo pants, and a white pleated shirt, open at the collar, with an untied black bow tie hanging loosely around his neck. *This is uncanny. That's exactly what Jack Robbins was wearing on the cover of* Revenge in Monte Carlo.

Bay slipped his shaking hands in his pockets in an attempt to hide his nerves and casually walked in King's direction. "Hey there," he said. "I hope I haven't kept you waiting too long?"

King pushed off the wall and straightened. He stuck out his hand. "Just got here a few minutes before you did. Good to see you, Bay."

"Likewise." Bay accepted King's firm handshake, dug his key card out of his inside coat pocket, and slipped it into the lock. He pushed the door open and held it for King to go ahead of him.

"Nice spread," King said.

Bay followed him into the living room. Room service was setting up a buffet. Earlier in the day, not knowing if King would be hungry or not, Bay had ordered a full bar and late dinner.

"All set, Mr.—"

"Thank you." Bay cut the guy off, not ready for King to know his last name. He signed the ticket and left the server a generous tip.

King leaned against the wall, smiled, slid his right hand into his pocket, and either deliberately or inadvertently struck a pose. Bay had no idea which, but it didn't matter. He simply watched in awe. *Being casual and debonair seems to come so naturally to him. It's like every pose is photographer-ready.*

King looked at Bay, sporting a crooked smile Bay had to admit was beyond adorable. "You know you're not required to buy an escort dinner when you're paying for sex, right?"

A thin layer of sweat started to form across Bay's brow. *Take a deep breath and play the game, Bay. How would Jack handle this?*

Bay flashed a smile that matched King's. "Is that what I'm doing?" he finally asked. "Paying for sex?"

"I sure as hell hope so," King answered quickly, his gaze unwavering.

"I thought we already established that I'm a straight man."

King's smile widened. "If I had a nickel for every man who told me he was straight while I was fucking him, I'd be a rich man."

Bay didn't reply. He walked over to the bar, filled two rocks glasses with ice, and poured two fingers of single-malt scotch in each, one of which he handed to King. Raising his glass, he said, "Touché."

King's smile morphed into a hopeful expression. "Does that mean I actually have a chance at being the first to take you on a trip to the wild side?"

Bay was starting to feel a little more confident. The tide was turning in his favor, and he was gaining the upper hand. "Who says you would be the first? I said I identified as straight. I didn't say I've never been on the wild side." *Where in the hell did that come from, Bay?*

King's eyes widened, and then his lips curved into a curious smile.

Bay relaxed a little. Sure, he'd bluffed his way through that hand, but bluffing or not, he'd won all the same, and he hadn't had to reveal his cards.

"In that case," King said, stepping in front of him, "you won't mind if I do this."

Bay had no idea what King had planned, but the relaxation he'd experienced minutes ago was quickly waning.

King unbuttoned Bay's tuxedo jacket, leaned forward enough for his cheek to lightly brush Bay's, and slipped Bay's coat over his shoulders. He folded it neatly and laid it on the couch. Bay inhaled deeply and took in the now-familiar scent of King's signature spicy cologne, and damn if it didn't smell intoxicating.

"That's better," King whispered. "Now this."

King slowly unfastened each of the buttons of Bay's vest and opened it, exposing the cream-colored shirt and suspenders beneath. He raised his hands to Bay's collar, slowly untied Bay's bow tie, and slid it gently from his neck. King added it to the coat. He looked Bay in the eyes and smiled. "Now that should be more comfortable," he whispered.

Son of a bitch! King was playing Bay like a fiddle. *So much for winning the first hand. Dammit. Jack Robbins never loses and nor will I.* He gathered his thoughts, smiled, and matched King's gaze. "Actually I am more comfortable. Thank you, King."

King's seductive expression quickly faded and was replaced with one of disbelief. Bay ignored the transformation and turned to the food. "Look at this spread. I didn't know what you liked, so I got a bit of everything. Come on, let's eat."

Back in control!

"MAN I'M full." Bay wiped his mouth with the white cloth napkin and dropped it on the table. "I didn't even realize I was hungry."

"That was very thoughtful of you, Bay. And it was delicious. Thank you."

King had been rather quiet while they ate, and to be honest Bay was grateful for that. He needed time to regroup. King *had* thrown him off-kilter, not that he would ever admit that to King. But he needed to figure out a way to keep King interested without giving away too much. Jack always loved a challenge, so he was going to take the chance that King was the same way. It was time for Bay to play what he called *hard to get.*

"Where are my manners?" Bay asked, motioning King to his feet.

King looked confused, but he stood hesitantly, locking eyes with Bay.

They were now facing each other, and Bay rose to his tiptoes, slipped King's coat off his broad shoulders, and folded it in half. Again, the faint manly aroma of King's cologne hung in the air as Bay laid the coat on the chair. *Why is this smell so intoxicating?* When King leaned the least bit forward, Bay felt King's warm breath on his neck and that, combined with the cologne, sent an unexpected jolt of something right to his groin.

Not wanting to lose his poker face, Bay ignored the sensation and slid King's bow tie from his neck, as King had done earlier to his. He dropped it on top of the jacket and rested his hands on his hips. "Now sit."

"Look, Bay—"

"Sit," Bay repeated.

King didn't move.

"You're mine for the next—" Bay looked at his watch. "—roughly hour and a half. Now sit."

King smirked, but he sat. Bay walked around to the back of the chair, rested his hands on King's shoulders, and began to knead his shoulders and neck. King's thick muscles under his fingers caused a reaction Bay hadn't anticipated.

King was looking forward, and it was a damn good thing. Bay's poker face was peeling away layer by layer, and if King saw his face now, he would see exactly what he was doing to Bay. No way Bay could have that.

King was now making little noises and moving his head from side to side, obviously enjoying the attention. Knowing he was bringing pleasure to King made Bay's heart flutter. After a few more minutes, Bay's resolve was fading quickly and he knew he had to stop. He squeezed one last time and patted King on his upper arms. "Did I do okay?"

King looked over his shoulder at Bay with lazy eyes. "You did great. But what I don't understand is why?"

"Why what?"

King rolled his eyes. "Don't play a player. You know exactly what I'm talking about."

Bay thought about it briefly. He had to admit in the beginning it was to throw King off-kilter, but then Bay was the one thrown off-kilter. *My God, Bay! You were getting into it.*

Bay heard his name, bringing him out of his head. "Ah. Well," he said, "in your line of work, I would imagine you're always the one doing the pampering, so I just thought you deserved a little pampering yourself."

King looked over his shoulder again and this time there was something akin to panic in his eyes. Bay was confused, but then King's expression changed again to something more relaxed. "Thank you," he said, sounding sincere.

"My pleasure. Now I need a drink." Bay walked over to the bar.

A couple minutes later they were seated side by side on the small couch, thighs brushing ever so slightly when one of them moved and each with a single malt in his hand.

Bay took a sip and proceeded cautiously. "Tell me a little bit about you."

"What do you wanna know?" King asked.

"Oh, I don't know. Like maybe how did you become an escort?"

"So you really don't know who I am?" King asked.

Bay looked at him quizzically. "Should I?"

"Huh," King said. "You really aren't gay."

Bay was doing his best to follow the conversation, but he was having a really hard time. "What does my sexuality have to do with anything?"

King shook his head and chuckled. "Because if I may say so myself, I'm a fairly popular gay porn star."

"No shit," Bay said. "Really?"

"Really."

Holy shit! Jack Robbins's doppelganger is a gay porn star.

Bay smiled. "I don't know what to say."

"Why do you need to say anything? Unless you're gonna judge me."

"Of course not," Bay said. "Who am I to judge?"

Bay got up and poured them each another glass of scotch. When he was comfortably seated again, he stretched out, leaned against the back of the couch, and put his feet up on the table. The scotch was starting to have an effect on him, and it was making him relaxed and very inquisitive.

"So tell me—"

Before Bay could finish his question, King was on his knees untying Bay's shoes. He slipped them off one by one, moved up to the couch, and turned Bay so his feet were resting in King's lap. Bay was taken aback at first. No one else had ever touched his feet. But when King started kneading and rubbing, whatever hesitancy Bay was feeling melted away. If the truth be told, it felt damn good. The pampering was adding to the scotch-induced calm, and Bay was becoming more relaxed by the minute. King's strong hands seemed to instinctively know where his attentions were needed, and Bay had to swallow a moan of pleasure on more than one occasion. The sensation of his feet being massaged by another person was odd but very pleasant.

"You were about to ask me something?"

"Oh yeah," Bay said as King continued to massage his feet. "How did you become a porn star? Is… there a school or something for that?"

King stopped massaging and looked up. "Are you making fun of me?"

"No. Really. I've never known a porn star or even watched porn, so I have no idea how any of this works."

King began massaging again. "Well, if you must know, a buddy hooked me up."

"A friend may have hooked you up in the beginning, but I'm sure your confidence, good looks, and charm are what made you successful."

King's face lit up. "You think I'm good-looking?"

"Come on, King. I don't have to tell you how attractive you are. I mean… I don't know anything about the porn business, but I can imagine your world gets pretty crazy. And you just don't seem like the crazy type to me. You actually strike me as a very levelheaded, intelligent, and somewhat normal guy."

King stopped massaging and squeezed Bay's foot. "But you didn't answer my question. Do *you* think I'm good-looking?" he asked, smiling playfully and pinching Bay's big toe.

Bay shifted awkwardly and tried to pull his foot back, but King had a firm grip. "A person would have to be blind to not see how handsome you are. I'm sure you have a lot of fans."

King started to rub again, and Bay held back a groan of pleasure. "I do now," King continued. "I mean… people recognize me, and mostly they just want to say hi or take a picture with me, but it's weird to me because I don't get it. I didn't always look like this, so when I look in the mirror, I guess I still see the old me."

"What do you mean the old you?"

King didn't answer right away, almost as though he was considering his response. But his expression morphed into one of a little boy's innocence mixed with a lot of pain. An expression Bay knew all too well, and one that told him more than any words could.

"Before puberty," King said, "I was one lanky mess. I was over six feet tall at thirteen years old. I was a fucking freak, and I stuck out like a sore thumb. And that wasn't fun."

Bay felt for him before the words left King's mouth. "Did you get picked on?" he asked.

"Oh, I got picked on all right—a lot. And to top it all off, I was going through puberty and my voice was changing, so I literally squeaked when I talked. I was a mess."

He could be telling my story. Why didn't I turn out like him?

"I'll bet you get lots of attention now. In a good way," Bay said.

"The weird thing is… for me, the attention is the worst part of my job."

"Then why do you do it?"

King hesitated but only for a second. He looked directly at Bay. "The money."

"Is the money that good?"

"The porn? Not so much," King said. "But the exposure I get from the porn beefs up my popularity and seeds the escort business, which in turn allows me to command five hundred or more an hour."

Bay took a sip of his scotch, swallowed, and enjoyed the burn that accompanied the taste. This time when King hit a certain spot, Bay was unable to swallow the moan that escaped his lips, and in turn King smiled with satisfaction.

Warmth crept up Bay's face, but he ignored the sensation. "Can I ask you another question?"

"Sure."

"Does it bother you that people only want you for sex?"

King chuckled. "Like you?"

Bay swallowed the lump in his throat but didn't answer.

"You'd be surprised how many people don't want sex from me," King said. "The guys who want sex are the easy calls. For many of the guys who come to me, sex is not the most important thing. They just want to be consequential. They want to be wanted and made to feel attractive and desired. Like you. You're the hard ones."

Bay quirked an eyebrow. "Is that what you think I'm doing?"

"I think I've got a pretty good read on you. So yeah, I think so."

Bay thought about King's summation, and he concluded King was right. Bay was enjoying feeling attractive and knowing that someone wanted him. Funny how that had never been important to him before.

But right now the foot rub, the attraction hanging in the air, it was all having some sort of an effect on him. *But this is not about you. Keep him talking.*

"Look," King said. "It's not about getting people off, it's about the experience and making sure they get what they need for their money. You say you're not gay, so I'm gonna do what I can within the boundaries you set to give you your money's worth."

"Like a foot rub," Bay said, wiggling his toes.

"Exactly," King replied. "You said you don't want sex, so I'll pleasure you another way."

Okay. He's talking again. Now just keep him talking.

"So. Did you go to college? Have a degree?" Bay asked.

King nodded. "Yeah. In sales and marketing."

"Have you put that to use?"

"A little. I was in sales for a while, and I did pretty good with it, but when the economy tanked, I had bills to pay, so I started doing the porn. Then that started going really well, so I decided to post an escort ad. I just planned on doing both to get back on my feet and build a little nest egg, but I found out I was good at it." King flashed a rueful expression. "Who knew having sex with a lot of guys could be a good thing?"

"After you started escorting,"

King nodded. "And before as well."

Bay cocked his head and waited for him to elaborate.

King smiled. "Let's just say I have some demons to conquer in that department and leave it at that. That's a topic for another night."

Bay didn't argue, but he wanted to. He wanted to know every detail of King's life, but he would wait until the time was right to ask again. *There's a story there.*

King continued. "I found out that being a good listener and reading people was a big part of the job. Much like in sales. Hell, I'm still in sales, I'm just selling a different product—me."

That made perfect sense to Bay. "Were you always this intuitive?"

"Who knows? If I was, I got it from my grandmother. I spent a lot of time with her when I was a kid and she could read people very well. She taught me about body language and how important that was."

"How so?"

"Oh, I don't know… like maybe if a person looked you in the eyes or not. Or what they did with their hands. She used to say it was all about the little things."

"I think she was a wise woman," Bay said.

"That she was," King agreed.

King hit a ticklish spot on Bay's foot, and Bay jerked it back as a little giggle escaped his lips.

"Everyone has a spot," King said with a laugh. "And I'm committing yours to memory for later use."

Bay flashed a nervous smile. The "later use" part both scared and intrigued him.

"So," Bay continued. "What do you do for fun?"

"Now?"

Bay nodded.

"I do this," King replied. "But in high school and college, I did some theater work."

"Like acting?" Bay asked in surprise.

"Yeah. And don't act surprised," King teased. "That's where I first started to shed the tall, skinny nerd persona and come into my own."

"Were you any good?"

"I was told I was," King said. "I won a couple of awards."

"Did you enjoy it?"

"I did."

King looked off into the distance like he was remembering that time in his life.

Bay had a million more questions, but he didn't want to interrupt King's memories or scare him off by playing rapid-fire Q and A, so he paused and took another sip.

"Hey," King said. "Enough about me. It's time to tell me something about you."

Damn. I should have kept asking. Bay! Don't ask him what he wants to know because you'll have to tell him. Just pick something.

"Well, I guess we were very similar as kids. I, too, was tall and very skinny. Simply put—I was one awkward kid. A real nerd. When everyone else in school was no more than five feet, I was almost a full foot taller and weighed in at 135 pounds."

"We're you picked on?" King asked.

"Tormented," Bay said. "I mean... by the time I was thirteen, I was a six-foot nerd kid wearing hand-me-downs and getting free lunch. Might as well have tattooed a target on my forehead. But the funny thing is...." Bay paused and did his own reminiscing. "If I had had any confidence at all, I could have beaten the crap out of those bullies. I was twice their size, but instead I ran."

A chill ran down Bay's spine as he mentally relived the torture. "But thank God—at least I stopped growing."

King squeezed Bay's foot one last time and leaned back, rested his arm along the back of the couch, and laid a hand on Bay's. "I'm sorry. I remember all too well what that feels like."

The sensation was oddly comforting. Bay rarely had human contact, and he seldom talked about himself because then people would know the person he appeared to be in public couldn't have been further from who he really was. But here he was, speaking freely to a gay escort.

Still, he guessed it was worth talking about this stuff to avoid the things he really didn't want King to know.

King's voice broke into his internal dialog. "We're you a good student?"

"Bs and Cs," Bay said. "I think I was pretty smart, but I was really introverted, so I couldn't get up the nerve to participate in class or ask any questions... and I didn't want to call any attention to myself, so I just kept quiet. And besides, I lacked the social skills required to make friends, so I was alone a lot."

"That must have sucked," King said sympathetically, now stroking Bay's hand tenderly.

Bay leaned his head back, closed his eyes and allowed himself to go back in time. Something he rarely did. Pain and regret washed over him as he remembered a time he thought he'd made peace with. "Thinking about it now, yeah, it sucked. But then... I didn't realize how bad it was and what it would eventually do to me. I know that sounds weird, but after struggling through miserable days of school, I came home and locked myself away from my parents' fighting and the world, and I didn't interact with anyone. My mother finally left, and my father was pretty much incoherent when there was beer in the house, which was almost always, so books and the television became my companions. I loved crime shows, and I immersed myself in them. And then when I'd exhausted all the television shows, I read—a lot. But on television and in books, one thing was consistent—I never found any characters I could identify with. On the television everyone was macho and handsome, and that's the way they all seemed in the stories I read as well, so out of desperation, I started writing my own stories. In my stories I could write tall, skinny, nerdy, ugly heroes who always saved the day—and themselves. Then at some point my characters starting coming into their own and blossoming, almost like I wish I had. And then I started writing me as I wanted to be. Handsome, well versed, and a fun-loving and outgoing guy. I could even travel the world if I wanted to. Take out the bad guys, save the heroine, and do it all without wrinkling my tuxedo. The transformation all sort of happened subconsciously. One day nerd hero, the next, Jack Robbins."

Loneliness, fear, and isolation slowly crept back into Bay's consciousness. He hadn't thought about this stuff in years, and he was surprised at how much bringing up all of this was affecting him. When he opened his eyes, a single tear escaped and slid down his cheek. But before Bay could wipe it away, King leaned over, rested his hand on Bay's chest, tilted Bay's head back, and brushed the tear off his cheek with his thumb. He then pressed his lips on the exact spot of Bay's cheek where the tear had been and held them there. No one had ever brushed away even one of the many tears Bay had shed as a young boy, and here he was being comforted by a stranger. It was probably one of the single most caring things anyone had ever done for him.

When King pulled back, Bay locked eyes with him, and King's expression was etched with undeniable concern. Bay lost all control of his senses, gripped King behind the neck, and pulled him closer until their lips met. King melted into the kiss and deepened it at once. All sorts of things were going through Bay's head, but he was unable to stop himself. King tasted of scotch and chewing gum, and the combination was like a soothing medication. King started unbuttoning Bay's shirt, but when he got to Bay's waist, Bay panicked, came to his senses, and stopped him. He pushed King away. "I'm so sorry. I can't do this."

King's expression was one of obvious hurt, and he turned away, but before either could speak again, there was a knock on the door.

CHAPTER FIVE

KING LOOKED away as Bay jumped to his feet, seeming grateful for the interruption. Bay headed for the foyer. King stayed put on the couch, still feeling like a wounded puppy.

Jesus, King! He doesn't want you. Just get the hell out of here.

But King didn't move.

You have no idea what's going on with this guy. He says he's straight, but his actions say otherwise. And more importantly, why do you care? He doesn't want you!

King leaned forward, rested his elbows on his knees, and ran his fingers through his hair. But he still didn't get up.

Why do I care? Maybe it's because we shared the same type of upbringing. We were both bullied, and it seems to have left its mark on us. Could it be I just feel sorry for the guy? No. Come on. You like him, King.

That realization set off a siren in his head. An alarm that wailed and warned, *A trigger. No emotional involvement! It's a trigger. Get out now!*

About to stand, King was arrested by voices. He looked over his shoulder to find Bay talking to a handsome guy in a tuxedo and some type of headdress. A kaffiyeh, King thought it was called. And there were three big, burly guys standing behind him.

The man looked over Bay's shoulder and must have noticed King sitting on the couch. He stopped talking and smiled knowingly. Hands on his hips, he glanced back and forth between King and Bay.

Bay looked nervous and embarrassed, and that hurt King more than he cared to admit. Even to himself.

"I realize what this must look like," Bay said, looking down at his open shirt and socked feet. He wiped at the perspiration forming on his brow again and bounced from foot to foot, obviously very uncomfortable.

"No wonder you shunned my advances earlier, you dirty boy," the man said, looking Bay up and down seductively. "You obviously had other plans."

"I'm sorry. I did have plans," Bay said. "But not the type of plans you are insinuating. King, this is my poker companion, the crown prince of Najirah. Your Highness, this is King Slater."

King was still sitting on the couch, leaning forward with his elbows on his knees, but that didn't stop the prince from blatantly undressing King with his eyes.

"No need for introductions," the prince said. "I know who this man is. And no need to apologize, Bay. I would have shunned me too if I had this waiting for me in my suite."

The prince brought his finger to his chin. "You are a very lucky man. I have been a huge fan of Mr. Slater, and had I known he was in town, I would most definitely have beat you to the punch."

"Oh no!" Bay said, sounding defensive. "It's not what it looks like."

"Uh-huh," the prince said. "I'll just let you gentlemen get back to what you were doing. Unless you... maybe wouldn't mind a ménage?"

Bay stammered. "I, uh...."

King wasn't going to take any more. It was bad enough he was crossing a line in his recovery by still being here, but Bay had led him on and then rejected him, and now the man was embarrassed to be seen with him.

And then King saw his way out. He got to his feet and covered the space between him and Bay in less than a second. "No ménage," King said quietly, glaring at Bay. He turned to the prince. "But I'll do you one better. For five hundred an hour, you can have me all to yourself."

The prince's eyes widened, and he glanced at Bay. "Are you sure?"

"No need to ask his permission," King said. "My services are no longer needed here." He locked eyes with Bay. "We're done."

"I don't mind sloppy seconds," the prince said. "And I'll do better than that. How about ten grand for the rest of the night?"

"No!" Bay said. "It's not like—"

"Deal," King said. "Lead the way."

The door slammed behind them.

BAY WAS in total and complete shock. *Did that really just happen?*

He didn't know what to do. He hadn't wanted King to leave, especially like that, but he had no right to stop him. And he certainly didn't want King selling himself to the prince because Bay had hurt his feelings.

Bay opened the door and stepped out into the hall. "Wait! King!"

King looked over his shoulder. "You *were* finished with me, weren't you? Besides, you're straight. Remember?"

"Straight?" the prince said through a big smile. "Seriously?"

"That's what he says," King said, loud enough for Bay to hear.

Bay rolled his eyes. "At least let me pay you."

"Keep it," King yelled. He leaned in and kissed the prince deeply, right there in the hall. When the kiss ended, King looked back at Bay. "The prince is happy to have my company, and *he* will take good care of me. Let's go."

Just like that, they disappeared around the corner, leaving Bay standing in the hall with his mouth gaping.

He shook his head in disbelief. "What in the hell just happened?"

BAY LOOKED at the clock on his bedside table for what felt like the twentieth time. The green LED lights glowed 9:46 a.m. As dawn had slowly approached, Bay had lain awake, watching the small bits of light creeping in from under the blackout draperies.

In bed for over six hours now, Bay had not had one minute of sleep. The events of the evening had played over and over in his mind. How sweet and sensitive King had been. The foot rub. The kiss. Bay's panic attack when things got a little heated. But mostly how guilty he felt after he'd rejected King, especially given that Bay had initiated the kiss. It had obviously hurt him, but Bay couldn't figure out why. King had said many of his calls did not involve sex, so why should this one matter? The thought popped into his mind that maybe King did like him, but he immediately decided against it. King was doing his job, pure and simple. And he was damn good at it. And besides, King had already said he did it for the money.

After Bay had analyzed the evening from every angle, he moved on to his feelings regarding King. Trying, at the very least, to be honest with himself as he sorted through what he *was* and *wasn't* feeling. The problem was he was feeling a lot. King may not be into him, but Bay was without a doubt into King. Bay had enjoyed King's touch and the kiss. It was the *why* that bothered him. He was definitely attracted to King sexually, something he was unfamiliar with. Was it because King reminded him so much of Jack? Was it because King was confident and self-assured and everything Bay wasn't? Or was it as simple as chemistry?

Bay really didn't care whether he was gay, straight, or bisexual. Over the years he'd never really given much thought to his sexuality. He wasn't wired that way. Certainly not in terms of choosing which sex he was attracted to. He had only engaged in sexual activity with women on those few occasions because that was what presented itself. He hadn't gone out looking for it; it had just sort of ended up in his lap, and he'd felt like to keep up his alter-ego charade, he'd had to go with it. He wouldn't say they were bad experiences, but he hadn't felt like he did when he was with King. Intrigued. Interested. Engaged. Aroused. All things that were never a part of his life. Especially the last one.

Bay sighed and hopped out of bed, trotted across the bedroom, retrieved his laptop, and crawled back under the covers. He was about to give in to something he been restraining himself from doing all night. His laptop came to life, and the light of the screen filled the dark room. With trembling fingers, he typed *King Slater* into the Google search window, and within seconds King's handsome face stared back at him. As he scrolled, all sorts of pictures filled the screen. King posing with tons of obvious fans, most of them drooling over him. King smiling broadly as he held some type of award. King posing with other scantily clad guys who were probably other porn stars. But the one that caught his eye was King dressed in a gladiator costume. His body was way more developed than Bay remembered from the strip-poker game. Clothes did not do King Slater justice. His body was an amazing work of art, crafted and sculpted to perfection.

Again, Bay wondered why someone like King would want someone like him. It *had* to be the money, didn't it? But King had turned down his money last night. Of course he was getting a lot more from the prince than Bay had agreed to pay him, so he was definitely covered. But if it wasn't the money, there could only be one other option: King saw Bay as a challenge. Had anyone ever initiated an encounter and then rejected King before? Could it be that his ego was bruised? Or…. Another possibility popped into Bay's mind. Bay had quickly declared he was straight because, well, he thought he was. Could King be out to prove him wrong?

With a still-trembling finger, Bay clicked on a site called RedTube that advertised unlimited free King Slater videos. A full page of thumbnail images of King with various other guys filled the screen. Bay spent the next hour or so scrolling through the videos, clicking on each of them, watching King fuck one good-looking guy after another. One particular video titled *King and Jared Flip Fuck* caught his attention. Curious as to what *flip fuck* meant, Bay clicked the video.

The scene opened with King and some guy seated on a couch in a very nice suite, fully clothed and looking very relaxed. Someone from behind the camera introduced King and then his costar, Jared Walker. He did a brief interview with both men, and Bay thought King's confidence and charisma came through loud and clear. Jared, on the other hand, seemed shy and a little reserved.

After some small talk, King finally reached over, pulled Jared close, and kissed him gently. Then King deepened the kiss, and Jared's shyness seemed to quickly fade. Jared gripped King at the base of his neck, pulled him closer, and wrapped his arms around King's back. For a split second, Bay remembered what King's kiss had felt like, and he experienced a pang of jealousy that surprised him. He pushed it to the back of his mind and kept his eyes glued to the screen. King and Jared removed each other's shirts without ever breaking their kiss as the scene unfolded in front of Bay. Jared unbuckled King's belt and unfastened King's pants. They fell to the floor, and King was down to his underwear.

Jared broke the kiss long enough to drop to his knees and remove King's shoes and socks. King stepped out of the pants pooling at his feet, and in one fluid movement, Jared reached up and pulled King's underwear down. Bay gasped as King's length broke free and Jared took it into his mouth. He moved slowly and deliberately, drawing long and continuous moans out of King, and King's already impressive length seemed to grow each time Jared withdrew and then swallowed him again. A few more moves and King's skin was pulled so tight it looked as though he might pop at any second. King pulled Jared to his feet and finished undressing him, then ended up on top of Jared on the couch.

King took Jared into his mouth and repeated what Jared had done to him. Then with the greatest of ease, King had Jared's legs over his head and was licking him in places Bay had never considered licking or being licked. Bay suddenly felt like he'd been living under a rock for most of his life and then quickly realized that was pretty close to the truth.

As King licked and prodded Jared with his tongue, Jared threw his head back and closed his eyes, but he gyrated under King, almost trembling. The next scene, apparently cut and edited, had King's sheathed length positioned at Jared's opening, and King slowly pushing in.

Jared had a tight grip on the back of King's thighs, seemingly guiding him. When King was totally seated, he held that position for a few seconds and then started moving slowly in and out of Jared. Bay had a hard time believing, even as it unfolded in front of him, that Jared was actually taking King's length. He didn't know a body could stretch that much. King picked up speed gradually until he was moving with vigor and pounding Jared relentlessly. Jared, in turn, seemed to be enjoying the beating and responded with continual grunts and whimpers.

King finally withdrew from Jared, removed his condom, and stood. He leaned over and kissed Jared deeply, then walked around, climbed onto the back of the couch, and positioned himself on his knees, spread-eagle, his long arms supporting his upper body on the couch cushions. King was essentially offering his ass to Jared, and Bay suddenly didn't want to watch any longer, but he couldn't look away.

King turned his head back and Jared kissed him as Jared rolled on a condom. He positioned himself behind King and slowly pushed in. King moaned and arched his back as Jared entered him. Something about King in that position—arching his back, submitting to Jared, and making those sounds—made the blood rush to Bay's groin.

Jared seated himself and then pulled out again. He leaned over and ran his tongue over King's opening as though he was trying to soothe a sting or pain associated with the intrusion. King moaned as Jared entered him again. This time Jared didn't withdraw. He slid back a bit and then plowed in again. King's head hung down, and he grunted as Jared pounded his ass.

Bay pictured himself in Jared's position. With each thrust, Bay's cock stiffened until he was harder than he'd ever been. Jared suddenly withdrew, walked around the couch, and lay down. King climbed on top of Jared and impaled himself on Jared's awaiting rock-hard length.

King rode Jared, grinding and moving rhythmically, keeping time with Jared's movements. Jared was stroking King's cock in slow, steady strokes, and before Bay even realized it, he had his own erection in hand and was pumping in time with King and Jared's actions. King finally threw his head back and grunted repeatedly as he came on Jared's chest. Bay pumped himself harder and was soon milking his own release as Jared milked King's. But while Bay's orgasm was over, King's lingered. King closed his eyes and shuddered and trembled for a couple of minutes more, with Jared still moving inside him.

When the effects of King's orgasm were finally over, he lifted off Jared, stripped Jared's condom, and stroked Jared until he came. King leaned over and kissed him deeply, and the scene faded away.

Bay went into the bathroom and cleaned up. When he came back, he sat on the edge of the bed and rested his head in his hands. He was even more confused now. He'd just gotten off to a gay porn video staring King Slater. *Yup, Bay. You're definitely bisexual at the very least.*

After a few long, agonizing minutes, Bay looked at the clock again. It was nearing noon, and he had to meet Rachel, his assistant, downstairs in just over an hour for a two o'clock book signing at the Barnes & Noble at Caesars Palace. *At least the book signing will be a distraction.*

Bay marched back into the bathroom and turned on the shower. While he waited for the water to warm, he stared at his reflection in the mirror. *Jesus, Bay, you look like shit.* He patted the circles that had formed under his eyes and sighed. *Maybe a shower will help.*

An hour later, Bay was dressed and in the foyer, looking in the mirror, practicing his mantra. Unfortunately the shower hadn't helped his appearance, and after trying every facial cream his stylist had forced on him, he'd given up. But it was time to transform from the nerdy Bay Whitman to the confident Jack Robbins before he ventured outside his suite. *Deep breaths, Bay. You can do this.*

When he made it downstairs, his assistant was waiting for him.

"What the hell happened to you?" Rachel asked.

"A long night," Bay said. "And don't ask."

CHAPTER SIX

KING WOKE with the prince's lips still wrapped around his flaccid dick. He tried to clear the fog from his head so he could decide how he was going to get out of this one without the obvious consequences, but after a few minutes of deliberation, he gave up and slowly shifted his weight and inched his midsection away from the prince. The prince stirred, and King froze. Thankfully the prince didn't wake. King eased out of bed, gathered his clothes and shoes, and tiptoed across the room. He quietly opened the bedroom door, closed it behind him, and blinked against the daylight filling the large hotel suite.

After dressing, King opened the door to the hallway, and of course the three thugs were still standing guard. They eyed him suspiciously, frisked him, and sent him on his merry way. This was one job King was happy to see end.

The prince had turned out to be one voracious lover—not a bad lover, but a hungry one—and he had put King through the wringer until late morning. King's original plan was to get the hell out of Dodge as soon as the prince had finished with him and his obligations had been fulfilled, but it was now apparent they had both fallen asleep out of sheer exhaustion—midaction.

It was now after two in the afternoon, and King was fighting to keep his eyes open as he drove down the Las Vegas Strip. To make matters worse, he had one more shoot before he returned to New York tomorrow afternoon. The sex part of the shoot was scheduled for six o'clock tonight, and the last scene was scheduled to be shot in a secluded little park a mile or so off the Las Vegas Strip tomorrow morning around ten.

Maybe—just maybe—if King hurried, he might be able to get a couple hours of sleep before the film crew arrived.

King pulled up in front of Caesars Palace, handed the keys to the valet, and took his claim check. As he sauntered through the casino toward the elevators, his stomach growled loudly, reminding him that he hadn't eaten anything since last night in Bay's suite... and he'd certainly worked that off by 6:00 a.m.

The thought of Bay squashed his appetite. He was still a little pissed off and quite honestly hurt at how Bay had led him on and then rejected him. *The nerve of that guy.* It was obvious to King that Bay was attracted to him. Bay might not want to be gay and that was why he'd rejected King, but Bay was at least bisexual, whether or not he'd ever acted on it. King had no doubts about that.

If the truth be told, though, none of that was why he'd left with the prince. He'd left for self-preservation. He'd connected to Bay on a level he normally didn't connect with a john. He'd allowed Bay to get to him—to get under his skin. When he'd realized that, he knew Bay could be dangerous to his recovery—*strictly business, don't care, don't want*—and he had to get out of there.

On an emotional level, King didn't like the way he'd felt when he realized Bay was embarrassed to be seen with him. For the first time since he was a kid, he'd felt small and undeserving, like with those bullies back in school. King picked up his pace as if to distance himself from his emotions. *People pay damn good money to be in your presence. You don't need this guy, King. Fuck him. Just fuck him.*

"Get yourself a sandwich and go to bed," King mumbled to himself. "Maybe when you wake up, this will all seem like a bad dream."

On the way to the food court at the Forum Shops at Caesars, King slowed when he saw a crowd of people surrounding several Greek statues posed in the middle of a fountain. The people were staring at the statues as though they were waiting for something to happen. Curiosity got the best of him and he stopped and stood along with them.

Just then, the forum lights dimmed, and the statues, one by one, seemingly came to life. Then he remembered where he was. *The Fall of Atlantis. You read about this in one of those tourist magazines in your hotel room.*

As the statues began to speak and move, he was entranced by the animatronics. When other statues rose from the depths of the fountain's pool, surrounded by mist and fog, swords flaming and fireballs exploding, he *ooh*ed and *aah*ed in amazement right along with the rest of the crowd.

The show ended about ten minutes later, and King felt lighter somehow. He waded through the crowds walking past one high-end jewelry or clothing store after another and then hit a brick wall of people gathered in front of the Barnes & Noble bookstore. They were all standing in some sort of line that stretched out into the mall area, and King realized it must be some celebrity book signing or something. In addition to all the people, three news crews were filming the entire thing.

He made his way through the crowd and stopped dead in his tracks when he saw a large poster on an easel outside the door—with Bay's picture on it. "Meet *New York Times* best-selling author Bay Whitman from 2:00 p.m. to 4:00 p.m. today."

"Bay *Whitman*?" King mouthed. *What the fuck?* King searched the depths of his memory and vaguely remembered either reading or seeing something about Bay and his novels a while back. Why hadn't he made the connection?

Curiosity got the best of King. He pushed past the stanchion guides holding back the hundreds of waiting people and walked into the bookstore. In the center of the store was a large table covered with Bay's books. King picked up the first one he came to and looked at the cover. The title was *Midnight Run*, and it had a picture of a guy in the distance running toward darkness, a pistol in his hand, looking back over his shoulder as if someone were chasing him. The guy looked vaguely familiar but his face was shaded in the darkness. The subtitle read *A Jack Robbins Novel*.

King walked to the register, paid for the book, and tucked it under one arm while he looked for a place where he had a good view of Bay but Bay couldn't see him. Bay was obviously in PR mode. He was totally animated—smiling, interacting with his fans, taking pictures, and signing books. He was dressed in a dark gray suit with a light gray dress shirt and a silver-and-gray tie that accentuated the silver at his temples. He looked incredible, and it was apparent from the faces of Bay's adoring fans that King wasn't the only one who thought so.

But King's mouth dropped open and he sucked in a breath when he focused on the life-size cardboard cutout of someone who looked an awful lot like him, positioned next to Bay's table. As King studied it, he realized there were a few subtle differences, but the hair color, the height, the eyes, the dimples, the beard, even what the image was wearing, were all him. It was uncanny. Had he been duped? All sorts of scenarios ran through his head, and he became angrier and angrier. Had Bay Whitman stolen King's identity to create a book character? Had their chance meeting been arranged? Could Bay have been lying to him all along?

All the adoring fans and everyone else in Barnes & Noble faded away, and it was just he and Bay. King's hands trembled, and he clenched his fists tightly as his heart rate steadily rose.

King straightened his shoulders, and his feet began to move before he even consciously made the decision to walk. Before he knew it, he was standing in front of Bay's table. When Bay looked up and saw him, he froze midsignature, and the blood drained from his face. The woman whose book Bay was signing did a double take. She looked at the cardboard cutout and then King and then the cutout again. Surprise and shock consumed her face, but before King could say one single word, she yelled, "Oh my God! It's Jack Robbins."

In a split second, every eye in the place was fixed on King. Another fan yelled, "She's right. Jack Robbins *is* here." In an instant, King was surrounded by men and woman waving their books and magic markers in front of him.

"Please sign my book, Jack."

"No," another fan said. "Sign mine. I'm your biggest fan."

King looked from the crowd to Bay, and Bay seemed to be as shocked as he was.

What the fuck?

Bay's eyes seemed to be pleading for King to go along with this charade, and suddenly King wasn't sure what to do. He didn't know why, but for some stupid reason he sympathized with Bay. Besides, these fans were sort of crazy, and if they turned on him, it could get ugly. For him and for Bay.

He hadn't given Bay a chance to explain, so he didn't want to jump the gun, but damn he was still pissed. King finally sighed in defeat and turned to the crowd. He flashed a big smile and threw his hands up. "Okay, everyone. There is no need to rush. There's enough Jack Robbins to go around."

King's eyes briefly met Bay's, and Bay smiled nervously. He appeared to be caught between *go with this* and *run like hell*, and King didn't know which. But it was too late now. King was all-in. Oh, King wasn't letting Bay off the hook this easy. He had some serious explaining to do when this was over.

A professional-looking woman standing behind the table pulled up a second chair, and King sat next to Bay. He signed Jack Robbins's name on book after book, until his fingers felt like limp noodles. When the last man stepped up to the table and handed his book to Bay, Bay signed it and slid it over to King.

"Hi, guys," the man said, looking at King. "You looked awful familiar to me when you walked into the store. I couldn't quite place you, but now I know who you are."

King looked at Bay nervously. Bay seemed as close to the verge of panic as King was. It was obvious to King this guy was gay, and now he was going to bust King.

"I thought Jack Robbins was a made-up character," the guy said. "But the minute you stood next to the life-size cutout, I knew exactly who you were. Knowing you are real is going to make this read a lot more enjoyable for me. If you know what I mean."

The guy winked at King, and King *did* know what he meant, but Bay still seemed to be oblivious. *Bay* must *be straight—and blind if he's not picking up on this.*

It was after four when the woman who'd seated King thanked everyone for coming and whisked King and Bay off to an employee lounge. "What the hell, Bay?" she asked, smiling at King. "Who is this, and why were you holding out on me? I could have publicized the hell out of this."

"Rachel, meet King Slater." Bay looked at King. "King, this is my assistant, Rachel Leonard. I'm sorry, Rachel, but... I... well.... Oh, never mind. I'll explain later. Would you mind giving King and me a minute to talk in private?"

Rachel glanced back and forth between Bay and King with a confused expression, but she nodded and seconds later slipped out of the door, closing it behind her.

King folded his arms and waited.

"King," Bay said, "I know what this must look like."

King didn't respond, but he kept his gaze plastered on Bay's, waiting for an explanation.

Bay looked around before he spoke. "I certainly don't want to get into this here, but I want you to know I had no idea you existed until a couple of days ago when you showed up at my suite. I really did win you in a poker game."

King felt a little relief at Bay's admission, but the skeptic in him wouldn't allow him to take Bay at his word. *I mean... come on. This is a very big coincidence.*

King simply stared at Bay.

"Can we get out of here?" Bay asked. "I'd like to explain further."

Looking at his watch, King realized he had under two hours before the shoot. *There goes my nap.* He sighed. "Come on."

King opened the door, and Bay smiled weakly with apparent relief. Bay said a few words to Rachel and then nodded at King, who led him to the front of the store and out into the mall.

"When we get back to my hotel room, you owe me food" was all King said.

"Whatever you want," Bay said.

"*Whatever* I want?" King clarified.

Bay sighed. "Yeah. Whatever you want. I owe you—big-time."

King smiled. "And I'm certainly gonna cash in."

King suddenly had an idea that might confirm his thoughts about Bay's sexuality, and now that he had Bay eating out of his hand, why not see where it led?

BAY'S HANDS shook so badly, he stuck them in his pants pockets as they rode the elevator in complete silence and then walked down the hotel hallway. Bay swallowed the lump in his throat when King slid his keycard through the door lock and paused. The light turned green, and King pushed the door open and walked in.

Bay followed, and when King stopped abruptly and turned, Bay almost ran into him.

King cupped Bay's face and kissed him deeply. His tongue roamed every part of Bay's mouth, and although Bay was definitely turned on by it, it was still a bit strange.

When the kiss ended, King simply said, "The down payment. Oh, and you look great by the way. That tie brings out the silver in your hair."

Bay smiled halfheartedly, suddenly understanding the full gravity of what he'd agreed to earlier. But if he didn't go through with this and King decided to go public, it could ruin everything. If King claimed Bay somehow stole his identity and it came out that Jack Robbins was based on a gay porn star, it could quite possibly put an end to his movie deal and the Jack Robbins series.

Bay heard King talking in the background, and he walked into the room expecting to see another person, but King was on the telephone ordering food.

King hung up, took off his jacket, and kicked off his shoes.

"King," Bay said, holding his hands up.

"Not a word until I get a shower," King snapped.

Bay nodded, realizing King must have just gotten back from his night with the prince when he'd walked into Barnes & Noble, and he was suddenly very happy King was going to shower.

King disappeared into the bedroom, and Bay took a seat on the small couch and looked around the room uneasily. It wasn't near as big as his suite, but it was nice enough.

Bay's heart raced, and his knees bounced, both things that happened when he was extremely nervous. His hands were still trembling, and he plastered them on top of his kneecaps and forced his knees and hands to still. *You've got to calm down, Bay! Get a hold of yourself. What's the worst that could happen?*

When Bay thought about all the possibilities, his condition deteriorated drastically. *You've got to find a way to make him understand Jack was just a character you developed a long time ago. But how?* The fact that Bay had hit it big with Jack was just a fluke. Before he could come up with a plan, King appeared wearing nothing but a towel wrapped around his hips. His hair was wet and hanging loosely over his forehead, and his broad chest glistened.

"Well?" King said.

CHAPTER SEVEN

BAY STOOD and bounced from one foot to the other, anxious to try to explain, but King walked over to him, smiling seductively as he grabbed a handful of Bay's package and then kissed him again. Bay jumped at the unexpected groping, a little weak in the knees, then felt King smile against his lips. *Fuck. King is toying with me. He's actually enjoying this.*

King stepped away and walked over to the mini fridge. He retrieved a bottle of beer and held it up in Bay's direction. "Sorry I don't have scotch."

Bay nodded. He needed *something* to take the edge off. King twisted off the cap, handed the beer to Bay, and got another for himself. He held the longneck up to his lips, tilted his head back, and downed the entire beer without pause, his Adam's apple bobbing with each gulp.

King tossed the empty bottle in the trash, turned to Bay, loosened the towel, and let it fall to the ground. "I guess I'm ready."

Bay again swallowed what seemed to be a permanent lump that had formed in his throat since he'd met King Slater. "Don't I even get a chance to explain?"

"They'll be time for that later," King said. "Right now I have other things in mind."

Bay's heart dropped to the pit of his stomach. King walked to him, slid Bay's suit coat over his shoulders, and tossed it on the couch. He then loosened Bay's tie, unbuttoned the top button of Bay's shirt, and patted his chest. He leaned in close and whispered, "That's better. Don't ya think?"

Before Bay could answer, there was a knock on the door. King stepped away, still completely naked, and opened it. "Hey, guys. Right on time. Come on in."

King watched four guys with large black carrying cases invade King's suite and begin to set up what looked like cameras, monitors, and lighting. "Fellas, meet Bay Whitman. He's a buddy of mine, and he'll be observing today's shoot."

Each of the guys acknowledged Bay with a nod but continued setting up their equipment.

"Can I have a word with you?" Bay asked. "In private?"

King walked into his bedroom, and Bay followed. "Yeah?" King asked.

"What's this all about?" Bay asked, trying to disguise the anger in his voice.

"Well," King said, "today I got to see what you do for a living, so I think it's only fair you get to see what I do for a living."

"Is this some sort of joke?" Bay asked.

"Not at all," King said. "But it's pretty interesting to me how you can go from 'I'll do anything. I owe you,' to 'is this some sort of a joke' in less than an hour."

King had a point. Although Bay certainly wasn't going to admit that to him. "So you're going to force me to watch gay porn?"

King smiled. "I can't force you to do anything. You're free to go if you like."

Bay was flooded with relief.

"But if you do," King said, "you'll be hearing from my attorney."

"Shit!" Bay hissed under his breath. "If you would just let me explain, I could clear all this up and be on my way, and you could do your shoot without an audience."

King smiled again. "I don't mind an audience."

"You're not serious?"

"I'm very serious," King said adamantly. "If you want to explain to me how my identity and likeness just happen to be the main character in your famous novels, I suggest you wait around, because right now I have a job to do."

"King?" a voice said from the living room. "We're ready for you."

"I'll be right in," King answered. He looked at Bay. "The choice is yours. Stay or go."

King started to walk past Bay, and Bay laid a hand on his arm. "And if I go?"

"To use language you'll probably understand, I guess the chips will fall where they may."

King shrugged off Bay's hand, which was still resting on his arm, and started for the living room.

"Damn," Bay mumbled, following him but not sure what to do.

King smiled and rubbed his hands together. "Let's get this party started, gentlemen. Oh and I hope you don't mind Bay's being here. He won't get in the way. I promise."

The crew looked at each other and shrugged.

Feeling like he didn't really have much of a choice now, Bay smiled weakly and took a seat in the corner.

A man with a large leather kit—undoubtedly the makeup person—stepped up and looked closely at King. "Jesus, King. Have you been up all night?"

"Maybe," King said, looking directly at Bay. "But you're the best in the biz, Joey. I'm sure you'll make me look extremely well rested."

Frowning, Joey said, "I am the best, but I'm not a miracle worker."

King rolled his eyes. Joey gestured for him to sit on the arm of the couch in easy reach. King sat, closed his eyes, and offered his face up to Joey.

As Bay watched nervously, Joey eyed King and nibbled on the tip of his forefinger, apparently trying to decide what King needed. He fumbled in his makeup kit, opened a small jar, and smeared something under King's eyes. Joey reached in again and came out with an airbrush tool. Bay remembered the makeup team at *Good Morning America* using the same device on him once. Joey pinched King's cheeks a few times, and then sprayed his entire face. He took a step back, then stepped up again, reached for another jar of something, rubbed it through King's hair, and picked at it a few times.

He stepped back again and stared. "That's as good as it's gonna get."

King opened his eyes and looked at himself in the hand mirror Joey offered him. "Nice," he said. "I look ten years younger. Thanks a lot, Joey."

"No problem," Joey said. "But get some rest before the next shoot. Okay?"

"Yes, sir."

Bay heard a door open, and a handsome and totally naked man walked out of the powder room.

King jumped to his feet. "Hey, Sam," he said, wrapping his arms around the guy. "It's great to see you."

"Ditto," Sam replied with an easy smile.

Turning to Bay, King said, "Bay Whitman, meet Sam Steele. He's an old friend."

"By 'old,' he means we met a year ago," Sam said to Bay as he crossed the room. "Nice to meet you, Bay."

"You know what I mean," King explained. "A year is like a lifetime in our business."

"True dat," Sam said with a fist bump.

Bay stood and shook Sam's hand. He was amazed how comfortable these guys all seemed to be, walking around naked as jaybirds.

"Bay... Whitman? Bay Whitman?" Sam mumbled. "Oh shit! Bay Whitman! You're *the* Bay Whitman. I've seen you on television. I love your Jack Robbins novels." He pumped Bay's hand several more times. "I've read every one."

"Thank you," Bay said shyly, backing away and taking his seat again, wanting to disappear or at the very least fade into the background.

Sam looked between Bay and King. "How do you know Bay?" Sam asked.

King eyed Bay again. *Oh no. Please don't let him go there.* Bay tried to plead his case with his eyes.

King looked back at Sam. "Long story, but I'll fill you in sometime."

Bay sighed with relief. But that relief was short-lived.

Sam smiled at King and patted him on the back. "You whore dog, you."

"Yeah. That's me," King said, smiling at Bay. "The old whore dog."

After studying Bay again, Sam winked at King. "Man, you're one *lucky* whore dog is all I'll say about that." Seeming satisfied now, Sam rubbed his hands together. "So what's the gig? All they told me was it was a two-day shoot."

"Not two full days," one of the crew, who Bay assumed was the director, said. "We shoot here tonight and then in a small park we found off the Strip tomorrow morning."

"Got it," Sam said.

The director continued. "The premise of the shoot is that you and King are longtime friends, but you're straight, and King is openly gay. In the first scene, you're playing touch football with some friends in the park and having a great time. Except you tackle King, and he gets up with an obvious erection. He tries to hide it, but you see it before he can adjust it. See, King has had a crush on you, and later when you press him about his erection, he finally confesses. You say you're flattered but straight and not interested in him that way. But—when you get home, drink a beer, and relax, you start thinking about King's admission. You eventually fall asleep on the couch and have a sexual dream about King. Today we're shooting the dream sequence, and tomorrow we'll shoot the scene in the park and the admission."

Bay shook his head and looked at the floor. *Are you kidding me? It's as if King planned this whole straight guy, gay guy thing.*

"I see," Sam said, wiggling his eyebrows. "You mean all I have to do is lie back and let King seduce me?"

"That's it," the director said.

"Yes! I've been dying to bottom for King. Besides, in my last six shoots, I've been stuck on top, and frankly I'm tired of doing all the work."

"A man after my own heart," King said. "You know how I hate to bottom."

As Bay observed King and Sam having a random conversation buck naked, he wondered if this was the norm for porn stars.

"Put these on, guys," Joey instructed, interrupting Bay's thoughts as he handed Sam and King tank tops, gym shorts, socks, and sneakers.

After both men were dressed, Joey sprayed what Bay thought was water on their shirts near the underarm and chest areas; he guessed it was to make it look like they'd been sweating.

"So, Sam," the director said, handing him a gym bag, "you're gonna walk in the door, drop your gym bag on the floor, grab a beer out of the fridge, take a seat on the couch, and put your feet up. I want you to take a few swigs of your beer and then place it on the table, lay your head back, and close your eyes. You'll be remembering King's confession. Don't worry, we'll drop in the scene from tomorrow when he actually tells you, and then you fall asleep. From there King will take it."

King rubbed his hands and flashed a sinister smile.

"King, I want you to position yourself at the ottoman, and we're gonna fade you in," the director said. "You'll start by removing Sammy's sneakers and slowly massaging his feet."

King looked at Bay sitting silent in the corner. "I've done that a time or two."

"Man. This is getting better and better," Sam added.

"Now Sam, you're gonna stir and moan a little but not really wake up. And then when King removes your socks, he's gonna lick the bottom of your foot from your heel up to your toes and that's when you're gonna wake. You're gonna jerk your foot and try to pull it away, and King is gonna tell you to relax, it's all gonna be okay."

"Got it," Sam said.

"I sure hope you washed your feet today, Sam."

"Showered about an hour ago," Sam admitted. "So you're in good shape."

Bay was shocked. He'd never even dreamed of licking someone's foot. But this was clearly a world with which he was, in no uncertain terms, unfamiliar.

"Positions," the director said. Sammy picked up his gym bag and went into the hall while King stayed out of camera range.

"Action."

CHAPTER EIGHT

SAMMY WALKED in the door, looking flustered and a little tired. He dropped his gym bag, opened the mini fridge, removed a beer, twisted the cap off, and sat on the couch. He propped up his feet and took a few gulps of his drink. For a moment, he stared off into the distance, and then he took another long pull off the beer and put the bottle on the table. After he swallowed, he leaned his head back and closed his eyes.

"Cut!" the director called. "Nice job, Sammy, but remember. One of your best friends has just told you he's been secretly in love with you for years. Think about how that would make you feel."

Sammy looked like he was considering the question. "At first I think I would be angry."

"Why?" the director asked.

"Because now that I know how he feels, nothing will ever be the same again. And I'll feel differently toward him."

"Exactly," the director said. "Now take it one step further. What if you actually consider it, just for a second, and then dismiss it right before you fall asleep?"

"I can do that," Sammy said. "Let's try this again."

"Okay. Positions."

Sam went into the hall again, and the director called, "Action."

After repeating his earlier actions, the actor plopped down on the couch and put his feet up. He gazed at the wall in front of him. "King? In love with me?" he mumbled. "How did that happen? When?"

He furrowed his brow, appearing to mull it over without reaching any conclusion. Finally Sam cursed, "Oh hell. Fuck him. Now he's ruined everything. Now that I know, how can anything ever be the same between us?" Sam laid his head back and closed his eyes. "King and me? Na. That's ridiculous."

"Cut," the director yelled. "That was perfect. Now King. Get on your hands and knees at the ottoman and we'll fade you in."

King did as he was told.

"Action!"

After slowly untying Sam's sneakers, King gently slipped one off and then the other. Sammy stirred a little but didn't wake.

King started to massage Sam's feet. He used his thumbs to knead Sam's arches while he squeezed and worked the rest of his foot with his fingers. From his vantage point, Bay couldn't see Sam's face, but the little sighs and moans escaping Sam's lips indicated he was enjoying the attention. Bay knew all too well how good it felt, having already been on the receiving end of one of King's foot rubs, and a wave of jealousy washed through him.

Sam then shifted a bit, and Bay finally caught a glimpse of his face. Judging by his euphoric expression, he was definitely enjoying what King was doing.

"That feels so good," Sam whispered to no one in particular.

King peeled one sock off and then the next. He leaned over and, starting at Sam's heel, ran his tongue all the way up the sole and sucked on Sam's big toe.

"Oh God," Sam said, opening his eyes. "What the hell?" When he saw King staring back at him, he freaked a little and tried to jerk his foot back. But King had a strong grip on him and held on tightly.

"Relax," King whispered. "It's all gonna be okay, Sam. I've been waiting for this for a long time."

Sam's expression indicated he was having some sort of internal debate. He eventually slowed his struggles but eyed King warily. King placed a kiss on the top of each of Sam's feet and continued the massage. Sam slowly relaxed into King's touch.

"Cut!" the director yelled. "Really good, guys. Really good. Now King. In the next scene, I would like you to massage Sam's feet a little more, until Sam realizes he's getting hard and starts playing with himself. Then I want you to push the ottoman out of the way and undress. Slowly and deliberately. And I want both you guys to hold eye contact until King is totally naked. Then Sam, I want you to slowly move your gaze down King's body until you get to his cock and stop there and hold until I cut again."

"Just give me a second to get ready," Sam said, slipping his hand down his shorts.

Bay was sort of fixated on Sam massaging himself, but he began to feel eyes on him. When Bay turned, King was watching him watching Sam. He saw something hiding just behind King's stare, but King looked away too quickly for Bay to identify it.

"Okay," Sam said. "Let's go before the old boy goes to sleep again."

King took his position at Sam's feet.

"Action!"

King started massaging Sam's feet again as Sam looked on, seemingly confused about why he was enjoying this.

Before last night, Bay hadn't seen any gay porn, but he thought Sam was doing a pretty good job of conveying what he was thinking and the director's vision.

Bay looked between the scene unfolding in front of him and the monitor as the camera zoomed in on Sam's erection. Sam started fondling himself as King continued to massage his feet. King finally stood, found Sam's eyes, locked on to them, and pushed the ottoman out of the way. He pulled his T-shirt over his head slowly and allowed it to drop onto the floor. Bay watched, mostly in awe, as King's chest filled the monitor. His chest and arms were impressive, and Bay could clearly see why King was so sought after. He looked great on camera.

King toed out of his shoes, removed his socks, and pulled down his gym shorts and underwear in one quick move. Completely naked, he stood before Sam in all his glory.

As directed, Sam dropped his eyes to King's midsection and held there. At first, Bay thought his expression was one of fear, but on second thought, he decided it wasn't fear at all. It was pure intimidation. Bay felt his pain. King was very well endowed, and Bay was sure he would feel the same way if he were in that position. And if King had his way, that might happen very soon. Bay forced that thought out of his head.

Bay turned his attentions back to King. He half expected the director to yell cut when King was naked, but King had already moved into position, kneeling in front of Sam.

"It's okay," King whispered, trying to reassure Sam.

Gripping Sam's shorts and underwear at the waist, King pulled them down and over Sam's feet and tossed them to the side. Bay knew then that Sam was a great actor because there was no way in hell he would have been intimidated by King's size. If at all possible, Sam was even more impressive than King. But to be fair, Sam was completely erect, and King was not all the way there yet.

King leaned forward, never breaking eye contact, and took Sam into his mouth. Sam sucked in a breath, threw his hands back, and gripped the couch, looking on in surprise. As King moved up and down his length,

Sam's expression became unreadable, which in Bay's opinion was very realistic. Having something feel so good when he wasn't sure he should be liking it would have Bay confused as well.

As soon as King slid all the way down and held that position, Sam's eyes seemed to roll back into his head, and he closed them and threw his head back. King fondled Sam's balls with his fingertips and teased, from what Bay could see from the monitor, the little patch of skin under them. Sam was now moaning and thrusting his hips forward. Whatever apprehension Sam had at the onset was now waning, and Sam finally looked as though he'd decided to let go.

Bay wondered if it would be that easy for him. Could he really enjoy someone pleasuring him solely for the way it felt? Regardless of who was giving the pleasure? He had apprehensively enjoyed the foot rub and King's kisses—after the initial shock, that is—but could he do more?

One of Sam's louder moans brought Bay out of his own head. When Bay looked closer, King had a finger in Sam, and Sam was not protesting. In fact, he seemed to be enjoying it, gyrating and pumping on King's finger. Then King inserted a second finger, and Bay's eyes widened in disbelief. *Oh shit!* Bay was suddenly starting to perspire. He loosened his cuffs and rolled his sleeves up a couple of turns.

In one quick move, King lifted Sam's legs, pushed them back, and held them there by the backs of Sam's thighs. Before Sam could protest or even react, King's face was buried in Sam's asscheeks, and Sam was purring like a big kitten. King licked up and down Sam's crack and then focused on Sam's opening with his tongue. Sam seemed even more animated now, and from the look of it, he was enjoying the attention immensely.

Bay wondered how Sam could give in so easily and then remembered he was watching two men act for a porn video. Of course he was going to give in. They had a limited number of minutes to make on-screen magic.

"Cut!" the director yelled again.

"Are you sure you just showered?" King said in a teasing tone.

Sam raised a hand, and King tried to dodge it, but Sam was too quick and caught King on the side of his head.

"Ow!" King said. "You are so gonna pay for that in the next scene."

"Promises, promises," Sam said.

The director handed King a condom and some lube. King prepared himself and Sam, and they both resumed their former positions.

"Action."

At some point during this sex show, Bay had changed locations to get a better look with no clear recollection when he'd done so. But now he was looking at King's back, and he could clearly see Sam's face.

King, still on his knees, held Sam's legs back and brushed his erection up and down Sam's opening. Sam appeared apprehensive, but he closed his eyes and gave himself over to King. King then positioned himself against Sam's opening and pushed in. Bay winced. Viewing it online and in person were two entirely different things. Bay was amazed that King's girth was able to fit inside Sam without ripping him wide open. But Sam wasn't bleeding to death, which Bay took as a good sign.

Sam gave a barely audible hiss at the penetration, and King apparently picked up on it and paused before easing all the way in, giving his partner time to adjust. Once King was deeply seated, he held his position for a few seconds and then started moving slowly. By this point, King was standing over Sam, his legs spread wide, holding Sam's ankles as Sam gripped the backs of King's thighs and guided him in and out. The discomfort on Sam's face morphed into something between pleasure and ecstasy.

King leaned down, and Sam gripped the back of his neck and pulled their lips together in a crushing kiss. When the kiss ended, King again straightened and picked up speed and vigor until he and Sam seemed to move as one. Sam's head rolled from side to side, one hand against King's chest while the other pumped his own length. From his new position, Bay saw King's ass muscles tighten and retract with each thrust. Bay was now hard as a rock himself. *What the fuck?*

Sam moaned louder and tensed as he shot his load onto his abdomen in several spurts, still pumping his cock feverishly. Seconds later, King pulled out of Sam and ripped off the condom. Something like a guttural moan escaped his lips. He started to shudder—almost convulse—as his release rushed through him and escaped, mixing with Sam's. King's orgasm seemed to go on and on, until his shudders became a tremble. King again leaned over and rested his forehead against Sam's, still breathing heavily, apparently trying to gather himself.

"Cut!" the director yelled.

"Man, I wish I could experience an orgasm like you," Sam said. "The damn reverberations seem to go on forever."

Before King could respond, the director interrupted. "Hey, guys. We have a shot here to finish."

"Oh yeah," Sam said. "Sorry, Mr. Director Man."

"Yeah right," the director said, rolling his eyes. "King, please put the ottoman back in place and step out of the frame. And Sam, put your feet on the ottoman, lean your head back, close your eyes as if you are still sleeping, and hold your cock in your hand. When you wake, you are alone and realized you just beat off to King in your dream."

"Got it," Sam said.

"Action!"

Bay tugged at his erection, which was now obvious through his tented suit pants. When he looked up, King was watching him and smiling sarcastically. *You are so busted, Bay!*

Sam finished the scene as described, and the director yelled, "Cut. That's a wrap. Great job, guys. Thank you."

King walked over and offered Sam a fist bump. "Good job, man."

Sam returned the gesture. "Hey. You did all the work."

"But you did the acting," King added. "And you were damn good at it."

Fifteen minutes later, Sam and the film crew were packed up and saying their goodbyes. They finally departed, leaving behind Bay and King and a lot of silence.

CHAPTER NINE

KING TOOK Sam's former position on the couch, breathed deeply, and tried to calm his heart rate as the residual waves of his orgasm lingered. From across the room, he could feel Bay's eyes on him, but neither of them spoke.

As the silence stretched out, King thought about Bay's reaction to the scene he'd witnessed. Near the end, Bay had had an erection that could have rivaled King's own. *I knew it! My plan worked perfectly.* All that insistence about being straight was just part of whatever game Bay was playing.

Although King had to admit he'd been on set with a couple of straight cameramen who by the time the scene was done had massive erections. He figured it must be the amount of testosterone flowing through the room. But none of those cameramen had ever initiated a kiss or had their tongues down King's throat. Bay's expression had given him away. He was actually getting into it.

"Do all your orgasms last that long?" Bay finally asked in a quiet voice.

King raised his head and looked at Bay. "As a matter of fact, they do. What of it?"

"Just curious. It looked rather intense."

King pushed himself up from the couch and started for his bedroom. "It was. They all are."

He stopped when he heard Bay's voice again.

"Can we talk now?"

"I need another shower first," King said, loving toying with Bay. He knew he was probably being vindictive, but hey—what's good for the goose. Bay had been cruel to him by leading him on with no intentions of following through, so it was time he paid the piper.

King would never force Bay to have sex with him whatever the outcome of their conversation, but it was sure fun making Bay think he might. "After I shower I'll listen to what you have to say before we... uh, you know."

Bay's expression of surprise and discomfort was gratifying. King smiled and headed to the bathroom.

When King returned ten minutes later, still naked, Bay was pacing the small living room like a caged tiger.

Bay turned and saw King standing in the doorway. He looked King up and down, stopping again at his midsection wide-eyed. King didn't miss the gesture and even felt a little proud. *Fuck yeah! A straight man is staring at my junk.*

King chuckled to himself and pointed to the couch. "Sit."

Bay sat without question, and King continued. "You now know I'm a celebrity of sorts. And to be truthful, I'm not sure you haven't known that all along. But I have a brand. And you, my friend, have infringed on my brand by using my likeness to sell your books."

King took a seat next to Bay.

"You've got one shot to tell me what the hell is going on here and convince me to not call my lawyer."

Bay sighed. "Can you at least put some clothes on?"

"No, I cannot," King said. "I'm very comfortable naked. Am I making you nervous?"

"Yes!" Bay said.

"Good. Now talk! Unless—" King wiggled his eyebrows and reached over and squeezed Bay's knee. "—you'd rather do something else until you find your voice."

"King," Bay said with obvious hesitation. "Jack Robbins is and always has been a character of my imagination. A character I created out of—well… I created. And let's just leave it at—"

"A character out of your imagination who just happens to look exactly like me. Same height. Same build. Same hair. Same eyes."

"Yes!" Bay said. "But that book cover was a computer-generated model based on my description of Jack in the first book."

King shook his head. "A description that looks almost identical to me. That's pretty damn hard to believe."

"But it's the truth," Bay pleaded. "I swear to you, King. When I opened my suite door that night and saw you standing in the hall. I was dumfounded. I couldn't believe I was looking at a living, breathing Jack Robbins."

Considering Bay's admission, King had a hard time believing this was simply one hell of a coincidence. On the other hand, Bay didn't seem like the kind who could lie that easily. But he wasn't convinced yet.

Before King could speak, Bay stood and started pacing again. "King. The thing is, most people think the character of Jack Robbins is based on me and my life. The *me* they see on talk shows and at book signings. But the truth is, it's totally the other way around."

Bay paused.

"I'm listening," King said.

"Well. When I signed the contract to publish my first Jack Robbins novel with a top-tier publishing house, I was mostly in shock. I couldn't believe they thought a lot of people would want to read my stories, but they were right. The book took off practically overnight. I was elated that I could now do what I loved and might even be able to support myself." Bay stopped and looked at King. "Perfect, right?"

King opened his mouth, but before he could respond, Bay started talking again. *I guess that was a rhetorical question.*

"And it *was* good in the beginning," Bay went on. "I was making a decent amount of money, and I could write full-time. But it was all about to come crashing down around me."

"Wait a minute! You're famous. So how did it come crashing down around you?" King asked.

"By becoming just that. Famous."

King couldn't believe his ears. "Wait! What?"

"With the huge amount of success of the first novel, and the second one scheduled for release in six months, my publisher wanted me to go on a national book tour."

Bay stopped talking, grabbed a beer out of the minibar, and held it up to King. King nodded and Bay tossed it over to him and took out another. He popped the top and downed half, stopped and caught his breath, and downed the other half.

"I already told you I was a shy, nerdy kid. What I didn't tell you was I was a tortured shy, nerdy kid who sort of turned into a recluse. And needless to say, the thought of a national book tour kept the recluse in me awake night after night. How in the hell was I going to travel the country, manage the stress of meeting the public at book signings, and appear intelligent while being interviewed on radio and television shows?"

Bay sounded sincere, and King's original anger was beginning to wane. Was he actually starting to feel sorry for the guy?

"Anyway. That's when the idea came to me. In all fairness, I have to mention I was also in a panicked drunken stupor. Lying on my couch three sheets to the wind, I realized I'd created Jack Robbins. Why not be him? I mean… I knew the man inside and out. I was him and he was me. He was the better me, of course. The me I dreamed of being. So why not?"

Bay stopped pacing and sat next to King. He looked him in the eyes. "That night I slept for the first time in weeks. When I woke the next morning, I laughed off the entire idea—initially. But then I began to think about it seriously. And my conclusion was *why not?*

"In preparation for the tour, my publisher hired a stylist and a trainer for me, and I started going to the gym daily. I had my hair expertly cut and highlighted, got new tinted contact lenses, and bought a whole new wardrobe. I imagined how Jack would speak and practiced endlessly, and then I got to work on the mannerisms. With each passing day, Bay Whitman became Jack Robbins. At least in public. So you see, the idea was born strictly out of necessity, not vanity. It was out of desperation. The only way to keep my sanity and keep my success going."

King raised a skeptical eyebrow.

Bay sighed. "Come on, King. Think about it. My first Jack Robbins novel was written just under eight years ago. How long have you been in the public eye?"

King sat motionless while he considered the ramifications of the question. *Good point. If the dates check out—that is.* "A little over four years," he finally said.

"Shit. I don't know why I didn't think of this before. Do you have a laptop?"

"Yeah." King pointed to the desk across the room.

Bay retrieved the laptop and again took his seat next to King. "When did you first start doing porn?"

King did the math in his head. "May of 2013."

Bay tapped on the keyboard. "Before then, were you in the public eye at all?"

"No. Like I said, I was in sales."

Bay turned the laptop screen to King. "Look at this."

King studied the screen. It was an Amazon page with all of Bay's books listed. Bay clicked on his first Jack Robbins novel and pointed. "Look at the publication date."

King followed Bay's finger and read it. November of 2009.

"This proves I couldn't have modeled Jack Robbins after you."

Bay had a point. King *was* a nobody when Bay was first published. And who knows how long ago he'd started writing the novel before it even got published.

King sighed but didn't respond. The logical side of him was relieved, but the ego side was almost disappointed.

"Even if I watched lots and lots of gay porn, when Jack Robbins was created, you were not even on the scene."

King nodded. "You have to admit, though, this is a pretty big coincidence and very farfetched."

"I know. And I know what it all must look like to you," Bay admitted. "But I swear it's the truth. Even if you don't want to believe me, you can't ignore the facts."

King took a sip of his beer and swallowed. "I'm not quite sure what I believe," he admitted. "But I guess you're right."

"I swear to you, when I saw you standing outside my hotel room, I was dumbfounded."

"But…," King said, "you knew then and didn't say anything until I stumbled across you at Barnes & Noble."

Bay's gaze dropped to the ground. "I know, and I'm sorry for that."

"Are you?" King asked. "Or are you just sorry I found out on my own?"

Bay looked at King with the biggest puppy-dog eyes King had ever seen, and his heart started to melt.

"I know I should have told you right away, but I didn't quite believe it myself. I was so intrigued by all of this."

"Intrigued?" King asked.

"Look at it from my point of view? Just for a second?" Bay asked. "All these years you were a character in my head, and then one day you're real and standing in front of me. As I told you already, I created Jack as the man I wished I could be. From his looks and build to his confidence and swagger. I gave him the poise and socialization skills I lacked. And I was looking at that person. You. Me. Or a combination of both. It was a bit daunting."

King shook his head. "But you still could have said something."

Bay stood and started pacing again. "I know. I should have. I realize that now. But I wanted to know more about you. As a writer, I create characters all the time. But most of them are bits and pieces of me or people I know. When I create a new character, I usually take the best parts of the people I've met or even admire. And for an evil character, I do the same thing but multiply the bad ten times over. But as writers, we can only take a two-dimensional character so far. To have a living, breathing person standing in front of me—especially Jack Robbins—was too intriguing to pass up. And I blew my opportunity. And I disappointed you in the process. I'm sorry."

King considered Bay's explanation. It sort of made sense. "Then I guess I should apologize for jumping to conclusions."

"No," Bay said. "I would have done the same thing. And that's one of the things I was most worried about. I mean… I didn't really think this thing through. My original plan was to get what information I could from you and see if I could use any of it."

"And now?" King asked.

Bay stopped pacing and sat next to him again. "Now? I genuinely like you and I see how much of an ass I was for even considering that option. I'm really sorry."

King looked away and then back to Bay. "The problem is… where do we go from here? It's pure luck that no one has made a connection between me and Jack Robbins before now."

"I don't think anyone would make the connection unless you were seen or associated with me."

"Like at the bookstore." King admitted.

"Exactly. And if my publisher found out Jack Robbins was a gay porn star and escort, I don't know how they would react," Bay added. "My next three novels were just contracted to be made into movies."

"How many of your readers are gay?" King asked.

"I don't really know the answer to that," Bay admitted. "But no one has linked us so far. I know based on the fan mail I get that Jack has a huge following of women, and I'm sure there are some gay men out there too. But I seriously believe that if we hadn't been in the same place at the same time, no one would have put two and two together."

"Makes sense. So again. Where do we go from here?" King asked.

Bay seemed to be considering the question. "I guess you got your answers, so we can go back to our own separate lives."

Once more, silence lingered between them for a long time, and King wondered if Bay had said all he needed to say. Or was he waiting for King to respond or protest and ask him not to leave? A short time passed, and Bay still wasn't making a move, so maybe he *was* waiting for King to react in some way.

But what should he say? At this point King knew Bay's leaving would be the best thing for both of them, so why wasn't he asking Bay to go?

He'd been all set to stay angry at Bay and let the man walk out of his life, for both their sakes, but when he'd learned why Bay had created Jack Robbins, it struck a chord with him. A deep chord. Maybe that was why he wasn't throwing Bay out.

When Bay stood with a sigh, King realized he had to make a quick decision. Either say something or let Bay walk out. Bay had shared some pretty heavy shit with him, and Bay's honesty alone already made him more of a man than King was. Yup. He owed him at least an acknowledgment. *Fuck! This was all so much easier when I was pissed off at him.*

"Wait" was all King could think to say. Bay sat back down.

King rubbed his eyes in frustration. He was mentally and physically exhausted, and his emotions were all over the spectrum. As the anger had morphed into understanding, he'd realized he had been wrong to torture Bay by making him watch the scene between him and Sam. So what if Bay was gay or straight? It was none of King's business. Bay was a job. Nothing more. Nothing less. He'd had lots of calls that involved just kissing and conversation. But Bay had been giving him mixed signals—leading him on and then pulling back when things got heated.

He'd been angry. Pure and simple. But if he were being honest with himself, he also knew his ego had been bruised, and he was even a little hurt. At the moment, it was the *hurt* part of the equation that was most disturbing. Why did he care? Because he and Bay seemed to be fighting a lot of the same demons? Four years ago, King would have given anything to have a fictional character to hide behind. To be anyone but who he was. He knew how Bay felt, and that was having a deep and profound effect on him.

King slowly turned and locked eyes with Bay. The expression on Bay's weary face told King the truth was the only way to go at this point. Bay had been honest with him, and he owed the man at least an acknowledgment.

"I'm sorry you were forced to hide behind a fictional character," King said softly, looking away again. "I know a thing or two about hiding and wanting to be someone else."

Bay sighed. "Thank you for saying that, King. I have a feeling there's a lot of history behind that statement."

King's own words had betrayed him, exposing more than he'd intended. His expression must have conveyed his uneasiness because Bay looked like he was about to comfort him.

"You're right," King said before Bay could speak. "The normally confident King Slater is human after all."

Bay reached over as if to lay a hand on King's leg but hesitated. "I'd love to touch you right now," he said, "but I don't see how I can without escalating this tension that always seems to stretch between us."

King didn't move, and after a moment, Bay mumbled something under his breath, laid his hand on King's knee, and squeezed. After he'd stared at Bay's hand for the longest time, King looked up and met Bay's eyes again. He could feel the presence of unshed tears threatening to spill, and he prayed he could hold it together. Why was his past catching up with him now? Here? With Bay?

Bay's next move took King by surprise. Bay placed a hand on King's chest, leaned in, and gently pressed his lips against King's. King closed his eyes and bent into the kiss. Bay's lips were as soft and warm as he'd remembered, but this time the softness was mixed with the slightest taste of beer, which only seemed to add to King's struggles. But neither King nor Bay deepened the kiss, and somehow that seemed even more intimate. When Bay pulled back, a single tear slid down King's cheek, and Bay reached up and brushed it away, as King had done for Bay.

With the confrontation now behind them, King was relieved, but they had somehow gone off in a totally different direction and King had no idea where any of this was heading. He just knew this was not good. Not good for Bay and definitely not good for him.

King closed his eyes and laid his head on the back of the couch. He could feel Bay's eyes on him, but for some reason he couldn't meet his gaze.

Bay spoke softly. "I still can't believe how much you resemble Jack. Your build, your hair, your beard, your skin tone. Even down to the right amount of chest hair. You are definitely a mirror image of what I created Jack Robbins to be."

King opened his eyes and met Bay's gaze. They held steady for the longest time, each simply regarding the other. Then King broke eye contact by looking away. He'd acquiesced to Bay, and he was unnerved by his own sudden lack of self-possession. He wasn't used to giving in to anyone. The King Slater he'd become would never give up control. Or would he? Was he suddenly struggling with his confidence again, after all these years?

Bay laid a hand on King's forearm, and King winced at the simple touch. What had just happened between them? Mentally, King was off in some distant place, a place Bay wasn't a part of, and he needed to sort through all of this.

"You can go now," King finally said, turning to look at him. "I believe you, and I won't cause you any trouble."

Bay closed his eyes and sighed. His expression was one of relief, but the relief quickly faded, to be replaced with something akin to dread or fear. Bay hesitantly stood and slipped both hands, which were now trembling, into his pockets.

King sighed. Was this the end for him and Bay? In truth, there was no real beginning. There *was* no him and Bay. King was a gay escort, and Bay had won him in a poker game. End of story.

Then in a frustrated tone, Bay said, "That's it? Just like that? You're dismissing me?"

CHAPTER TEN

KING NARROWED his eyes but didn't speak. An uncomfortable silence lingered, and the tension in the room was so thick it could be cut it with a knife.

"Just tell me your game, man," King demanded. "At least that way we will be on an even playing field."

Bay took his hands out of his pockets and rested them on his hips. "What's my game? What's… my game?" he repeated, more indignant each time. "There is no game."

"Come on, man. This entire shit show is too weird to even comprehend. One minute you're telling me you're not gay and the next you're kissing me."

Bay groped for an explanation. On the one hand, he could hardly deny the attraction, regardless of however he had identified—or refused to identify—in the past, On the other, he wasn't yet ready to admit to it, let alone act on it.

King glared at Bay, his arms folded tightly across his chest. "I'm waiting for an answer."

Bay dropped his head. "There is no game. I swear it. But you're right. I can't explain the kiss or the attraction."

Bay sat next to King again. He reached out to touch King's arm, and King followed the motion with a defiant stare. Bay quickly pulled his hand back and rested it on his own leg.

"King," Bay said in almost a whisper, "I told you I'm basically a recluse when I'm not promoting my books. I don't go out. I don't date. I hardly leave my apartment. I always assumed I was straight."

"And now?" King asked.

Bay ran his fingers through his hair and shook his head. "All I know is there's a very strong attraction I can't explain. And maybe…."

"You can't even say it, can you?" King hissed.

Bay lowered his head again.

"Tell me this," King asked, "are you in some kind of convoluted relationship with your fictional character or something?"

"Of course not!" Bay huffed. "That's ridiculous."

King glared at him. "Is it?"

Bay hadn't thought about that angle. Could the lines be blurred between Jack, the man Bay wanted to be, and Jack, someone to whom Bay might be attracted?

"Well?" King said.

Bay chewed on the end of his fingernail nervously. "I don't know," he finally admitted.

King glared at him again, raising an eyebrow. "At least you're being honest," he groaned. "I'll ask again, Bay. What do you want from me?"

Bay stood, paced for a moment, and then stopped and gazed at King. "I don't know that either," he said, "but I do want to figure it out."

King stood, grabbed Bay by the wrists, and held them tightly. "Figure *what* out?"

"Figure out what's going on with me," Bay finally said. "Why I'm so attracted to you."

"You don't need me for that," King said through clenched teeth. "You're a rich, successful writer. You can afford the best psychiatrist in the world."

Bay saw where this was heading and got that panicky feeling again. "That's where you're wrong. I do need you. I just can't explain why. I'll pay—I'll pay as much as I have to."

"What?" King tightened his grip on Bay's wrists and narrowed his eyes. "Whaddya mean you'll pay?"

"You're an escort, and I'm a customer," Bay said, breaking his wrists free from King's grasp defiantly.

"Fuck!" King threw his hands in the air. "Are you kidding me right now?"

Bay stood tall. "I'm as serious as a poker game. Oh shit!" Bay looked at his watch. *A poker game. I'm gonna be late.* "How do you feel about poker?"

"What in the hell kind of question is that?"

"Put on your tuxedo. We're going to a poker game."

"I will do no such—"

"I'll pay double your normal rate," Bay said. "A grand an hour."

"No!" King snapped. "It doesn't work like—"

"Okay, then, two grand an hour."

That seemed to get his attention.

"And a guaranteed four-hour minimum," Bay added. "That's eight grand."

"Did you do that in your head?" King asked sarcastically.

Bay smiled. "I'm a mathematical genius."

King looked like he was caught somewhere between wanting to laugh and wanting to kill Bay. "You do know escorts can count, right?"

"I'm sure you can do anything you put your mind to."

"Flattery? How shallow do you think I am? No, wait! Don't answer that."

"Why?" Bay asked.

"Because it doesn't matter."

Bay felt that dread again. "Why doesn't it matter?"

"Because fortunately I'm on a red-eye back to New York tonight and can't play along with your stupid little experiment."

Bay breathed a sigh of relief. *New York? Jesus! He lives in New York.*

"You *are* not," Bay said.

"Yes, I am."

"No! You're not," Bay repeated. "Do you wanna know how I know that?"

King didn't respond.

"Because you have a shoot at a park off the Strip tomorrow morning."

King looked down at the floor and turned his head away, but Bay heard the whispered curse. He was sure King had forgotten he and the director had discussed that little tidbit during the shoot he'd been forced to watch. *Payback is a bitch!*

"Fine, then. I'm leaving tomorrow right after the shoot. You happy?"

"Yeah. I am," Bay said, trying not to sound smug but feeling like he'd played that hand well.

He must not have succeeded in hiding his smugness because King narrowed his eyes and glared at him. "Did you ever think that maybe I lied because I don't want to spend any more time with you?"

Bay flinched internally. That hit a little too close to home and smarted, but Bay knew where the attitude was coming from.

"Four hours. No more. No less," Bay said. "And I promise I'll have you back in plenty of time to get your beauty rest before your big shoot in the morning."

Bay had no idea what he expected to happen in the next four hours, but he sensed their time together would make or break their situation. He wanted King as a friend, or at the very least, not to make him an enemy.

More than that? All he knew was that he was extremely attracted to King, but he'd have to figure out how to deal with that later. "Okay. Now that we have a deal, get into your tuxedo. And please hurry. We're cutting it very close as it is."

King eyed Bay suspiciously. "Cash. Eight grand. Four hours. And then we're done."

Bay nodded but crossed his fingers behind his back.

King turned without saying a word and disappeared into the bedroom.

KING STOOD in front of the mirror tying his bow tie. He was already regretting his decision to play along with this little experiment. What was Bay's endgame? That was the question plaguing him. What did Bay expect to walk away with? After mulling that over, no valid conclusion presented itself, so he shoved the question to the back of his mind. For now, he would focus on the positives.

The first of course being the eight grand. On many occasions he'd worked a hell of a lot harder for a lot less money, so why was he even questioning this? Take the money and run. He told himself this was no different than any other call.

The second being his suitor was hot as hell, and he reveled in the fact that Bay challenged him. King had always loved nothing more than a good challenge, and when Bay hadn't instantly fallen for King's charms, it made him want to work even harder.

But if King were being totally honest with himself, he couldn't deny the fact that he genuinely liked Bay. A lot. And therein lay the problem. Bay was more than just handsome. He was also smart and could be charming, more so when he wasn't trying to be. King *had* to give him that. But beyond his looks, he seemed to have some heavy insecurities. He certainly wasn't without his flaws, and King liked that about him. The flawed side of Bay Whitman—that was something he could identify with. That was something they had in common. And for a split second, that simple thought made King feel like he wasn't as alone as he sometimes felt.

King straightened his bow tie and studied himself in the mirror one more time. *I guess we all have our issues. The last thing you need is to get distracted and thrown off your game by one Bay Whitman. Now get tonight over with and get your ass back to New York.*

When King reappeared, wearing the same white dinner jacket and black tie he'd worn on their second encounter, Bay was pacing and continually looking at his watch.

"Sorry. I only brought one tuxedo with me," King said.

Bay started for the door and then appeared to realize King had said something. He stopped and looked back. "I'm sorry? What did you say?"

"I apologized for only bringing one tuxedo with me."

"Oh. That's okay. I should be apologizing. I'm a little nervous, and we still have to get back to my hotel so I can change before cocktails and then the card game." Bay looked at King. "You look great."

"Save it," King said.

Bay rolled his eyes. "Well, you do."

KING AND Bay walked to the parking garage in a mostly uncomfortable silence. Bay seemed unusually nervous, and King wasn't in the greatest of a moods either.

When King pulled out onto the Las Vegas Strip, the flashing lights of the Bally's casino sign created a glare against his windshield and for a second or two nearly blinded him. He cursed under his breath. They inched along until King caught a red traffic light and stopped in front of Bellagio. Bay nervously tapped his fingers on the dashboard, and King tuned out the obnoxious noise and rolled down the window. Lee Greenwood was singing "God Bless the USA" as the waters swayed to the beat, lights brightening and dimming as they changed colors. He focused on the music and the dancing fountains while he continued to try to figure out Bay Whitman.

When the light changed, King rolled up the window and stepped on the gas. The only reasonable scenario he could come up with was that Bay was indeed gay and playing some kind of cat-and-mouse game. He was a gambler, after all. But why? What would he win? Certainly not King.

Traffic just about came to a stop when they reached Planet Hollywood. Judging by the sheer number of people gathered out front, something huge was taking place, and for a second, King wished he was there. Anywhere but here.

When they finally started moving, King was again deep in thought, still analyzing his situation. He halfheartedly took note of the Eiffel Tower of Paris, Las Vegas, the vigorous lights of Monte Carlo, and finally, in the distance, the MGM Grand. At that point he still had no idea what Bay was up to, so he gave up. *Oh, who the fuck cares? After the next four hours I'll have eight grand in my pocket, and tomorrow night I'll be on my way back to New York. I'll never have to see Bay Whitman again.*

"Just pull up to the valet," Bay said, interrupting King's thoughts. "I'll take care of it."

The valet opened the door. "Mr. Whitman. Welcome back."

"Thanks." Bay handed the guy a hundred-dollar bill. "Can you keep the car out front, please? I'm running late for an engagement, and I need to change."

"Certainly," the valet said, glancing at the folded bill and smiling. "It'll be right here waiting for you."

Bay made a beeline for the revolving door, and King was right on his heels. The elevator seemed to be moving at a snail's pace, and Bay looked like he was going to blow a gasket. When they finally reached Bay's suite and he opened the door, Bay started stripping in the foyer. Shoes went flying. He tossed his coat and tie on the back of the couch, and his T-shirt landed on the floor, as did his pants and socks.

"Can you get the garment bag labeled Prada out of the closet and lay it on the bed for me while I take a quick shower?"

King nodded. "Sure." Two grand an hour was his bottoming rate, so for that amount of money he could surely lay out a tuxedo.

He opened the closet door and smirked at the row of labeled black garment bags hanging neatly. Just for the hell of it, he counted, and there were an even dozen. He thumbed through the bags and said the names out loud as he searched for the Prada bag. Dolce & Gabbana, Hugo Boss, Versace, Burberry, Gucci, Canali, Armani, Z Zegna, and fourth from the last was finally the Prada bag. Just for shits and giggles he read the last three labels. Brioni, Ralph Lauren, and Ike Behar. *Damn, this guy has great taste in clothes.* He removed the bag marked Prada and reluctantly closed the closet door behind him. He laid the garment bag on the bed and turned to leave the room, but something made him stop.

King walked back to the bed and unzipped the bag. He held back a gasp when he saw a gorgeous black tuxedo with a white shirt, white silk vest, and matching white silk necktie so neatly pressed it could have been brand-new. Attached to the shiny wooden hanger was a velvet pouch. King emptied the contents onto the bed and stared at an elegant set of white pearl cufflinks with matching studs and two silver collar stays. King removed the tuxedo from the bag and laid it out on the bed. For some unknown reason, he rummaged through the drawers and found a pair of underwear, a white T-shirt, and a pair of black socks. He positioned everything on the bed, stepped back, and studied his handiwork. *Shoes?*

He returned to the closet and saw a half-dozen felt shoe bags lining the shelves. He remembered a rule he'd read in *GQ* many years ago. Lace-ups with a suit and loafers with a sport coat. He opened each bag until he found what he was looking for, left the closet, and laid the highly polished black shoes on the floor next to the bed. For some odd reason, he felt a sense of accomplishment preparing Bay's clothes.

Bay cleared his throat, and King turned to see him standing in the doorway of the bathroom, a towel hanging loosely around his hips. King bit his lip. Bay's half-naked body was a sight to behold. He wasn't ripped by any means, but he was fit and muscular in all the right places.

Bay looked at the bed and then back at King. He flashed the warmest smile King had ever seen. An hour ago, King had been ready to strangle Bay, and now his heart was warmed beyond capacity.

"Thank you," Bay said. "I think this is one of the nicest things anyone has ever done for me."

"Seriously?" King asked, feeling a bit sad, but still extremely happy he'd done it.

"Yeah," Bay said. "Seriously."

"Well," King said, "this game is obviously very important to you, and I'm glad I could help."

"Oh shit," Bay said. "The game. We can't be late."

"Then let's get you dressed."

Bay stepped up to the bed and dropped his towel. King knew he should look away, but he couldn't bring himself to do it. Bay's cock was a sight to behold. When Bay saw him staring, he blushed and turned around, which was okay with King because his ass was equally impressive. Round and firm, which went perfectly with his narrow hips. But the show ended as soon as Bay slipped on his underwear. He then pulled his T-shirt over his head, slipped on his socks, and took the tuxedo pants King was holding out to him.

King slipped Bay's shirt over his shoulders, clipped on the suspenders, and then added the vest. As soon as Bay finished fastening all the buttons, King turned up Bay's collar, wrapped the tie around Bay's neck, and began to knot his tie.

"I feel like I have my own personal valet," Bay said. "And I do believe I could get used to this. Hey! How much would it cost to take you home with me?"

"Too much," King said, tucking Bay's necktie inside the vest and handing Bay his coat. "Where are we going anyway?"

"A private penthouse suite at the Bellagio."

King whistled. "We better get a move on, then."

Once in the lobby, Bay stopped at the casino's cashier desk and got a twenty-thousand-dollar advance against his black American Express card. He counted out eight crisp one-thousand-dollar bills and handed them to King. "As promised."

King accepted the money, but instead of putting it in his pocket, he simply stared at it. He suddenly felt guilty taking it. But why? This was a business deal. No different than any other call, or so he kept telling himself. But he knew better, and that's what was starting to scare him. Before he changed his mind, he folded the bills and slipped them into the inside pocket of his coat. "Thank you."

"It's a business doing pleasure with you," Bay said through a smile.

King's rental car was waiting for them as the valet had promised, and within minutes the two men were navigating the Vegas Strip again.

"Have you ever been a companion during a poker game?" Bay asked.

"Nope."

"Okay. So when we're seated at the poker table," Bay explained, "you'll probably be able to see my hand very clearly. But please—try not to make any facial expressions that might enable my opponents to draw any conclusions."

"You mean like maybe when you're bluffing or something?" King asked.

"Exactly."

"Got it," King replied. "I'll do my best."

"Thank you."

"This poker stuff really gets you going, huh?"

"Almost like a drug," Bay said. "It's the only pleasure I allow myself. Just for me."

The words *just for me* echoed in King's mind. He hoped one day he, too, could allow himself to do something *just for him*. But as in the past, that was usually dangerous.

"I know it sounds crazy," Bay said, "but it's the truth."

"There's one thing I don't understand," King noted. "If you hardly left your apartment, how did you get involved in gambling?"

"Online," Bay said.

"How did you make the transition to actual games?"

"That's where Jack Robbins came into play. Gambling was right up his alley. So I just did what he would do. I started out small, mostly poker tables with a five-dollar minimum bet, but as I started to realize a little success and made more money, I slowly upped the ante, and now I do high stakes."

"What do you consider high stakes?" King asked, suddenly very curious.

"Oh I don't know—anywhere between two and five thousand dollars as opening hands."

"Get out of town," King said as he turned into the Bellagio Hotel. This was going to be one interesting night.

Chapter Eleven

Bay headed for the elevator bank that went directly to the penthouse and checked in with the guard. "I'm Bay Whitman, and this is my guest, King Slater. I am expected in Mr. Devlin's suite this evening."

"May I please see your ID?" the guard said.

Bay presented his driver's license, and King did the same. The guard nodded and flipped through some pages on a clipboard, running his finger up and down each page. "Ah yes. I see your name here, Mr. Whitman, but I don't see Mr. Slater's."

"Of course," Bay said. "I just ran into Mr. Slater and invited him to join me. If you would be so kind as to call Mr. Devlin's suite, I'm sure it will be authorized."

The guard did as asked, and in less than a minute, they were riding the elevator to the top of the hotel.

"I've been in this suite before," King admitted.

"Really?" Bay said. "Is it nice?"

"Very."

Bay simply nodded.

"Aren't you gonna ask me why?" King asked.

"I'm pretty sure I already know the answer to that question."

"I guess you do," King said with a grin.

"Anyone I know?" Bay asked.

King nodded. "Without a doubt. But I don't kiss and tell."

"I see," Bay said. "Since our lips have met on more than one occasion, I'm very happy to hear that."

Before King could respond, the elevator doors opened into a round marbled foyer. Laughter and piano music came from the suite. And then he heard footsteps and blinked twice when Rich Devlin stepped into the foyer with a drink in his hand.

"Bay! It's about time you got here. We were starting to think you stood us up."

"And pass up an opportunity to kick your sorry asses at poker?" Bay replied. "Not on your life."

Rich stuck his hand in King's direction. "Rich Devlin."

"Oh crap! Where are my manners?" Bay said. "Rich Devlin, meet King Slater."

Rich tilted his head and studied King closely. "Have we met?" he asked. "You seem very familiar to me."

King smiled. *Either Rich is gay or he thinks I'm Jack Robbins.* "I don't think so," he said. "I think I would have remembered that. But it's great to meet you."

"Is that Bay?" a voice called right before Zeke Cambridge joined them in the foyer.

King did another double take. *Holy shit! It's Zeke Cambridge. I wonder who in the hell else is in here.*

"Hey, Zeke," Bay said, shaking the man's hand. "Oh, and this is my friend, King Slater."

Zeke shook Bay's hand and then King's.

He, too, studied King. "Have we met?" he asked.

"I asked the same thing," Rich said. "He looks very familiar to me."

"I don't think so," King said. "But it's nice to meet you now."

"Oh well." Zeke shrugged. "You guys come in and get a drink before we start the game."

WHEN KING rounded the corner, the bright lights of the Las Vegas Strip became clearly visible through the wall of windows. He was as taken by them tonight as he had been the first time he was in the suite. The flashing lights seemed so close, as if a person could reach out and touch them.

He took a quick look around and stopped when he saw the white grand piano. Brian Addison, the wildly popular country singer, was sitting at the keyboard, tickling the ivories as two beautiful women sat on top of it listening to him play.

I feel like I've stepped into an alternate universe.

His thoughts were interrupted when an attractive woman walked up, slid her arm into Rich's, and held on. "Bay and King, this is my wife, Luciana."

Bay smiled. "Then *you* are one lucky man, my friend."

Rich looked at his wife with obvious admiration. "Tell me about it."

"Hey!" Zeke said, turning toward the piano and raising his glass to one of the ladies on the piano, who raised hers back. "I'm lucky too."

"That's an understatement," Luciana said as she gestured to the piano. "But I think even Jennifer would agree that Brian is the luckiest."

Bay and King followed Luciana's gaze back to the piano and stared at the gorgeous blonde sitting next Zeke's wife. She was making the sweetest goo-goo eyes at Brian.

"Hell," Luciana said. "I'd even do her."

Rich's face lit up. "Seriously? Man! I would so pay to see that."

Zeke raised his glass and looked at Luciana. "And I'll double whatever he pays."

"Let me check with Cristan," Luciana teased, "and I'll get back to you."

Everyone laughed.

Zeke took Bay and King over to the bar. "Give these men their poison, and then we'll get this party started." Zeke glanced over his shoulder and then looked back at them. "I'll see you guys at the piano. I don't want to neglect my wife too early in the evening."

King leaned over and put his mouth very close to Bay's ear. "You could have warned me, you know."

"Now where's the fun in that?" Bay said smugly.

"How do you know these people?"

"Relax. I just met them," Bay said. "I played cards with Rich and Zeke a couple of nights ago, and believe it or not, they are fans of mine and invited me to join them here for a friendly game."

"A friendly game with pretty high stakes, I would imagine."

Bay smiled. "Probably."

As soon as they got their drinks, Zeke waved them over, and when they reached the piano, Brian stopped playing and stood. "Bay." He offered his hand. "These clowns have told me a lot about you. But just so you know, I'm already a big fan."

"Likewise," Bay said and then gestured to Rich and Zeke. "How do you know said clowns?"

Brian chuckled. "I'm doing the soundtrack for their upcoming movie, and we just hit it off, I guess."

Bay smiled. "Yeah! They're pretty likable guys."

"Aw shucks," Rich said, ruffling Zeke's hair. He then made formal introductions, and everyone shook hands.

"Sorry I missed the game the other night," Brian said, looking at his wife adoringly. "Cristan was a little under the weather, and I didn't want to leave her alone."

"That's very admirable," Bay said, smiling at Cristan. She was drop-dead gorgeous, very pregnant, and was resting her hand on her stomach. "Pregnancy certainly agrees with you. You're absolutely glowing."

Cristan smiled. "Thank you. By the way, I read your last novel, *Revenge in Monte Carlo*, after Brian recommended it to me, and I must say I am very impressed. Jack Robbins is one intriguing man."

Rich snapped his fingers and pointed at King. "That's it," he said. "I knew I recognized you."

Oh shit! King's heart dropped to his stomach and he looked at Bay. Bay seemed to be holding it together nicely and didn't appear to be the least bit unnerved.

"You're the model on the cover of *Revenge in Monte Carlo*. You're Jack Robbins."

"You're right," Zeke said, looking back and forth between Rich and King.

King flashed a nervous smile, but before he could speak, Bay jumped in. "Well, King. It looks like your anonymity just got blown."

"Oh come on." Rich slapped King on the back. "You're safe with us."

"Great cover, by the way," Cristan said.

"Thanks," King replied, not at all comfortable being dishonest.

Brian offered his hand to Cristan as she slid off the piano. "Let's get this game started."

Bay helped Jennifer to her feet as well. When Luciana slid her arm in King's, and Jennifer took Bay by the hand, Rich and Zeke looked at each other with *what the fuck?* expressions.

Just before Luciana pulled King to the poker table, he heard Zeke say, "Apparently we didn't make the cut."

The table was set up with several decks of cards and stacks of chips positioned in front of four chairs. Brian, Rich, and Zeke took their seats at the table with their wives sitting slightly behind them, giving each woman a clear view of their husband's hand.

"King?" Rich asked. "Are you here as a player or an observer?"

"I think these stakes might be a little high for my taste," King said honestly. "Us mere cover models don't make as much money as you actors, so I'll just watch. If that's okay."

Rich slapped King on the back. "I think I like you."

King pulled up another chair and placed it directly behind Bay's in imitation of the women. No one had even alluded to the fact that he and

Bay might be here as more than friends, so it felt a little weird sitting like the other spouses. Of course, with the exception of a couple of odd kisses, they weren't anything more than friends. And not even that, really.

But surprisingly, King found that he liked thinking of himself as another one of the supportive spouses. It warmed him. He always had to be a loner where the heart was concerned, so he liked playing at being connected to someone. Even if it wasn't real and was only for the money.

While the guys got comfortable, King couldn't help but think of the one real relationship in his life. Like most things, he'd fucked that one up royally. But this—he could do this. He could be here to support Bay all night long. It was his job, and once he was off the clock, it was over. He would put no demands on anyone and none would be put on him. *The best of both worlds.*

Zeke's voice pulled King out of his thoughts.

"Since this is a friendly game, let's make this easy and play a little five-card draw to start. Everyone okay with that?" Zeke asked.

The guys all looked at each other and nodded.

"Two-grand ante?" Rich asked. He glanced around the table, and no one disagreed.

"High card for first dealer," Zeke said, fanning the cards across the table facedown. Each man drew one and they all turned their card up at the same time. Rich had the high card, so he scooped up the deck, shuffled, and dealt the first hand.

As King watched, Bay picked up his five cards and spread them out in his hand, then tilted them so King could get a clear view. King saw a six of clubs, a six of hearts, an ace of diamonds, a queen of spades, and a four of hearts.

Since Bay was sitting to the left of the dealer, the first bet was up to him. "Bay?" Rich asked.

"Three thousand," Bay said, tossing three chips to the center of the table.

King thought Bay was crazy to risk three grand on a pair of sixes, but he remembered what Bay had asked him and did his best to keep his face expressionless.

"You don't waste any time," Brian said, looking between his cards and Bay. "I don't know why, but I'm in." He picked up three chips and added them to the pile.

"Me too," Zeke said, tossing in the appropriate chips.

"And the dealer's in as well," Rich said, sliding his chips to the center of the table.

It was now back to Bay. King knew a little about poker, and if it were he, he would keep the pair of sixes and toss the rest. But King was shocked when Bay laid the queen and the four facedown on the table. "Two, please."

I guess he's hoping for two pair, ace high.

Brian asked for four cards, which probably meant he didn't have anything. Zeke threw three cards facedown on the table, which indicated he was keeping a pair.

After Bay, Brian, and Zeke's cards were dealt, Rich gave himself only one. *He must be going for a straight, flush, or full house. Bay better proceed with care.*

Bay picked up the two cards and added them to his hand. When he fanned them out, King saw a nine of hearts and a jack of diamonds. In other words, nothing. He was five grand in with a pair of sixes.

King watched Rich as he eyed Bay. Bay finally smiled coyly. "I'll raise five grand," he said, adding five chips to the pile.

"Too rich for my blood," Brian said, tossing his cards to the dealer.

Zeke looked between Bay and Rich, studied his cards again, and finally slid five chips to the center of the table. "I'll match your five grand and raise you five."

"Shit," Rich said. "I'm out. It's ten grand to you, Bay."

Zeke stared Bay down, but King was unable to read Zeke's expression.

Bay looked at his cards once more, obviously playing the game to the fullest, and then raised his eyes to Zeke again. Sweat built on King's forehead. And it wasn't even his money. But he came close to losing it when Bay counted out ten chips and slid them to the center of the table. "I'll call."

Bay was calm, cool, and collected, holding it together like a professional while King was about to pass out from holding his breath as he waited for Zeke's next move. The next few seconds seemed almost as if time had stopped. Everyone was looking back and forth between Zeke and Bay, and the place was so quiet you could hear a pin drop.

And then, much to King's surprise, it was all over almost as quickly as it had started. Instead of revealing his cards, Zeke looked away, cursed under his breath, and threw his cards onto the table. "Dammit," he hissed. "I got nothing."

King breathed a sigh of relief, pulled a white handkerchief out of his pocket, and wiped his brow. Bay, on the other hand, tilted his head, smiled, and said, "I have a pair of sixes."

"Son of a bitch," Zeke said through a smile. "Nice bluff, man."

Bay nodded as he cupped his hands around the pile of chips and pulled them toward him. He looked back at King and winked. King smiled and wiped his brow yet again.

Over the next few hours, the lead swung back and forth, each guy winning some and losing some, and by the end of the night, Bay was by far the big winner. King was glad it was over, exhausted from the emotional roller coaster he'd been riding. Over and over again.

To Bay's credit, throughout the night he'd included King in just about every play, either with whispered words, eye contact, or facial expressions, and King nervously realized he liked being there to support Bay. When the game concluded and everyone said their goodbyes, King and Bay stepped into the elevator. They waved one last time, and as the doors closed, Bay sighed heavily.

"You okay?" King asked.

"Yeah, I'm good," Bay said. "But thanks for asking."

"Are you sure?" King asked, trying not to sound judgmental. "That sigh I just heard says differently."

Bay was silent for a long time, and when he finally spoke, his voice was weary. "It's just so exhausting pretending to be someone you're not. Especially when the person you're pretending to be is sitting right next to you."

King's heart broke a little for Bay because he knew all about pretending. Shit! His entire life was one big pretend session, on camera and off.

CHAPTER TWELVE

WHEN KING pulled off the Strip at the entrance to Bay's hotel, Bay couldn't believe how fast the time had flown since they'd left the Bellagio. He and King had talked nonstop about the entire evening from start to finish. Covering everything from how down-to-earth and friendly their hosts were to the games and the amount of money that had floated around that table.

Bay started to get that sinking feeling in the pit of his stomach again. The same feeling he'd experienced when King had asked him to leave his hotel room earlier. He knew this was it. He'd had no idea what these few hours would buy him, if anything, but he was grateful when he saw the traffic moving toward the hotel's entrance at a snail's pace. It was only prolonging the inevitable. He knew his and King's time together was coming to an end. After all, he'd given King his word, and he was going to be expected to keep it. Fingers crossed behind his back or not.

Bay had so enjoyed having someone with him. Someone seemingly behind him. He'd included King in each play and enjoyed getting King's input. He'd always been such a loner, but he'd never felt lonely until now. King had touched something in him he hadn't know he was missing and now he wasn't sure he could go back to his old life. He'd gotten a little taste of what it was like to be one of two people. A team. And it felt good.

While they inched their way to the entrance, Bay wondered what it would be like to have King as a companion and even a lover. One option comforted him and the other excited him. But that was a stupid fantasy. King was a porn star and an escort, and Bay was a nerd and a recluse. What an impossible pair they would make.

When King finally pulled up to the main doors and stopped the car, he seemed hesitant when he looked at Bay. "We're here."

"How about a nightcap?" Bay asked, feeling a little desperate.

King looked at his watch and back at Bay. "Well, technically you paid for four hours, and by my account, you still have twenty minutes left. So sure. Why not? I certainly want you to get what you paid for."

Bay smiled. "I appreciate the sentiment."

On the way up to the suite, Bay stopped by the VIP concierge and ordered a celebratory bottle of that Boërl & Kroff Brut Champagne the prince had ordered the other night. After all, he *had* won a good bit of money, so why not enjoy some of it. It was his and King's last drink together, and Bay was going home tomorrow night, so this would be the end of his socializing until his next book release.

While they waited for the champagne, Bay took off his coat, vest, and tie and kicked off his shoes. King removed his coat as well, untied his black bow tie, and in a very Jack sort of way, allowed the untied ends to hang around his neck.

When the champagne came, Bay handed the bottle to King. "Would you do the honors, please?"

Bay signed for the delivery, tipped the room-service attendant, and closed the door. He watched as King worked on the bottle carefully and within seconds heard the familiar pop of the cork. King poured them each a flute, and Bay gestured toward the couch, where they sat side by side.

Bay held up his glass. "Here's to you, King."

"Me?" King asked. "Why me?"

"Because you're everything I'm not."

"Wait a minute," King said. "Don't put me on a pedestal. I get paid for having sex with strange men. How is that something to be proud of?"

"Because you know who you are and what you do, and you own it," Bay said. "You do what you do with confidence and, from what I've seen, never compromise your self-respect."

Fighting the quiver in his voice, Bay paused, wanting to make the rest of his point without losing it. "To me…," he finally said, "that makes the way I live my life seem weak and cowardly."

"Stop it," King said. "That's not true. I watched you tonight. You were outgoing, engaging, and a strong and confident man."

Bay looked away. "On the outside, maybe, but that wasn't me," he said. "I was simply playing a part."

King tilted his head to one side and stared at Bay quizzically. "Did you ever stop to think that maybe, just maybe, you are more like Jack Robbins than you think?"

Bay laughed heartily at that one.

"Laugh all you want," King said, "but I think I'm right. You created that character. That had to come from somewhere. And—" King tapped his finger against Bay's chest. "—I believe it came from in here."

"If only that were true," Bay said, looking away and feeling like he might lose his shit.

When Bay thought he was composed enough to keep it together, he turned back to King. He did his best to flash a sincere smile. "Man. You're damn good at what you do and worth every penny."

Bay realized how that sounded and wanted to take it back. He'd meant it as a compliment, but when the words left his mouth, they sounded disrespectful, condescending, and rude. Bay noticed a slight change in King's expression, and he cursed himself.

"Oh God. That sounded awful and was not at all what I meant. It was supposed to be a compliment," Bay tried to explain. "You *are* good at what you do. You read people and are intuitive enough to assess what they need at any given time and give it to them. *That* is a great skill."

King's expression lightened a little. He glanced at his watch. "For the record, I've been off the clock for thirty minutes. Which reminds me." King reached into his pocket, withdrew the money Bay had given him earlier, and placed it on the table in front of them. "I can't in good conscience take this."

"What?" Bay asked. "Of course you can take it. We made a deal."

"Yeah, well," King said, "I'm breaking that deal."

Bay picked up the money and tried to give it back to King, but King pushed Bay's hand away. "No. I'm not taking it."

"Why?" Bay asked.

"Because for some reason it no longer feels right. And in my experience, if it doesn't feel right, it isn't."

The two men locked eyes, and time stood still until King finally spoke again. "Look, I had a great time tonight. I really enjoyed myself socially for the first time in a very long time. It felt like…." He looked away.

"Felt like what?" Bay pressed.

King turned back and faced him. "I can't believe I'm saying this, but even if only for a little while, it felt like I belonged"—he shifted his gaze away again, but Bay heard his mumbled words clearly—"to you."

Suddenly, lust was clanging in Bay's head like church bells tolling on a Sunday morning. He didn't know what propelled him, but he gently slid his finger under King's chin and turned King's face back to his. And then Bay leaned forward, gripped King behind his neck with his other hand, and pulled King to him. They were so close Bay could feel King's breath on his face. King's expression was full of something Bay couldn't identify, but fuck it. He wanted this. He was suddenly tired of playing cat-and-mouse games.

Bay still had no idea what was fueling his actions, and he didn't care. Straight or gay, right or wrong, he wanted to kiss King. And he wanted to do it now. He pulled King closer and pressed his lips against King's. When King didn't pull away, Bay sought entry with his tongue, and King gloriously opened to him. With Bay's hand gripping King's neck securely and his tongue exploring that warm, wet mouth, Bay felt empowered. Something he'd never really felt as Bay Whitman.

Suddenly Bay was soaring to new heights. So high, in fact, the air was becoming thin and literally taking his breath away. Goose bumps broke out all over his skin as blood rushed to his groin. He was a bundle of nerves, riddled with fear but, surprisingly, excited as hell. Bay instinctively caressed King's chest and abs like a sick man finally getting the medication he needed. That was an unexpected revelation Bay tucked away in the back of his mind to dissect later.

When the kiss ended, Bay pulled back and looked into King's eyes. "Have you ever belonged to anyone?" he asked.

King's expression reflected uneasiness and pain. But to his credit, he didn't look away. "Once," he said. "But like most things, I screwed it up."

"I'm sorry," Bay said, shifting his gaze away. "But that's one more than I ever had."

When Bay looked back, King's eyes were filling with tears.

Bay's heart was suddenly breaking for King, and he had an overwhelming need to be closer to him. Bay leaned in again, but he froze when King stiffened.

"Stop," King whispered. "Please stop. I can't."

Bay wasn't hearing right. He couldn't be. He was offering something to King. He wasn't sure what, but something. Himself, maybe. And that was something King had said he wanted from the first time they'd met. Now King was rejecting him? But maybe what King had wanted all along was Jack—cool, sophisticated Jack, who oozed sex appeal—not shy, sensitive Bay, who came with emotional baggage and a need for connection.

"Why?" Bay asked. "I mean, I'm sorry. I've never done this before, and I'm sure I'm doing it all wrong, but—"

"No!" King said. "It's not you. I need to go."

Rejection flooded over Bay like a tsunami. He got to his feet and took his head in his hands. *Stupid, Bay! Why would King want you? He's a gorgeous, confident man and you're just an insecure, antisocial nerd. Now you know why you should never put yourself out there. You stupid fool!*

"I'm sorry," King mumbled, shaking his head and getting to his feet.

"I get it," Bay said, mustering every bit of pride he could. "It's okay. I understand. Just go."

King picked up his coat, his expression unreadable as he left the hotel suite. In the far reaches of Bay's conscious mind, he was screaming King's name, begging him to stop, but no real sound ever left his mouth. He lay on the couch, exhausted and forlorn.

BAY WOKE to the sound of his cell phone ringing. He stood, shuddered at the bright sun streaming in the balcony doors, and stumbled across the room to his tuxedo coat. He dug in the pocket, fished out his phone, and looked at the screen. *Rachel.*

He slid his finger across the screen. "Hey."

"Rise and shine, Mr. *New York Times* Best-Selling Author. It's gonna be a great day," his assistant said.

Bay rubbed his eyes with his thumb and forefinger. He wished he could bet against those odds. "What time is it, Rae?"

"Six o'clock," she said in her cheery early-morning voice. "Remember you asked me to call to make sure you were awake?"

"Oh yeah. I forgot," Bay said, already dreading the interviews and book signing scheduled for the day.

"Well, lucky for you, *I* didn't. And by the sound of it, I'm pretty sure I woke you up. Now get moving, and I'll meet you in the lobby at seven thirty sharp."

"'Kay."

"Oh, and Bay?"

"Yeah?"

"Wear that charcoal-gray Zegna suit with the light gray shirt. It'll look great on camera."

"Yes, ma'am," Bay said unenthusiastically. "What time is the first interview?"

"Eight ten. And then we have a little over an hour to get to the next network for the second interview at nine twenty. Unless we run into major traffic, it should all work out fine."

"And the book signings?" Bay asked.

"Two different locations, one o'clock and five o'clock. With plenty of time to get you to the airport." Rachel cleared her throat. "Speaking of the book signing, what are the chances you can get that Jack Robbins look-alike guy to show up again?"

"Zilch," Bay said with 100 percent confidence.

Rachel sighed. "That's too bad. He's quite the looker, and lordy, the crowd ate him up. I still can't believe you were holding out on me."

"I wasn't holding out on you, Rae. I told you, I just met the guy. This is all one big coincidence, and trust me when I tell you he doesn't want to get involved with any of it."

"Are you sure? I could call him. We'll pay, ya know."

"He's already on a plane heading home. You'd be wasting your time."

Bay knew he was stretching the truth, but he didn't want Rachel to know that King was probably getting ready to shoot the opening of a porn movie in a park. Or even worse, her trying to contact him. He would probably be at 36,000 feet by the time Bay arrived at his first book signing.

"That's too bad" was all Rachel said, sounding disappointed.

"Look, Rae. It's getting late, and I need to pack, get showered, and dress. I'll see you downstairs in a bit."

Bay ended the call and tossed the phone onto the chair. He stretched his back and mentally cursed the uncomfortable couch. The half-empty bottle of champagne and the two flutes sat there mocking him, so he took them to the bar. Then he took a seat on the couch.

Staring at the empty spot next to him, he remembered that just hours ago King had been seated there, in living color. And to make matters worse, Bay had kissed him again. His face heated. He'd made a complete fool of himself. As usual. He'd preached to King about how straight he was and then kissed him. Again. "What in the hell were you thinking?"

When the shock subsided, the pain creeped in. The hurt. The rejection. All coming to the surface. Bay pushed everything to the depths of his mind. He had one more day of promotional work to get through, and he'd be on the red-eye tonight and back in New York by tomorrow morning. Bay stood, and a picture of him and King kissing on the couch flashed in his mind's eye. An array of emotions from embarrassment to shame and everything in between flooded him. *Am I really gay?*

Shaking his head to get the image out of his mind, he walked into the bedroom, perplexed. He mulled that question over and over in his head as he packed, stripped, showered, and dressed again. In the end, as he tied his tie, he decided it didn't really matter. He was never venturing out of his comfort zone again. He'd taken a chance, and it had blown up in his face big-time. If nothing else, he was a man who learned from his mistakes.

Bay slipped on his suit coat, sprayed on a little cologne, shoved the bottle into his carry-on bag, and zipped it up. He walked to the foyer, looked at his reflection in the mirror, and realized how absolutely horrible he looked. He wanted to curl up into a ball and sleep for a week, but he had commitments, and he couldn't let Rachel or his publisher down. So he straightened his tie, brushed his hair out of his eyes, and began his ritual of shedding Bay Whitman and becoming Jack Robbins.

CHAPTER THIRTEEN

KING PUNCHED his pillow and huffed with frustration as he looked at the clock for what seemed like the hundredth time since he'd crawled into bed sometime after midnight. *Three minutes after eight.*

He knew the time had come to get out of bed and give up on any chance of capturing the sleep that had eluded him throughout the night. Besides, he had to be showered and ready to leave by nine fifteen to make his shoot. After lunch, he'd agreed to do some promotional stills in the studio, and then he could go home.

King pulled the covers back, exposing his naked body to the chilly, air-conditioned room, which was still quite dark courtesy of the blackout drapes hanging in front of the balcony doors.

He sighed, turned, and then planted his feet firmly on the floor. After a quick stop in the bathroom, he sat on the foot of the bed and aimed the remote at the television. King would do anything to avoid thinking about Bay Whitman, and at this point, the morning news was his only option. Besides, he was absolutely sure the president of the United States had done or said something offensive the night before and would once again be making headlines.

King flipped through the channels, pausing on the national news networks only to see they had already done their morning rundown. So next he surfed the local shows and stopped when one news anchor appeared to be in the middle of his recap.

"And that's the morning's latest news," the anchorman said as he straightened his papers on the desk and smiled at the camera. "Now over to you, Jessica."

Damn. I just missed it.

The camera cut to another set, and King's mouth dropped to his knees. There in front of him was exactly what he'd spent the entire night trying to forget. Bay Whitman. Looking dashing in a dark gray suit and smiling broadly into the camera. He was sitting next to a life-size cardboard cutout of Jack Robbins, and the interviewer was holding a copy of *Revenge in Monte Carlo* in her lap.

The bouncy blonde with the bright white perfect teeth held the book up in the air. "We at KTNV are very pleased to welcome, as our very special guest, *New York Times* best-selling author Bay Whitman, who's with us this morning to talk about his latest Jack Robbins novel, *Revenge in Monte Carlo*."

She turned to Bay. "Good Morning, Bay, and thank you so much for taking time out of your busy schedule to spend a few minutes with us."

The camera zoomed in on Bay. "It's my pleasure, Jessica," he said. "Thanks for having me."

King did a double take. "Jesus," he whispered to himself. "He looks like shit."

Suddenly feeling guilty, King did his best to push his concern to the far reaches of his mind. "Better yet, he looks like I feel," he added.

Bay's face was plastered with the usual pancake makeup, but it did little to conceal the deep dark circles under his eyes. King had looked into those very same eyes yesterday, and man, what a difference a day made.

Bay appeared to have gotten about as much sleep as he had. "I did that," King admitted to himself, no longer able to hold those feelings back. "I saw him as a challenge. And after I wore him down and he gave in, I rejected him."

The interviewer's annoyingly perky morning voice broke his concentration. "Okay. So I'm gonna get right to it," she said. "Man oh man is Jack Robbins one sexy hunk of a character."

Bay chuckled. "Yeah, I hear that a lot."

"It's been said on more than one occasion that Jack Robbins is based on you and your life. Is that true?"

Bay laughed this time. "That, Jessica—couldn't be further from the truth."

"Come on, Bay," Jessica pleaded. "You can be honest with me. Do you truly expect me to believe you make this stuff up in your head?"

"I do. It's all fiction. I swear it," Bay reiterated. "If you knew where and how I write, I think you'd be extremely disappointed and unimpressed."

"How so?" Jessica asked.

"Well, for starters, I write in a small dark room with no outside stimulation. I find it better to not have any distractions. Some writers like to have great views as inspiration, but I prefer to make up my views in my head. I picture Jack Robbins in every scene. The scene unfolds in my head from a blank slate, and I build upon it until it's where it needs to be."

"And what about the plots?"

"They, too, unfold in my head," Bay explained. "I start out with a premise and then let that premise naturally unfold into a story."

To King, Bay seemed relaxed and at ease in front of the camera, but now that King knew him a little better, he picked up on a few subtle nuances that gave Bay away. Like the way he scratched his chin a few times or the way he tilted his head. They were subtle, but there. And the way he answered the questions seemed almost rehearsed. *Yup. Bay is definitely nervous.*

Jessica looked down at her notes. "What's so interesting to me is many writers say their stories take on lives of their own. Have you ever experienced that?"

"Absolutely. You can strong-arm a character into doing what you want them to do, but the story never really holds together in the end when you try to force it. I know it's hard to understand, but the story you've imagined in the very early stages of development needs to play out naturally."

"Taking that into consideration," Jessica said, "has he ever disappointed you in a path he chose to take?"

Bay looked away as if to consider the question. Then he turned back and stared directly at the camera, almost as if he were looking right into King's eyes, and spoke. "To be absolutely truthful, no. He hasn't. Jack is solid as a rock. He knows who he is, and he always stays true to himself. I, on the other hand, have probably disappointed him a time or two with paths I tried to lead *him* down. Paths that rang true in my head, seemed natural, and felt right at the time, but in the end would have probably ended up as a blasted suicide mission."

Jessica didn't respond right away, but when she did, her response was solid. "I don't know if I agree with that," she said. "As an avid reader and a fan of yours, I instinctively trust you and Jack. You both seem like the type of guys who go after exactly what you want in life, and neither of you would ever do anything you didn't want to do." She paused. "But hey, that's just me."

Bay appeared stunned by her comment, but he quickly regained his footing. "I'll take that opinion into consideration," he said, winking.

"Wow!" Jessica nodded. "I always assumed someone sat down and simply wrote a book. The fact that the story sometimes, for lack of a better phrase, *writes itself* is so interesting to me. I could talk about this all day, but unfortunately we are just about out of time."

Bay smiled weakly and nodded.

Jessica looked at the camera. "*Revenge in Monte Carlo* is on shelves now, and I suggest you pick up a copy. You won't regret it. Bay, it's been a pleasure. Please stop by next time you're in town. We'd love to catch up with you and Jack Robbins again."

Bay dipped his head. "I'll do that, Jessica. And thanks again for having me."

"John, back to you."

King clicked off the television and hung his head in sheer exhaustion. The fact that he was intrigued by Bay Whitman, in spite of the short amount of time he'd known him, said something. It said a lot, actually. Volumes, which King hadn't allowed himself to think about. Bay challenged him. He treated King with respect, regardless of his chosen profession, and didn't make him feel like a piece of meat. In a normal world, a world other than King's, that might be enough to spark something. Dating? A relationship? Who knew? But maybe….

Unfortunately, to use a term Bay would understand, caring for someone wasn't in the cards for King. *That* was his reality. But those reasons still didn't keep Bay's words from ringing loud and clear in his head. *"Paths that rang true in my head, seemed natural, and felt right at the time, but in the end would have probably ended up as a blasted suicide mission."*

"Maybe we could have had a shot," King said to the blank television screen, "if things were different. In another place and time. If I wasn't so fucked up. And that is a big *if.*"

In a fit of anger, King stood and threw the remote control across the room. The sound of the plastic hitting the wall and shattering into pieces, batteries flying in every direction, echoed through the quiet hotel room. "Fuck," King sighed in desperation. All the fits, broken remotes, and wishing wouldn't change the way things were. *You have a problem, man. You took a chance once, you lost, and it nearly killed you. You won't survive that again.*

CHAPTER FOURTEEN

BAY MADE it through his next interview, a meet-and-greet luncheon, and both two-hour book signings on autopilot. He smiled, signed books, and made small talk with hundreds of people and was finally done. In a way it had been a great distraction, but alas, it was over.

Rachel, who was staying behind one more day to pack up all the promotional items and get everything shipped back to New York, pulled up to the Departures area of the airport and put the car in Park. "Are you okay?"

Bay turned to her. "Yeah, why?"

"You've not seemed yourself today."

Bay sighed. "I didn't sleep very well last night, and I'm pretty tired, so you're probably right. Nothing a little rest won't fix."

"Glad to hear it," Rachel said, leaning over and giving him a kiss on the cheek. "I'll be in touch tomorrow. Travel safely."

Bay did his best to give her a genuine smile. "I will, and you do the same. Good job, by the way. Bye, Rachel."

BAY FLAGGED down a porter, who loaded his bags onto a cart and took them over to the curbside check-in. After banging on the computer keyboard a few minutes, the porter handed Bay's identification, along with his boarding pass, to him. Bay slipped him a twenty and headed to security, where he was promptly questioned and patted down in a way that felt akin to being violated. All because of the bottle of cologne in his carry-on bag. He eventually made it through security, after gladly relinquishing his cologne and eliminating the very serious threat of smelling good, and went in search of a place for dinner.

He found an empty, dimly lit restaurant near his departure gate and, because he didn't want to be recognized, chose a small table way in the back. He was craving solitude, and he desperately needed time to think. The events of the past few days weighed heavily on him. Not only coming face-to-face with his fictional character, but their encounter and interactions bringing his sexuality into question. That in itself was enough to send him into solitude forever, but there was more on his mind. Something had been nagging at him, had been a dull ache in the back of his mind all day. Was it something he said during one of his interviews? Or maybe something one of the interviewers had said to him? He couldn't for the life of him remember, but he was determined to get to the bottom of it. Maybe a glass of wine, some dinner, and a little quiet time would help.

When the waiter appeared, Bay ordered a burger, fries, and a glass of pinot noir.

As he sipped his wine, he acknowledged that during every second of his day, he'd thought about little else but King. How had the man gotten so far under his skin in such a short amount of time? Was it King? Or was it what King represented, the fact that he was somehow now questioning his sexuality? Again the question nagged at him. *Am I gay?*

Being gay was never anything Bay had considered. But on the other hand, he'd never considered being straight either.

He'd always thought of himself as shy, introverted, and nerdy Bay. That didn't make him straight or gay. But he couldn't ignore his attraction to King. Their first encounter, during which King had come on to him, seemed so out of left field, he was unprepared for it. And his rejection of King's advances must have been what kept King coming back. He assumed King didn't get rejected often, and he must have seen Bay as a great big challenge.

Maybe at first. But he sincerely didn't get that vibe from King the more time they spent together. Especially at the poker game. King had seemed very into being his date. Was *date* the right word? No. *Paid escort* was more like it, but that was not right either, because King had given him the money back. He still didn't get that. Except for the fact that King had said he'd enjoyed, even if just for a little while, belonging to someone. Was that feeling worth eight grand?

Bay decided something deeper was definitely driving King's actions. He imagined that in King's chosen professions, having a relationship would be difficult. It would take a very strong and confident kind of man to be in a relationship with a porn star and escort. But even considering all that, he suspected King had some serious issues with intimacy. Strange that an escort would have intimacy issues, but the more he thought about it, how could he not? How did an escort separate work from a personal life? Bay understood both gave King pleasure, but one was purely physical and one was both physical and emotional. Then it hit him like a ton of bricks. *It's the money! As long as he was getting paid, you were a job.*

In the beginning, King was being paid to seduce him. And he'd done his best to do just that. For pay. And each time they were together, if Bay had given in to King's advances, he and King likely would have been intimate. But once King was off the clock and had given Bay his money back, he was no longer willing and had pushed Bay away.

That had to mean something. Had he given the money back because he was starting to have an emotional connection to Bay?

While he ate his burger, Bay rolled this over and over in his mind. His only conclusion—something had definitely changed between them. No great revelation. But King's simple gesture with the cash told Bay he was no longer a customer and had become something else to King. He was sure of it. The burning question was… *what*?

Bay finished his wine, wiped at the corners of his mouth, and laid his napkin on the table. The waiter reappeared to clear the nearly empty plate, and Bay ordered a second glass of pinot noir. Pushing back from the table, Bay wondered when all the other restaurant patrons had flooded in. The place was packed, and he hadn't noticed a single one of them enter or take a seat. He crossed one leg over the other and took a sip of his wine.

With one problem identified, another took over. The same thing that had been nagging Bay all day worked its way back into his consciousness. With idle time, he started to recount his day, starting with the first interview, but he'd talked to literally hundreds of people. How could he recall every conversation?

Okay. Start by focusing on the interviews.

The first interview had been early in the morning, and based on the circumstances of the previous night, Bay wasn't altogether there. But— he did remember Jessica had started off the interview by saying Jack Robbins was a sexy guy. He dug further into the recesses of his brain as he quietly tapped his fingers on the table. *Oh yeah!* Then she'd asked if Jack was based on him or his life. That was a joke. *Oh!* And if he'd made his stories up in his head? That was more like it. Bay took another sip of his wine and stared blankly at the backs of the couple sitting next to him. What came next? He listened to the steady tapping of his fingers. How he wrote and where? Yeah. That came next. And then something about the story taking on a life of its own?

It was coming back to him slowly. The problem was, those were all the standard questions. Bay could answer them in his sleep. What came next?

The question she'd asked next had surprised him. He'd had to really think about his answer. *Think, Bay.* Then as if a light switch had been turned on in his head, it came to him. *"Has Jack ever disappointed you in a path his character has taken, or do you think you've ever disappointed him by taking him down a wrong path?"*

Bingo!

The last part of the question and his response were what been nagging at him all day. *I was obviously thinking about King when I responded.* But more interesting was what he remembered next. Jessica had said she, as a reader, instinctively trusted him and Jack. She said they seemed like the types of guys who go after exactly what they want in life. And would never do anything they didn't want to do. *That's it!*

If King was right and Jack and Bay were one and the same, which he seriously doubted, then maybe it was time for him, like Jack, to go after what he wanted in life. He didn't know exactly what that meant for him and King, but he definitely wanted to explore this attraction to King. No one else had ever made Bay feel this way. That had to mean something. The connection he'd felt to King, fueled by Jack Robbins or not, was real.

Bay realized he was already missing King and made up his mind right then and there. When he got back to New York, he was going to reach out to King. He would beg if he needed to, but he wanted time to figure this out. The answer might be that King was an escort and was only doing his job, but the emotion and tears in King's eyes last night told a different story, and Bay wanted to get to the bottom of it.

At least with a plan, Bay felt a little better. He glanced at his watch and panicked. *Oh shit!* His plane was probably boarding already, and he needed to move. He left money on the table and exited the restaurant, dragging his carry-on behind him. No one was in line when he arrived at the gate, breathless from running down the terminal. He showed his boarding pass and ID.

"Glad you could join us, Mr. Whitman," the gate attendant said. "You're seated in 4B. Please feel free to board." She scanned his boarding pass, gave it back to him, and motioned toward the Jetway.

As he stepped onto the plane, Bay looked up in search of an open overhead compartment for his roller board. He found a place above 3C, shoved his bag in, and clicked the door shut. When he turned and looked at his empty seat, he stopped dead in his tracks. The man in 4A was looking out of the window, his head resting against the plexiglass guard. Even without seeing his face, Bay recognized those broad shoulders. King Slater.

CHAPTER FIFTEEN

OUT OF the corner of his eye, King saw someone standing in the aisle, fumbling in the overhead compartment, but he ignored the urge to turn, smile, and acknowledge his seat companion. The last thing he wanted was small talk. His day had turned out to be much longer then he'd anticipated, and he was truly exhausted, mentally and physically. His plan was to pull the airplane blanket over his head as soon as they took off and hopefully sleep all the way back to New York.

King closed his eyes and sighed. The shoot in the park had taken three times longer than it should have due to the crowds of people enjoying the sunshine and mild temperatures. They'd had to do take after take when someone would walk or run through a shot, so they eventually had to start getting people to sign releases. It had been way past lunch when they finally finished. And because of that, the photo shoot at the studio had to be pushed back to five o'clock, and it had taken several hours. King had arrived at the airport with barely enough time to return his rental car, fight his way through security, and get to his gate before they started the boarding process.

The flight attendant had eyed him strangely when she'd taken his drink order, and now King felt more eyes on him. But familiar eyes this time. The hairs on the back of his neck stood at attention as he gave in to his curiosity, slowly turned, and then blinked in disbelief when he found Bay Whitman looking back at him. *Damn he looks good*! was King's first thought. He was still in the same gray suit he'd worn for the television interview, albeit his shirt was now unbuttoned at the collar and his tie loosened, which gave him a more relaxed appearance. But there was something else. Bay's face revealed signs of weariness, and King was pretty sure he was responsible for that. Maybe not intentionally, but he'd done it just the same.

As soon as the initial shock of seeing Bay wore off, dread replaced all the other feelings he was experiencing.

"What are you doing here?" King asked, for lack of anything better to say.

"Great to see you too," Bay said, slipping into his seat.

King sighed. "Sorry. I'm just surprised to see you."

"As am I," Bay agreed, smiling weakly. "You told me you were on a flight right after the shoot in the park."

Heat crept up King's face. "In all honesty I didn't say 'right after,' I said 'after,' and well, technically… it's after."

Bay shoved his satchel under the seat in front of him and looked back at King. "Whatever."

King knew *whatever* in this case was slang for *fuck you*, and he guessed he deserved it. He had led Bay to think he was leaving right after the shoot, but he'd had good reason at the time. King was about to apologize when the flight attendant approached.

"May I get you something to drink, Mr. Whitman?"

Before Bay could answer, the woman knelt beside his seat, looked around, and leaned in close. "I'm a huge fan. I've read all your books and loved each and every one of them."

Bay smiled. "Thank you very much. So glad to hear it. In fact, I have one in my bag. I'll be happy to autograph it for you before the flight is over."

The flight attendant's eyes lit up, and she stood. "Really?"

"It would be my pleasure."

The woman glanced at King again, and her expression told him as soon as she'd put two and two together. *Here we go again.*

She flashed a broad smile at King and mouthed, "That's where I know you from. Jack Robbins. I knew I recognized your face."

King smiled but put his finger over his lips, "Shh…."

She nodded, covered her mouth with her hand, and looked back at Bay.

Bay crooked his finger in her direction, and she leaned in close again. "Yes. He is the cover model for my Jack Robbins novels, but he's not as used to the attention as I am, and he gets a little nervous when people recognize him."

She turned to King again, and he nodded. "Mum's the word," she said. She took a furtive glance around again and then twisted her finger in a locking motion in front of her lips.

"I'll have a Dewar's Black Label and water," Bay said.

"Another Tanqueray and tonic, please," King added.

The attendant nodded. "I'll be right back, gentlemen."

"Thank you for making her go away," King said. "There is a very good likelihood that at least one of the male flight attendants on this flight is gay and could very well recognize me. The last thing you need is a scandal involving Jack Robbins and a porn star-slash-escort."

Bay laughed. "You're right. But it sure would be interesting, wouldn't it?"

"So," King said. "You caught me stretching the truth, but why are you on this flight?"

"I've always been scheduled on this flight."

"Funny. I didn't know that."

"You never asked," Bay replied as he retrieved his satchel from under the seat. He dug through it and brought out a Sharpie and a copy of his latest book. He signed his name on the back cover, flipped it over, and offered the book and the Sharpie to King. "You sign on the front."

King didn't move. He simply stared at Bay. "Are you serious? I thought we just agreed you didn't need a scandal."

"Oh come on," Bay said. "It would make her so happy, and besides, it will keep her from wagging her tongue to the others. What if she opens her mouth to one of those male flight attendants you were speaking of?"

King huffed and rolled his eyes but finally took the book. He studied it, still amazed at how much the cover imaged looked like him. Again, King had a sudden twinge of guilt at the dishonesty of pretending to be someone he wasn't, but he shook it off. It was only one last time, to avoid any type of scene. He scribbled Jack Robbins's name on the bottom of the cover and gave the book back to Bay. "There."

"Thank you," Bay said.

When their flight attendant returned, she unfolded cloth napkins and laid them on each of their open tray tables. "I'll be right back with your drinks."

When she left, Bay slid the book under his napkin and waited. When she returned he whispered, "My napkin has a stain on it."

"Oh no," she said, looking down. He picked up the book covered by the napkin and handed it to her. She accepted the napkin and obviously felt the hard object underneath. It took her a second, but she smiled and winked. "I'll get you another right away, sir."

King took a sip of his drink. The bubbles from the tonic tickled his throat, but the tasty liquid slid down easy. He put the glass down. "Very smooth," he said, looking at Bay.

"A simple trick of the trade," Bay said. "Especially when you want to avoid drawing a crowd."

"Tell me something," King asked, "if you're so uneasy in your role as a well-known author, why do you do it?"

Bay didn't respond right away. He stirred his drink with his finger while he appeared to be carefully considering his answer. "The short answer—because I have to write," he said. "It's not only my creative outlet, but it's the way someone like me experiences life. The way we're heard."

King sipped his drink again. "What did you do before you became so successful? If you don't mind me asking."

"I've always written," Bay explained. "But believe it or not, before I became famous I was a copywriter and editor. I worked from home and paid the bills by writing ad copy and marketing materials for an advertising agency and editing newspaper articles."

"I see," King said. "When did you start writing fiction?"

"Like I said, I've always written fiction. What I thought was okay, I self-published. The rest sat locked away on my computer, never to see the light of day."

"Did they sell?"

"I sold some copies here and there but never enough to really amount to anything. Until—"

"The Jack Robbins novels?"

Bay nodded. "Shortly after I released *A Tryst in Thailand*, my first Robbins novel, someone from Random House read it, loved it, and contacted me to ask if I would be interested in having them rerelease it under their imprint, with new editing and a new cover. Of course I jumped at the chance, never imagining it would be successful. I mean… I couldn't really imagine so many people reading my work. I simply thought it would sell a few hundred copies and that would be that."

"Apparently that's not what happened," King said.

"Nope," Bay replied.

"I'm sorry to say I haven't read any of your work, but I will. I mean… I've been sort of caught up in my own tawdry success. Nowhere near your status but not too shabby in my world."

Bay held up his glass in a toast. "Here's to our shared success."

King touched his glass to Bay's and took a sip. "What do you think makes your work so successful?"

"I've been told one of the draws to my work is because I do a thorough job with my research. In my novels it's important to me that a reader can clearly picture a location by the detailed description of the scene. Using every tool at my disposal, I research images, history books, travel guides, the internet, etc. I piece together the location for a scene in my head as if I've actually been there, and then I describe it. Oh hell. I don't know. You're probably sorry you asked."

"No! Please go on," King said. "I find this very interesting."

Bay appeared to be gathering his thoughts, and then he spoke. "Well. Each of the Robbins novels takes place in an exotic locale. In my early twenties, when I was finally out of school and my phobias were at their height, I did massive amounts of research for each of my novels. It was good to get facts right, but it was also a way for me to leave my apartment without ever having to actually do it—"

"So that's what you meant by 'the way someone like me experiences life,'" King interrupted.

Bay nodded.

"Okay, sorry. Go on."

"So by the time I'd finished researching a locale," Bay continued, "I felt like I had actually been there."

King pointed at Bay's forehead. "I can't imagine the amount of knowledge that must be stored away up there."

Bay smiled weakly. "On the few occasions my father was sober, lucid, and feeling fatherly, he would say, 'If you know a little something about a lot of things, you'll always be able to contribute to a conversation.' The thing is, I never left the confines of my four walls, so I never had a chance to share anything I learned with anyone."

"Now you share it with the world," King said.

"I suppose."

"And you're here now," King said, "sharing your story with me, and you seem fine."

"The truth is I have about 340 days a year to prepare myself for the four weeks a year I have to do promotional work," Bay explained. "And because I take on Jack Robbins's personality, I can grin, bear it, and play the part. But once this is over, it's back home for me until the next book release."

King flagged down the flight attendant and ordered another round of drinks. They had been in the air for almost an hour, and he was enjoying listening to Bay's smooth, even voice. Bay was opening up to him about his personal struggles, and that, for some unknown reason, made him happy.

Dinner was served shortly thereafter, and with a little encouragement, Bay elaborated on his career, how he overcame his fears, and how absolutely scared shitless he'd been months before his first book tour. In fact, Bay had explained that he'd been very close to cancelling the entire tour and letting Random House sue the pants off him just to have it all go away. But then he'd come up with the idea to steal Jack's identity.

After the flight attendant had cleared their dinner, the cabin lights were lowered and everyone settled in for the rest of the flight. King smiled and turned to Bay. "So where were we?"

"Well, I think you were about to tell me what I said last night that brought you to tears and what I did to make you storm out of my hotel suite without an explanation," Bay said.

Ouch! A sucker punch. King's smile faded, and he looked out the window into the darkness. *How am I gonna explain this?*

King took a gentle elbow to his side, and he turned to Bay in response.

"Not so fun when the shoe's on the other foot, is it?" Bay asked.

The confident King Slater melted away, and he was sure the smell of fear was oozing out of his pores. He looked out the window again.

Bay rested a hand on King's forearm. "Look at me."

King slowly turned.

"It took me a while, but I figured it out."

A wave of nausea coursed through King. *Here it comes, man. Your secret is out.* "Figured what out?" he asked, not recognizing the voice that came from his own mouth.

"That all this has to do with money."

"Let me—wait! What?" King stuttered.

"Look, King. When you were getting paid, you were up for anything. You pursued me relentlessly, and when I resisted your advances and then you found out about Jack Robbins, you punished me by putting me in a very uncomfortable position and forcing me watch you have sex with another man. And you enjoyed the hell out of it."

Remorse again replaced his fear in just under a second. *He's right. It was unfair.* "You're right, and I'm sorry."

"Don't be," Bay said. "That was the cocky and always-in-control King Slater, putting me in my place for not being honest with him. I get that."

"But it was wrong of me to do that," King said. He touched Bay's arm. "I truly am sorry. At first I *was* just being King Slater and putting you in your place, but later I thought I might be helping you."

"Helping me?" Bay asked. "How?"

"I thought you were struggling with your sexuality, and maybe seeing two men having sex up close might help."

King's words hung in the air, and silence loomed between them.

Bay, looking straight ahead, spoke quietly. "Maybe it did. I don't know. But what I do know is last night when you gave me the money back, you were no longer just doing your job. You made me want to explore my attraction to you. But... something had already changed between us. Was it all just the challenge? When I was no longer a challenge, the attraction seemed to dissipate."

Silence again filled the space between them. Bay turned to King and looked him in the eye. "Come on, King. I've been brutally honest with you. I've answered your questions as truthfully as I can, and I think you at least owe me some sort of explanation."

"Owe you?" King hissed, quietly enough so as not to be overheard by the other passengers. "The night we met, I was an escort simply going on a call. That's it. Then I knocked on your door, and my life did a double flip. Where was this so-called honesty when you failed to tell me you were famous and I was the spitting image of your book character?" King turned away again.

"Yes, I wasn't totally truthful the night we met," Bay admitted, "but I came clean—"

"When you got caught at that book signing," King snapped.

This time Bay turned away. When he looked back, he looked even wearier. King again felt for Bay, but he didn't know how to explain his inability to get involved with him.

"Okay. You win," Bay said, sighing. "And we can just leave it at that. But for the record, I'm very sorry for whatever I did to offend or upset you. I'm gonna try and get some sleep now."

Bay reclined his seat, crossed his arms over his chest, and closed his eyes.

King turned back to the window and silently cursed himself and his life. He once again rested his head against the cool plexiglass window and closed his eyes, allowing the vibrations and the hum of the engines to lure him into a trance. How could he have let this happen?

Sometime over the last few days, he'd allowed Bay Whitman to get under his skin—something he'd not allowed another human being to do in a long time.

Avoid temptation, King. It was the first thing he'd learned in recovery, and he'd been able to do it successfully—until now.

He's right. I do owe him an explanation. But how?

King focused on the darkness as he tried to unclutter his mind and think clearly. Bay had gotten to him. There was no doubt about that. But how? Or more importantly, *when* had he let his guard down? It had happened so subtly he hadn't even noticed it. That was not like him. Since he'd started recovery, he been so guarded. But something in Bay made him feel safe. In an odd sort of way, they did have a lot in common. Even if all their likenesses screamed of dysfunctionality. Their insecurities. Lack of self-confidence. Their ability to hide behind an alternate personality. *You need a meeting, King. If you can just get to a meeting, this will all be better.*

SOMETIME LATER King was brought out of his own head by little whimpering sounds escaping Bay's lips. King reclined his seat, leaned back, and turned to face Bay. Their noses were now mere inches apart, and King studied his traveling companion. In slumber, his facial muscles were relaxed, and the weight of all he carried seemed to fade away.

If he dreamed, King hoped his dreams were good ones, not bad ones caused by King's actions. His storming out of Bay's suite had clearly hurt Bay, but he appeared at peace now, almost childlike, with a boyish look about him that made King smile. For the longest time, King studied him as he slept.

When Bay slowly opened his eyes, he was still looking so fresh-faced and cuddly that King wanted to wrap his arms around him and hold him. That desire surprised King. It wasn't sexual desire; it was emotional. One that didn't have anything to do with sex. *That* hadn't happened in, well—a very long time.

It seemed to take Bay a moment to focus, but when he did, he smiled. "Hey," he said.

King had an overwhelming longing to come clean. Before he had time to reconsider, he blurted out, "I'm a recovering sex addict."

King quickly looked around the first-class cabin to see if anyone had stirred or, even worse, heard him. He sighed with relief when everyone still looked to be asleep. He leaned back in his seat and closed his eyes in frustration. "Dammit," he said quietly. He looked at Bay. "That's not how I wanted to tell you."

CHAPTER SIXTEEN

BAY HEARD the words, but they didn't register at first. *Did King just tell me he's a recovering sex addict? What does that mean exactly?*

He was sure his face wore that deer-in-the-headlights expression, but that was exactly the way he felt. All sorts of questions ran through his mind.

Bay snapped out of his own head and studied King. His face bore obvious pain, mixed with relief and what looked like anticipation. Somehow Bay sensed this would be the turning point for them, and the way he reacted or what he said now would make or break any potential for a friendship, but he knew little about sex addiction. Only what he'd come across on television shows or online. He thought there was a 12-Step program, just like for alcoholics, but he couldn't be sure, so he was flying blind.

"Say something," King pleaded. "Please, Bay."

The shakiness in King's voice touched Bay. He decided the best course of action would be honesty. "I want to. But I want to make sure I say the right thing."

"There is no right or wrong thing to say," King explained. "Tell me how you feel."

How do *I feel?* "For starters I'm a little surprised that you are a recovering anything. You're always so strong and confident."

King groaned. "Maybe my confidence is an act." And then he added, "Just like yours."

"Maybe?" Bay said. "But you're awful good at it."

"And so are you."

"Okay. Point taken," Bay said. "I don't really have any experience in this area, but at first consideration, it doesn't seem to me that your chosen line of work might be the best fit for a recovering sex addict."

"That's where you're wrong," King explained. "It's exactly the place for me."

Bay cocked his head. "How so?"

King paused and then spoke. "Sex addiction is not like an alcohol or drug addiction. They can stop cold turkey, or at least try to, but sex addiction is different. It's like a food addiction. You can't stop eating, and you don't stop having sex. You find a way to moderate your behaviors."

"Okay," Bay said. "But I don't understand how having sex with a lot of guys is moderating it."

"That's the whole point," King said. "Because none of the sex I have is about me. It's not for my enjoyment. It's for theirs. It's always about their pleasure. Remember, these guys call me. They pay me. And it's my job. And the video work—it's the hardest work there is. There's nothing romantic about it. It's work. A lot of hard work."

A lightbulb went off in Bay's head. "That's why when you gave me the money back and I kissed you, you couldn't handle it, and you bolted."

King sighed. "It was no longer work." He turned to Bay. "Please hear me when I tell you that I haven't kissed a guy or had sex with a guy *for me* in over three years. That act would be what we call a trigger and could very well bring my walls tumbling down around me. The way I moderate it is to never make it about me. And you… were about me."

Bay was flattered and felt guilty all at the same time. "I'm sorry," he said. "I had no idea."

"I know you didn't," King admitted. "And I should have told you instead of running out, but I got scared."

"The other night when we were just getting to know each other and you referred to the amount of sex you'd had, I asked if that had been after you started escorting, and you said 'and before.' You were talking about the addiction. Right? I sensed you were alluding to something."

"Yeah," King said. "That same night I told you how gawky and awkward I was as a kid and that I had been picked on relentlessly. When I was a teenager, my self-image was really bad, but then in my midtwenties I started working out and bulking up, and guys started noticing me. Being attractive was not something I was used to, and man, the attention was like oxygen to a drowning man."

"And that's when you started having so much sex?" Bay asked.

King nodded. "I didn't handle the attention well. I mean… the city is full of hot guys, and they wanted *me*. So why not? It was all so new, and then it became an obsession to see how many guys I could get to sleep with me. And in the middle of all of this, I was becoming addicted to the sex, and I didn't even know it. I lost everything because of it."

"Everything?" Bay asked.

"During this insanity, I was in the first and only relationship I've ever had, and it was great for a while. It could have been life-changing. But I fucked it up royally and hurt a good guy."

"I'm sorry," Bay said.

"No. It's okay. Everything that happened to me back then made me who I am today. I'm nowhere near perfect, but I'm okay. As you once said, I know who I am. I struggle with self-confidence, but I think most people do. I walk a tightrope every day of my life, balancing what I am with who I am, and I've done an okay job."

"When did you realize you had a problem?" Bay asked.

"My best friends finally did an intervention," King explained. "I went to my first meeting, and within the first half hour, I knew they had been right. I kept going to the meetings, and I started seeing a therapist to help me figure out why I was behaving the way I was."

"And?" Bay asked.

King sighed. "I realized having a lot of sex had become my identity, and I no longer knew who I was without it."

Bay nodded. "And from there you were able to fix it?"

"I was able to start to live with it," King said. "It takes a long time to fix it, but like I said earlier, you moderate it. And eventually there *will* be sex for *me*. When the time comes, it will be built on emotional trust, respect, and a healthy passion. Recovery is different for everyone. For me, for now, it means no more compulsive behavior. I do my job, please my customers, and go home."

Bay laid his hand on King's arm. "Thank you for sharing this with me. I must say I'm very impressed by the way you've handled your recovery."

"Thank you," King said. "I'm a work in progress."

"But you know the one thing that surprised me while listening to your story?"

"What's that?" King asked.

"That sex addiction is not really about sex."

King smiled. "It isn't about sex at all. It's about a lot of things. It's about the hole in our lives and how we fill it—with alcohol, with drugs, with sex. It's about avoiding intimacy with the ones you love while making connections with strangers you perceive to be safe. It takes time to turn all that nonsense inside out. It takes time and help to right all the wrongs."

King turned and looked out the window again.

"King," Bay said. "Look at me, please."

When King turned back and their eyes met, King's were moist with unshed tears. "It sounds to me like you've ridden a tsunami and come out on the other side with your head above water. I know we just met a few days ago, but I feel a sense of pride in what you've accomplished, and I have the utmost respect for you. But more importantly—I feel a strong connection to you. I don't want the friendship we *were* building to end."

King smiled warmly. "Who would have thunk it?" he said. "A successful, straight *New York Times* best-selling author and a gay porn star-slash-escort become friends."

The *straight* part of that sentence caught Bay's attention. Based on his newfound attraction to King, he figured he had to be bisexual at the very least. And after everything King had just shared with him, the time for secrets between them was over. Bay cleared his throat. "Well, to be honest, King, based on my attraction to you, I don't know exactly what I am, but *straight* is not it."

King didn't look surprised. "I know that," he said. "But I was gonna let you figure that out on your own."

"I was really confused at first," Bay admitted. "I've never been so attracted to another person before, and the fact that you were a man made it all the more confusing, but to be honest, I figured it out pretty early on. I was just afraid to admit it, even to myself. I wanted you to know that."

"I think every gay or bisexual person has been where you are," King reassured him. "And... have experienced exactly what you're going through. You're just a late bloomer."

"It's like thinking you're American all your life and finding out you were born in another country," Bay said. "It's boggling my mind."

"Don't overthink it," King suggested with a supportive smile. "Have you never been attracted to another man?"

"Never," Bay admitted. "But for that matter, I've never really been attracted to women either, or anyone in fact. I mean, I notice attractive people, men and women, but the couple of women I've been with have sort of fallen into my lap, so to speak, and I just went with it. With you, the attraction was different. It caught me totally off guard, but it was strong and genuine."

King's smile faded. "Bay, I'm a recovering sex addict, porn star, and escort. What could I possibly have to offer you?"

"Friendship, for starters," Bay said. "My friends list consists of my assistant, Rachel, my editor, Jamie, and my publicist, Samantha."

"Really?"

"I told you I don't get out much."

"Don't feel badly," King admitted. "I have three really good friends and a lot of acquaintances."

"You?" Bay asked. "In your business I figured you'd have friends coming out the wazoo."

"Nah. In my experience, most guys in the business are pretty untrustworthy, and I stay away."

The lights brightened, the familiar *dingdong* that usually accompanied the flight attendant's voice sounded, and she announced their final approach into JFK.

Bay stuck out his hand. "Friends?"

King chuckled and shook Bay's hand. "That much I can give."

"Hey, where do you live?"

"Midtown. West Fifty-Sixth," King said. "You?"

"Lincoln Square. West Sixty-Third."

"We're close, but I would have figured you for an Upper East Side kinda guy," King teased.

"Oh, so now you think I'm a snob?" Bay asked. Without allowing King time to answer that, a thought hit him. "Hey. You wanna share a cab?"

"I'm going straight to a 7:00 a.m. meeting," King said. "But it's near my apartment, so sure. I'll share a cab."

CHAPTER SEVENTEEN

BAY WAS back at home and surrounded by the safety and security of his dark, closetlike office, where his thoughts and words usually became his stories. But not now. The first two days since his return, he'd focused on nothing but researching sexual addiction. He read everything he could find on the internet at least twice and was amazed at how much information was at his fingertips.

He learned that most men and women join Sex Addicts Anonymous and initially have no clue how to recover. They first deal with the problems that brought them to the meetings—their compulsive, dangerous, and often illegal behavior—and then hopefully grew from there. He also learned that in SAA, they develop "circles" that define the kind of behaviors that mark them as sex addicts. The "inner circle" represents the behaviors they'll never do again—like the drink for the alcoholic, the fix for the drug addict, the hamburger for the food addict. If they slip, they start counting their time again. They learn to avoid triggers and situations where they can potentially fail. He was surprised to learn that many of these men and women are in marriages or long-term relationships. Their lives are dysfunctional, and they know it. But once they seek help, they'll expect to spend months, if not years, in 12-Step meetings, individual therapy, and marriage counseling if they hope to save their relationships.

Once he'd memorized everything he could find on sexual addiction, he finally tried to write. He stared at his computer screen and stared. And stared. But nothing came. So instead he found his fingers typing King's name into Google, and once he started watching what came up, he couldn't stop. He watched and watched and… watched. Most nights until the wee hours of the morning. Anything to distract him from picking up the phone and calling King. Speaking of triggers, the more he watched, the more he wanted to see King in person. But he couldn't be King's trigger. King had made that perfectly clear.

Whatever had happened between them in Vegas had happened, but King had taken him into his confidence, and now that Bay knew King's struggle, it was his responsibility to keep King's recovery moving along. So the next best thing was the internet. When Bay had seen every movie he could find with King in it without having to join some pornography website, he watched them all over again.

Day after day for the next three weeks, he sat in his mostly dark office, which was lit by nothing but the glow of his blank computer screen, acting like a beacon to his fingertips, calling them, egging them on. But sadly, still no words came. Words that usually came to him so fast his fingers couldn't keep up. And what he did write, he'd rewrite and then eventually delete. At which point the process would start all over again. When the next attempt would ultimately fail, he'd give up and watch more porn, and then go to bed.

Since he'd been back from Las Vegas, all he'd been successful at was discovering gay porn, educating himself on sex addiction, and ironically enough, masturbating repeatedly to King's porn videos.

Restless and slouching from sitting week after week inactive and unable to write, Bay propped his elbows on the arms of his leather chair and rested his chin prayerlike on his intertwined fingers. Since he'd been unable to concentrate on anything remotely related to a story, the month had given him a lot of time to sort through some things regarding what had happened to him out West and his sexuality in general. After watching tons of gay porn and actually enjoying it, he'd come to the conclusion he was bisexual—at the very least. And surprisingly enough, he was okay with it. But King Slater was a very different story.

King had called him a couple of times over the last few weeks, according to King to simply say hello. They had shared what amounted to small talk, but King had offered no invitation for them to meet. Bay didn't think it was his place as the fact King had been close to sabotaging his recovery because of him still weighed heavily on Bay's conscience. He did not want to be the trigger King had so clearly defined. But finally, King had called and suggested they have dinner, and Bay's heart had skipped several beats. He said yes without hesitation. He simply didn't have the power to say no.

Taking King's addiction out of the equation, Bay would jump at the chance to see if there was anything between them besides the initial attraction. But it had to be at King's initiation. And wherever that led him, it led him.

Tonight was their dinner date. Date? Was it a date, or was it merely two friends having a meal together? The closer the day came, the more anxious Bay had become. What should he expect? Would King be the same guy he'd been in Vegas, or would he be different on his own turf?

Bay hadn't left his apartment since he'd returned, and normally he loved the isolation his cocoon provided—a place where he could hide away and do what he did best. Live someone else's life. But if the truth be told, for the first time he felt like he was going a little stir-crazy. Had he sampled a bit of what real life tasted like and now he wanted more? The answer was a great big *maybe*.

For the last thirty days, as he pondered the events that led up to his return, he realized Las Vegas had fundamentally changed him. And not in a subtle way. He wanted to make some real changes in his life. When and how had that happened? And more importantly, he'd decided he wanted King to be part of those changes. But wanting and having were two different things. Would King be on board if Bay wanted more? On the plane, King had said he had nothing to offer Bay, so that was probably a no to Bay's own personal pipe dream.

But if there was the slightest chance that in time King might have something to offer Bay after all, he would wait. Hell, he'd been alone all his life; he could wait for King to sort things out. But how long would that take? According the everything he'd read on sexual addition, it was normally at least a year before things started to get better, but King had been in recovery for at least three years. Maybe it was taking longer because of his profession. He was sure that made things more complicated. Which brought up another point. Was he okay with what King did for a living? If by some strange whim of the gods, he and King did start seeing each other, could he handle his boyfriend sleeping with other men? He would have to. That's how he'd met King. He couldn't ask him to give up his job. He would have to trust King to keep his emotions separate, which was really no different from what he was doing now.

Bay had to get his head in the game. Not just for dinner tonight, but equally as important, a book signing at the Barnes & Noble in Union Square in one week. And this one was a big deal. His publisher, as well as DreamWorks Pictures were going to be in attendance to formally announce that Jack Robbins was coming to the big screen, directed by none other than Rob Offernan. For this one—Bay would have to be front and center.

KING HAD made the decision to ask Bay to dinner an hour before he'd made the call. He'd debated internally for quite a while but in the end decided it was now or never. He'd chosen a little Italian restaurant named Brasso56 down the street from his apartment. It wasn't fancy, but it was quiet, intimate, and had great food. Bay was meeting him there, and King was ready early, so instead of taking a cab, King decided to walk. As he strolled down West Fifty-Sixth Street, he mentally prepared himself for seeing Bay again. Butterflies danced around in his stomach at all the scary possibilities, but he'd committed to this, and he was going to see it through.

Since he'd returned, he'd focused mainly on working and getting his recovery back on track, the recovery almost derailed because of one Bay Whitman. And reading Bay Whitman's novels. He'd started with *Midnight Run*, the book he'd bought in Vegas, and then read every book Bay had written. They were good. Damn good, and King could totally understand Bay's success.

Soon after his return, much to his own surprise, King had started turning down escort jobs. One here and one there at first, and after the first few, all of them. He didn't need the money now, and for some reason they no longer held his interest.

He'd thought of little other than Bay. The man had shaken his resolve to its core, and knowing Bay was only blocks from him made matters even worse. Bay was a trigger, and that scared the hell out of him.

They hadn't seen each other since they'd been back, mainly because King thought he needed some time to get his shit together, and luckily Bay hadn't suggested they meet either. King didn't want to fall into old habits. He needed to steady himself. He'd been to his SAA meetings every day and had met with his sponsor at least twice a week. The meetings were something he desperately needed to ground him, and they did their job. On his first meeting with his sponsor, King had filled him in on everything that had happened in Vegas, and since that meeting they had talked about little else. But what his sponsor told him after their last meeting wasn't at all what King had expected—he'd pushed King out of the nest. He told King he thought he was ready and reminded King that he'd been in recovery for a little over three years. The time had come to test the waters. His sponsor's words echoed in his ears. *"You've done the work. Now it's time to see if it paid off."*

The 12-Step program never stopped an addict from having sex; it changed the way an addict acted on and thought about sex. But in the beginning, this sponsor had taken King on reluctantly because King had said he wanted to address his issues but couldn't give up his profession to do it. The sponsor had explained to King that he was a very unusual case, and together they were going to take it a day at a time. In the beginning, the sponsor had imposed limits on the number of escort and porn jobs King could do and warned him that if he showed any signs of not taking his recovery seriously or did more jobs than allotted, King would either have to give up his job or get a new sponsor. King had never forgotten that. But his sponsor had assured King that if he held up his end of the bargain, they would work through it together. And apparently that's what they had done.

"Old habits die hard," King mumbled to himself, still unsure.

But I have done the work.

The question that kept ringing in King's ears was whether he could trust Bay with such a sacred step. Even though Bay was struggling with his sexuality, King was pretty sure Bay would never intentionally do anything to hurt him, but what if King let his guard down and then Bay decided he couldn't or wouldn't be associated with a porn star? Or even worse, what if something did develop between them? Could Bay handle what King did for a living? It would take a very strong and confident man to accept King's lifestyle, and in Bay's own words, he was neither. Would King ever consider giving up his profession? He seemed to have more questions than answers, and that frightened him.

He and Bay had chatted a couple of times since they returned, and each time they'd spoken, Bay had seemed excited to get the call, albeit a little reserved. King assumed Bay was respecting King's boundaries and allowing him to make the first move, so after his last scheduled meeting with his sponsor, he'd done that. And when King had asked Bay to dinner, Bay hadn't appeared to have any hesitation, which made King hopeful. He would feel Bay out tonight and make the decision on how to proceed.

When King arrived, Bay was already seated at a table for two, wearing a black turtleneck and what looked like black jeans. Bay hadn't seen him yet, so King studied him. He looked more casual and relaxed than he'd looked in Las Vegas, but nonetheless stunning. He was a handsome man, and black emphasized every attractive feature.

Bay spotted him, smiled broadly, stood, and waved. King moved in his direction, mustering all the swagger he could get. When King extended his hand, Bay accepted it and pulled him into a hug.

"It's good to see you," Bay said, sounding sincere.

King stepped back and looked at him again. "You look great. Black is definitely your color."

Bay flashed a silly grin. "That's the same thing my stylist says, but I'm sure if it were up to me, I'd go around looking like a circus clown. I've never had any sense of style."

Bay sat, and King followed his lead.

"Well… you'd never surmise that by looking at you."

"Let's not test that theory," Bay teased. "And look at you. Not too shabby yourself. That green shirt makes your eyes sparkle, and may I add that it hugs you in all the right places." Bay held up his arms and gestured to King's biceps.

"You think so?" King said, smoothing the front of his shirt.

"I do. Oh, and I hope I'm not being too forward, but I ordered a bottle of pinot noir."

"Sounds perfect. Thanks."

When the wine came, King leaned back in his chair and studied Bay again as his dinner companion inspected the label and the sommelier opened the bottle. He seemed like he was on the mark, looking calm, cool, and confident, but King knew him well enough by now to see that some nerves were simmering below the surface. They'd only had a few days in Las Vegas, but those days were intense, and he'd seen Bay at his best and at his worst. But knowing he wasn't the only one with butterflies made him feel better.

The sommelier poured a small amount of wine into Bay's glass. Bay tasted and nodded, and the sommelier filled King's glass and then topped off Bay's. Bay held up his glass. "Cheers. It really is good to see you."

King touched his glass to Bay's and nodded. *So far so good!*

"Oh hey, before I forget," Bay said. "Next Saturday afternoon at one o'clock, I have a thing at the Union Square Barnes & Noble. My publisher and a representative from DreamWorks will be there to announce that *Revenge in Monte Carlo* will be the first of three Jack Robbins novels to hit the big screen. Please say you'll come."

"Is that wise?" King asked. "Me looking like Jack and all."

"Oh, that," Bay said. "Hell. We've already established your resembling Jack is all a coincidence, and besides—you are my friend and someone I care about. I want you in my life."

King smiled. "Okay, then. I'll be there." *He wants me in his life.*

OVER DINNER, the conversation was comfortable and flowed back and forth with ease. Bay took the lead, and King listened intently as he became animated and funny describing his writer's block and the frustration that came with it. But something was a little off with Bay. King detected a subtle difference in him. He couldn't quite put a finger on it, but it was definitely there. Not bad. Just there.

As the dinner progressed, King paid special attention to Bay's behavior. Bay was undeniably the same person he'd gotten to know in Vegas, but with an understated hint of someone else. Could the real Bay Whitman be joining the persona Bay normally wore when he was in public? According to Bay, there was no such person, but King knew there had to be. King decided he liked the mixture. Bay was still a little "Jack" in his gestures and mannerisms, but that could have been habit. The unfamiliar part of him had an easier wit mixed with a little sarcasm but was fun and way more relaxed. King decided he liked the new Bay even more.

It was King's turn to bring Bay up to speed on what had been happening in *his* life.

"So I finally got around to reading your books," King said, resting his arm on the back of his chair.

Bay's smile said he was pleased. "Which ones?"

"All of them."

"Really?"

King nodded proudly. "Yes, sir. And you're damn good."

Bay reached over and squeezed King's hand. "I don't know what to say. And thank you."

"Don't say anything. Just hurry up and release *Assassination in Argentina*. I can't wait to see what Jack gets into next."

"It's finished and in editing," Bay said. "Tomorrow I'll have Rachel send you a beta copy."

"Seriously? That would be great."

"Consider it done."

King went on to tell him about his daily meetings, the shoots he'd done, and about the times he'd spent with his sponsor. Not all the details, of course, not just yet. But the minute he'd seen Bay sitting at their table, he'd known he was going for it.

While they ate, King waited patiently in hope Bay would give him a lead-in to talk about them, but instead Bay nervously chatted away about New York theater, Las Vegas, and any number of topics. For someone who never left his apartment, Bay was knowledgeable about a great many things. When King made that comment, Bay blamed it on research.

"Ah yes," King said. "I remember you telling me you do massive amounts of research. You have a plethora of knowledge."

Bay laughed. "Yeah, but unfortunately most of it is useless."

After dinner they casually sipped port and shared a hunk of chocolate cake while enjoying a lull in conversation and a surprisingly comfortable silence. During dinner, Bay had not mentioned anything that had happened between them in Vegas, and King was starting to think Bay had decided he didn't want to explore their opportunities and was avoiding the topic.

King's hopes were beginning to fade, but then Bay said his name. And something in the way he said it got King's attention.

King looked up in anticipation. "Yeah?"

"You remember how I said I like research. Right?"

King nodded.

"When I got back from Vegas, I did a lot of research on sexual addiction," he explained. "I wanted to know everything I could."

King arched an eyebrow. "And…?"

"I understand a lot more about it now," Bay said. "I learned more about triggers and about how you should never put yourself in potentially unsafe situations. And the last thing I want to do is ruin or affect your recovery."

"I know that," King said. "And I appreciate it."

"But…," Bay said hesitantly, looking up through his eyelashes. "Am I a trigger? A dangerous situation?"

King sighed. "Yes. You are a trigger. And a potentially very dangerous situation for me."

Bay's expression turned to one of disappointment.

King reached across the table and took Bay's hand. "But you're a trigger and a potentially dangerous situation I'm willing to risk."

Bay tried to slide his hand out of King's, but King held on tightly. "No. I can't allow you to do that," Bay babbled. "I know if you mess up, you have to start counting your sobriety all over again. You've come too far—I can't be a part of that."

"Jesus," King said, "you have done your research. But Bay, this is not your call."

Bay studied King. "Of course it's my call," he said finally, yanking his hand out of King's, wadding up his napkin, and dropping it on the table. He pushed back and got to his feet.

"Wait," King said. "I didn't mean it like that. Just please sit down and listen to me."

Bay hesitated, but he eventually sat again and stared at King.

"Okay. I already told you I met with my sponsor three times this week. But what I didn't tell you is what we talked about."

"Isn't that confidential?" Bay interrupted. "Your conversations between you and your sponsor, I mean."

"On his part, yes," King explained. "I can share what we talk about if I want to, but he cannot. Bay, that's not the point."

"Then what is the point?"

"The point is," King said, "he thinks I'm ready to take the next step. To move forward in my recovery. With someone—with you."

The blood seemed to drain out of Bay's face. "What?" he asked, surprised.

"A sex addict's goal or purpose is to eventually get to a good, healthy place sexually," King said. "If not, what's the point of recovery? I've been in the program so long, I was afraid to dip my toe in the water. I mean… I'd gotten used to the norm."

Bay looked down. "I don't understand any of this."

"Here's the bottom line," King said. "I want to see where this thing between us is going, and I got the green light from my sponsor. The real question is—do *you* want to go down this road with me?"

Apparently Bay heard that part. He smiled and took King's hand this time. "Yes. I do. I mean… I think about you all the time. I only stayed away because I didn't want to be the one to—"

"I figured as much," King said. "And you have no idea how much I appreciate that. But it's okay. It's really okay."

Bay's gaze dropped to the table again.

"What's wrong?" King asked.

"I know what I want," Bay said softly. "What if you take a chance on me, and I screw it up?"

King chuckled. "I'm not worried about that. Hell, I'm more likely to screw this up than you are," he added.

"I am worried," Bay said. "I have no idea what I'm doing. What if I do it wrong? I mean… I've watched your videos. I know *what* to do—I just never did it before."

Did he just say he watched my videos? King's first thought was that Bay had scammed him. That Bay had known all along who King was and had been playing him.

King stood, and his chair flew backward. "You watched my videos? When?"

Bay looked startled and stood as well. "I'm sorry. While I had writer's block, I was thinking of you, and I got curious."

King lowered his voice and looked around the small restaurant. Everyone was now staring at them. But King didn't care. Right now he needed answers.

"When?" King demanded.

"When I got back to New York," Bay said. "Well, first after I met you in Vegas, but mostly since I got back. Why? Is that important?"

King cursed under his breath, overcome with embarrassment. He righted his chair and sat again. Why had he gone there first? He didn't really think that Bay would play him.

Bay sat as well, but from his expression, it looked like his wheels were already turning. King figured he was probably putting two and two together and coming up with what King had been thinking.

"Wait!" Bay said. "You still think I already knew who you were before we met in Vegas? And that I'm some kind of player?"

"No, I don't think that," King said, reaching across the table and trying to take Bay's hand again, but Bay pulled back and dropped it under the table.

"And yes, I went there for a second, but I was wrong. Honestly," King said, "I think I'm nervous and a bit scared."

Bay leaned back in his chair and crossed his arms over his chest. "Of me?"

"Not you exactly."

"Then what?" Bay demanded.

"You didn't even know you might be gay until recently," King said. "I'm taking a chance. What if you don't like it? Don't like me?"

Bay's expression softened. "King," he whispered, "you're right. I don't know what I'm doing here, but I do know if sex with you is anything like kissing you, I don't think you have anything to worry about."

King smiled. He wanted badly to give Bay another sample, but as he looked around the restaurant, people were again staring at them with a renewed interest. "I really want to kiss you right now. Can we please get out of here?"

Bay nodded. He flagged the waiter, and King grabbed the bill before Bay could. "I got this." He laid cash on the table. "It's the least I can do for being an ass and jumping to conclusions. Now let's go."

CHAPTER EIGHTEEN

ONCE THEY were outside and away from the prying eyes of the restaurant patrons, King quickly scanned the area and then pushed Bay into a nearby alley. He pinned him against the wall, and Bay read the desire and need in King's eyes. King smiled briefly and then angled down and laid his lips over Bay's.

Bay's heart raced as King's warm tongue pressed against his lips and then slowly slipped inside. It moved against Bay's tongue, and Bay gripped the back of King's neck and pulled him closer. He wanted him closer. Needed him closer. King broke the kiss and gazed into Bay's eyes again. "My place."

He took Bay by the hand, and they hurriedly walked, almost ran, down the street until they reached King's apartment building. King nodded at the doorman and led Bay up to the elevators. He pressed the Call button and waited. Then, as if he could wait no longer, he shook his head, cursed, and led Bay to the stairwell. Once inside the cement-enclosed shaft, King took two metal steps at a time, with Bay right behind him. When they reached the first landing, King stopped and again pressed Bay against the wall. He pulled Bay's turtleneck down and mouthed Bay's neck. Bay tilted to give him better access, and King nibbled and bit lightly and then licked. Bay's entire body shivered with pleasure. King's erection pressed against Bay's. Only thin layers of fabric separated their mutual need. Bay had seen King in action on-screen and off, and he knew what King had to offer him.

A wave of dread overtook Bay. Could he satisfy King? Or worse, could he even begin to compete with what King knew in the romance department? Then as King pulled away and tugged him up the next landing, he pondered how ironic it was that *he*, Bay Whitman, was in a stairwell making out with a porn star and male escort. Bay, the nerdy introvert, was doing exactly what Jack would have done with a conquest. But he wasn't Jack, and King wasn't a woman. It suddenly dawned on Bay that he hadn't been Jack all evening. He'd been mostly himself, and that revelation shocked him even more.

Another six floors and they were both out of breath, partly because they were climbing stairs at a very fast pace, but more because they were stopping at every floor to make out like teenagers. When they finally reached King's floor, King flung the stairwell door open and dragged Bay through it. They almost ran down the hall until King stopped in front of a door. He pulled out a key, fumbled to get it into the lock, and then in seconds they were inside King's apartment. King slammed the door shut, and the rest of the world was finally locked out.

King yanked Bay's turtleneck out of his jeans and pulled it over his head. He angled down, covered one of Bay's nipples with his mouth, and bit lightly, then licked the sting away. Bay flung his head back and gripped the back of King's head as if he'd done this a thousand times. The slight bit of pain mixed with the pleasure and warmth were sensations Bay had never experienced before, and he quickly realized how a person could get addicted to this. *Oh shit! King! How is he handling this?*

Bay pushed King back gently. "Slow down for a second," he whispered.

King gave him a questioning glance. "Are you okay?"

"Yes," Bay said. "But I'm worried about you. Are *you* okay?"

"Hell fucking yeah," King said. "Jesus, this is so good, but...."

"But what?" Bay asked.

"Why did you stop? Did I do something wrong?"

Bay pulled King to him and kissed him hard. He withdrew. "No. Everything's right. So right. But I want to slow down. You always take care of everyone else. For your first time since your recovery, I want to take care of you. I'm flying blind here, but I want to try to do this."

When King opened his mouth to speak, Bay was sure he was going to protest, so Bay stopped him. "It's important to me."

King acquiesced. He took Bay by the hand and led him into a living room, large by New York standards and stylishly decorated, with a small kitchen on one end and a door Bay assumed led to a bedroom on the other. King held his arms out to his sides. "I'm all yours," he said. "Have at it."

Bay rubbed his hands together and smiled, mischievously. No, not mischievously—more like giddily. He'd written about women being giddy because they were with Jack Robbins, but he had never actually experienced it for himself. The feeling was empowering, intoxicating, and a little overwhelming. King was giving himself over to Bay to do whatever Bay wanted.

Fear and apprehension replaced excitement. *Where do I start? What do I do?* But Bay cleared his head of all the clutter, stepped up to King, and allowed himself for the first time in his life to be guided by his senses, by lust and desire. The hows and whens, he thought, would present themselves. A little voice in the back of his head spoke to him. *"Do what you saw in King's videos. That's a good place to start."*

King smiled at him curiously. Bay kept his gaze locked on King's as his hands instinctively moved to King's emerald shirt. King took Bay's hands by the wrists and held him there. "Wait. Before we go any further, I want you to know I'm HIV negative and very healthy. I'm on the HIV preventative drug Truvada, and because of my work I'm tested for HIV and STDs every thirty days, using the latest RNA and p24 tests. They are the most accurate tests out there. And I use protection with everyone."

Bay dropped his forehead against King's chest. "I don't know what any of that means, and I'm so stupid because I never even thought to ask."

King cupped Bay's face in his hands and pushed Bay's head back until their eyes met. "You're not stupid. You're just inexperienced." King kissed him. "I just wanted you to know."

"Thank you."

King nodded. "Now, where were we?"

"I think I was about to do this." Bay slowly released each button of King's shirt. He tugged the shirt out of King's pants, slipped it off his shoulders, and let it fall to the floor. Bay broke eye contact and lowered his gaze. As he'd remembered, King's chest was tan, broad, and muscular. He ran his hands over King's naked skin, and it was soft and warm to the touch. He did as King had done to him—covered one of King's nipples and repeated King's actions. He bit gently, sucked, and then licked. King moaned, and Bay hoped that sound signaled pleasure and not pain. He got his answer when King pressed against the back of *his* head, forcing Bay's mouth harder against his nipple.

Bay kissed his way up King's chest to his neck. He buried his face there, licking and teasing King's soft, warm skin. King tilted his head, and Bay took full advantage of the added access. He breathed in the heady mixture of King's sweet cologne and his musky natural smell as he mouthed across King's Adam's apple, where he sucked, nibbled, and nipped a little more.

King's moans were getting more intense, which drove Bay to want to do more and do it better. With both hands on King's chest, Bay gently backed him up until they reached the couch. He pushed King down, his ass landing on the couch with a thud.

King looked up at him in surprise, and Bay simply smiled. He knelt at King's feet, removed King's shoes, and briefly rubbed his feet as King had done for him. When he looked up, King had rested his head on the back of the couch, and his eyes were closed.

"You okay?" Bay asked. "If you need me to stop...."

"No!" King said. "Please don't. It's been so long since I've experienced real feeling. Real emotions. This is so good."

Bay moved up to the couch and straddled King, kissed him, ran his hands through King's hair. It almost felt like someone else had taken over his body. He'd never dreamed in a million years he would be here—in a place like this, with a man like this. But here he was.

King's erection pressed against Bay's ass, and it both terrified and excited him. Driven by pure instinct, Bay wiggled. King opened his eyes in surprise, and Bay smiled and kissed him. Without their lips parting, Bay rose to his knees enough to reach between them, grip King through his tented pants, and squeeze. King moaned into Bay's mouth as Bay tightened his grasp and moved his hand up and then down again, repeating the motion several times. Bay's actions surprised even him.

With the overwhelming urge to taste King's skin again, Bay slid down a little farther and took King's other nipple into his mouth. King gasped loudly and gripped Bay behind the neck again, pulling his mouth closer. Bay circled King's nipple, bit lightly, and soothed the bite as he had before, by licking it. King moaned again, and the sound made Bay want to go further. Anything to please King, a man who had pleased so many but had denied himself for so long.

Bay then slipped off the couch onto his knees, positioned himself between King's legs, and spread them. He vaguely heard his name being spoken, but he ignored it, driven by a force he'd yet to experience in his life. Something bigger than he was. He wasn't sure what it was because nothing compared to the emotions coursing through him. The drive and determination to pleasure another was first and foremost in his mind. He unfastened King's pants, unzipped his fly, and pulled his underwear down, exposing his hardened length.

Bay had seen it during the shoot and on the internet, but being up close, having it right in front of his face, made what he was about to do all very real. But that didn't come close to stopping him.

His erection at full extension, King in all his glory was truly a sight to behold. Bay noticed the white, pearly liquid gathering at the tip and instinctively licked at it. King gasped and stiffened, and that reaction was intoxicating to Bay. He wanted more sounds like that, needed them.

Savoring the unfamiliar taste, Bay decided it was bitter, sweet, and salty all mixed together. King's essence on his tongue was like an aphrodisiac that aroused and empowered him beyond anything he'd ever known. He closed his eyes and nervously took King into his mouth. Bay had no preconceived notion what he expected King to taste like, but the reality of what he experienced didn't disappoint. King's skin was warm and silky, and when Bay moved his mouth lower, he caught an aroma he could only attribute to King. His own unique scent. He again realized what it might feel like to be addicted to something. This signature, this aroma, was pure King.

"Oh, Bayyy," King moaned, drawing out his name. Bay slid his mouth up and down again, but then King pulled him off. King's arms were under Bay's armpits, raising him up.

"Stop," King whispered.

Bay panicked. *It's Las Vegas all over again. King's not ready, I pushed too far. What was I thinking?*

Bay got to his feet. "I'm so sorry, King. I pushed you too far."

"No, baby," King said, getting to his feet, his pants falling to the floor at his ankles.

Bay stepped back, and when King stepped forward, his pants caught his foot, and he fell right into Bay's arms. Bay caught him, and they stood face-to-face. "It's not you, baby. I was about to come. You brought me so close, so fast. I didn't want to… I want to make this last."

Bay sighed with relief. "I thought…."

"I'm sorry," King said. "I should have been clearer. You are doing everything right."

King kicked his pants free, pulled his socks off, took Bay by the hand, and led him to the bedroom. He kissed Bay deeply and fumbled at Bay's belt buckle. Seconds later King broke the kiss and dropped to his knees. He pulled Bay's jeans down, untied each of Bay's shoes, and slipped them off, then peeled his socks off next. He lifted Bay's feet at the ankles, one at a time, pulled the jeans away, and flung them to the side.

Bay was self-conscious standing there in the nude, but not enough to run and hide or attempt to cover himself up. He wanted this. Wanted

King. When King got to his knees and took Bay into his mouth, Bay heard a thousand instruments in his head, strings and horns all playing the same chords at once. He slipped into a new world of wonder. So this was what he'd been missing all his life.

King released Bay and got to his feet. "You're beautiful," he whispered. "Your body. Your mind. Perfect in every way."

Bay flushed, but King didn't give him time to demur. Instead, he pushed Bay backward until his legs hit the bed. With a shove from one big hand, King laid Bay on his back in the plush bed and climbed on top of him. King pressed his lips against Bay's in a hungry and deep kiss, and Bay's erection throbbed between them. Wanting this to be about King more than him, Bay quickly raised one knee, pushed up, and had King on his back in one fluid move. King laughed, his eyes wide in disbelief.

Bay smiled down at him. "This is about you, remember?"

King pulled Bay down, wrapped his arms around him, and held him tightly. Bay eventually wiggled free and slid down once again to take King into his mouth. He did what he'd seen on-screen and moved slowly up and down King's solid length while he used one hand to play with King's balls and the soft skin underneath. When Bay looked up, King's eyes were closed, and his arm lay across his forehead. He was whimpering.

Bay might have been doing this for hours or only minutes; he didn't know, and it didn't matter. For the first time in his life, he felt truly alive. King stiffened, and he grabbed Bay's head and pulled Bay off him. He groaned out Bay's name, took himself in hand, and pumped one time. Warm, thick liquid landed on Bay's face and mouth. Bay licked his lips, and then King gripped him under the arms and pulled him up until they were face-to-face. King gazed into Bay's eyes with an expression Bay couldn't identify and then kissed him deeply. He shuddered and trembled for another few minutes, and Bay stayed right there with him, stroking his hair, kissing him, and holding him.

When King opened his eyes, he smiled. "That was incredible, Bay. You must have watched a lot of movies."

"A few," Bay teased. "But so much of it came naturally. It's as though I've been waiting my entire life for this very minute. It all felt so right."

King kissed Bay again and then flipped them over once more. "And it's gonna feel a lot more *right* very soon."

King repositioned himself at Bay's midsection and took Bay's still-hard length between his lips. The instant warmth of King's mouth surrounding him sent waves of pleasure up and down his body. King was doing something with his tongue that was driving Bay close to losing it, but he wanted more. As if King could sense Bay was close, he let Bay slip from his mouth.

Bay missed his warmth until King pushed Bay's legs back and licked at the skin between his ass and balls and he was again taken under. The area was so sensitive that Bay's nerve endings fizzed like they were being electrified. When King moved his tongue to Bay's opening, Bay froze. This was an area so personal, but King's intrusion sent waves of pleasure through his body. He put those self-conscious thoughts out of his mind, gripped the sheets, and held on for the ride. When King's tongue pushed in, that orchestra went off in Bay's head again. If he thought his nerves were on fire before, that was nothing compared to this.

King's hand moved up and down Bay's length as his warm, wet tongue teased his opening, bringing him almost to orgasm from all of the overwhelming sensations at once.

Bay's orgasm started to build deep within him. He stiffened and arched his back, and King's mouth was on his cock again, encircling him as his release raced to escape his body. When he came, it was longer and harder than he'd ever come in his life, and King had quite literally coaxed it right out of him. When King had drained Bay of every drop, King climbed back up to face him. "Was that okay?"

Bay couldn't speak. Tears stung the backs of his eyes, but he refused to allow them to escape. He nodded, and King chuckled.

When Bay could again form words, "Fucking A" escaped his lips before he could stop it. *Where did that come from?*

King laughed enthusiastically. "If you think that was good, wait for round two."

BAY OPENED his eyes to the brightest sunshine he'd ever seen. It streamed in through massive floor-to-ceiling windows, and the rays illuminated the dust particles dancing in the air. King's long, solid body was pressed firmly against Bay's back with one arm wrapped tightly around his midsection, gripped firmly in Bay's hand. King was snoring lightly, and the sound was comforting.

If he died this very minute, Bay thought, he would die happier than he'd ever been in his life. Again he wondered how all this could have happened to him in just over a month. Seemingly straight right on past bisexuals to obviously gay in thirty days must be some sort of record, but it just went to show that people were not always what they seemed, including him. In public he was never who he seemed to be, but personally he was not who he thought he was either. He didn't want to tempt the gods with too many questions, though. He figured he'd have lots of time to analyze all this later.

"I can hear you thinking," King whispered. "Please tell me those aren't regrets?"

Bay tightened his grip on King's hand. "Not on your life. You?"

"No, sir," King said. "I think I need to see my sponsor this morning, to talk through some of the emotions, but no regrets on my end either. Overall, I think I'm doing pretty well."

King released Bay and stretched. "I wonder what time it is?"

Bay looked at his watch. "Just after seven."

Bay had never stayed over the times he'd had sex, so he had no idea what the protocol was for this kind of thing. "Should I go?" he asked quietly.

King snuggled up behind him, his morning erection nestling in the crack of Bay's ass. He briefly wondered what it would feel like to have King inside him. Sam had seemed to enjoy it, as had every one of King's partners in his videos.

"Of course not," King said. "I have a shoot at eleven. I'll try to see my sponsor before then, and if you want we can grab a late lunch."

He has a shoot. Bay fought a pang of jealousy. *It's his job, Bay. You knew that before you got involved.*

"Bay?"

"Yes. Yes," Bay said, "I would love that."

"Then it's a date," King said. "We still have an hour or so before we have to get moving, and I know just what to do to fill that time."

King rolled over onto his back and Bay turned and slid next to him. Their lips met in a crushing kiss, and it was ecstasy, but King's shoot was still lingering at the back of Bay's mind. They probably should have spoken about this before, but now it was too late. Bay closed his eyes and decided to put that out of his mind until later.

He looked down at King. "Let's see what I can do to alleviate that hard thing poking my thigh."

CHAPTER NINETEEN

TWO HOURS later, King walked Bay down to the street, hugged him tightly, and put him in a cab. He showered and hopped in a cab himself to meet his sponsor at their usual coffee shop. On the way over, many emotions ran through him, but mostly he felt alive. For the first time in so long, he felt whole and normal. But a nagging apprehension had him scanning the sidewalks and nearby cars, paying special attention to every good-looking guy he could find. Much to his surprise, he had no desire to have sex with any of them. *That has to be a good sign.*

When King reached the coffee shop, his sponsor was already there, and without hesitation he slipped into the booth, said hello, and started talking. It was as if his mouth had a mind of its own, and the words flowed easily, without conscious thought. King realized he was a big bundle of emotions as he described his and Bay's evening. In a couple of days, he'd gone from seriously questioning his sponsor's suggestion that he act on his feelings for Bay, to nervousness for both himself and Bay, to cautious optimism at the restaurant, and then finally to elation.

As they talked, King's sponsor reassured him that everything he was experiencing was a normal part of recovery. Most of the emotions he was sorting through were brought on by fear—the fear of relapse, of trusting himself again and trusting the strength of his recovery, but mostly the fear of taking that first leap of faith.

King knew he was right. The man had been through it all himself and had survived with the help of a supportive wife and a good understanding of his demons. Now hopefully King would have Bay to help him maneuver this new territory. If all went well. But even if Bay didn't stick around, King could make it on his own. He felt stronger somehow.

By the time he said goodbye to his sponsor and got back in a cab, he was regretting the morning shoot. It was stupid and irrational, but he wanted to be with Bay. Not for sex, although that wouldn't be a bad idea, but he wanted to really get to know him. He wanted that emotional connection they'd had last night. A connection he hadn't allowed himself to develop in many years. But King again cautioned himself. He was a gay adult-film star and escort. That was his job. Was a real relationship sustainable? How he made a living would be difficult for anyone to handle long-term. What if the situations were reversed? He'd only known Bay Whitman for a month, but could he handle Bay going off to work each day to have sex with other men? Just the thought of someone else touching Bay made him crazy, so that answer was a great big no.

Added to Bay's own apprehensions and personal situation, asking him to get involved with a man who was in King's line of work was asking an awful lot. None of his friends in the business had been able to hold on to serious relationships. Why did he think he might? He decided that as soon as his shoot was over, he would go to Bay's place, and they would have this discussion. No need moving this *thing*, for a lack of a better word, between them forward without an open, honest, and direct conversation. If they were both being mature adults, it should have happened before anything else, but once everything started moving last night, it had gone so fast they'd both gotten caught up in it.

The thought of having to walk away from Bay because of his career was heartbreaking, but Bay deserved someone who made him feel safe and secure. If King's job didn't give Bay that security, he couldn't in good conscience let this move forward.

The shoot was proving to be awkward and draining, but King was doing his best. The director kept cutting, changing positions, rolling, cutting again, changing angles, rolling, and King was getting tired of it. This was nothing new to him, and he normally took directions well, but today it was getting on his nerves big-time.

Something was off with him. He was uneasy, like he was doing something inappropriate or wrong, like he was cheating in some way. But that was silly. Right? Bay knew what he did for a living. That was how they'd met, after all. Maybe it was because they hadn't broached the subject since they'd taken their relationship to the next level. Hopefully once they'd discussed it, everything would get back to normal. Whatever that was.

When the shoot was over, King showered, dressed, and called Bay.

"Hey, handsome," Bay answered cheerily.

"Sorry. I must have the wrong number."

"Very funny," Bay said.

"I'm done here. We still on for lunch?" King asked.

"Sure. I've been looking forward to it all morning. Why don't you come by here and we'll decide what we want then?"

"Perfect, but I need the address again."

Bay gave him the address and apartment number and told him the doorman would be expecting him.

"See you in a few."

King ended the call and flagged down a cab. He gave the driver the address and sat back to try to figure out a way to bring up the subject.

"We're here," the driver said in a strong unidentifiable accent, interrupting King's thoughts.

King looked up. They were indeed at the right place. *Man, that trip went fast.*

After paying the driver, King studied Bay's building. It was impressive, and Bay was on the twenty-second floor. *His views must be killer.*

The doorman held the door for him. "King Slater to see Bay Whitman."

"Yes. He's expecting you, Mr. Slater."

King rode the elevator to Bay's floor and looked at the set of numbers on the wall, which told him to go right. He walked all the way down to the corner unit, read the number on the door, and rang the bell.

He heard footsteps, and then Bay opened the door.

Each time King saw him, he was reminded of how handsome Bay was. Even more appealing, Bay had no idea what a devastating effect he had.

"Hey there," Bay said. "Come in."

Bay closed the door, pinned King against the back of it, and kissed him hard. "I've waited hours for this," he said breathlessly.

"Me too," King said, meaning it.

Bay took King by the hand and led him into the apartment. "Welcome to my humble abode," he teased.

"Humble abode?" King said, gazing around. "Jesus, Bay!"

Straight ahead was an enormous living room, with an equally large terrace and huge sliding doors. The living room alone was probably twice the size of King's entire apartment. To the right was a fully updated kitchen, and to the left was a powder room.

"I don't need this much space," Bay explained. "But my publisher strongly suggested I have a place large enough to entertain a few members of the press and other important muckety-mucks for each of my book releases."

"It is that," King said, still looking around in amazement.

He saw a ball-and-claw-footed desk positioned at an angle facing the terrace. "Is that where you write?"

"Oh no," Bay said. "I write in here."

Bay led him into the bedroom, and it was equally as impressive as the living room.

King looked around for a desk, but there was none. "You write in bed?"

"No, silly," Bay said, opening a door. "The place came with two walk-in closets." King looked in. All of Bay's clothes were as neatly hung as they had been in Vegas. Shoes lined up according to color, shirts folded and showing through glass-front, built-in drawers.

Bay opened a second door and pointed. "I write in here."

King stuck his head inside. The room was no bigger than eight by ten. There was a small desk, a lamp, a laptop computer, and a printer. "Man. You weren't teasing when you said you didn't like stimulation."

Bay smiled sheepishly. "Not that a lack of stimulation has done any good *lately*."

King frowned. "Still no luck, huh?"

"Actually this morning was much better," Bay said. "I think I'm heading in the right direction. And a lot of that has to do with you."

"With me?" King asked in surprise.

"Indirectly," Bay explained. "When I had no life, no stimulation, and lived through Jack, there was nothing to distract me, and I wrote like I was living his life, but now that you are in my life, I have to learn to function like every other writer who has distractions and needs to differentiate fact from fiction."

"But I don't want to be a distraction," King said.

Bay squeezed King's hand and kissed him on the cheek. "You can't help it. But you're gonna be a good distraction."

"How is that?"

"Before you, my writing was my life, which also just happened to be my job," Bay said. "But because of *you*, I want them to be separate now, and I'm gonna have to learn to do that."

"I think I get it." King paused. "Hey, while we're talking about jobs, I guess we need to discuss mine."

Bay's expression turned to one of obvious concern. "Okay."

"Can we go into the living room and sit?" King asked.

"Oh man," Bay said. "If we have to sit, this must be serious."

King took Bay's face in his hands and kissed him softly. "I hope not, but it's something we need to talk about."

"Come on," Bay said, leading King to the living room. They sat side by side on the couch, and Bay felt King's eyes on him.

"I think we should have had this conversation last night at dinner," King started, "but I—we—got carried away."

Bay gave him a knowing glance. "I think I have an idea where this is going."

"You do?" King asked.

"You probably want to know, after what happened last night, if I'm still okay with what you do for a living?"

King nodded. "This affects us both now."

Bay stood and started pacing. "Can I be completely honest?"

"Please," King replied.

"Is it my first choice?" Bay asked rhetorically. "Hell no. The last thing I want is my boyfriend sleeping with other men for a living. And I'm probably gonna be jealous and pissed."

King's stomach did a backflip.

"But...," Bay said, "it's your job. It's what you do, and I knew this before I got involved. I will do my best to keep my jealousy under control."

King felt instant relief. "I'm sorry," he said. "I know it won't be easy."

"Easy?" Bay asked. "That's an understatement. King, you're dealing with a man who has very little self-esteem and self-confidence. It's gonna take everything I can manage to keep from killing someone."

King reached out, took Bay's hands, and pulled him close, then kissed him.

When the kiss ended, Bay pulled back. "I can't in good conscience ask you to quit your job, no more than you can ask me to quit mine. But you're gonna have to be an open book to me. There can't be any secrets between us."

"Well, in the spirit of that," King said, "I want you to know I haven't taken on any escort jobs for the last few weeks."

"Why?" Bay asked.

"I don't know," King said. "I'm still trying to figure that out. But it didn't feel right. Right now I'm okay on finances, and I'm still doing the porn shoots, but if I have to start escorting again, I promise I'll tell you as soon as I decide."

"The only thing I will ask, and I realize this is all new and we have no idea where's it going, but please don't ever use this against me," Bay said.

"How do you mean?"

"For instance," Bay said, "if we get in an argument and you're angry at me, please don't take an escort job to piss me off or hurt me. If you used that against me, I don't think I could ever trust you again. And oddly enough, I do trust you."

"I'm glad." King frowned. "But I'm not a vindictive guy."

"I don't think you are," Bay assured him. "But I want everything on the table. Complete honesty."

"You referred to me as your boyfriend," King said with a smile.

"I did?" Bay asked. "It just came out. I'm sorry?"

"Don't be. I like it."

"I'm not naive enough to think this is gonna be easy or perfect," Bay admitted. "But I do want to see if we have something here."

"So do I." King angled his head down and kissed Bay again. He pulled back and looked into Bay's eyes. "I have a boyfriend. Who knew?"

"That makes two of us," Bay chuckled. "Having a boyfriend is exhausting. Can we get something to eat now?"

"Tired of me already?" King asked.

"Not on your life. The sooner we eat, the sooner I can show you how not tired I am of you."

"I'm gonna hold you to that."

CHAPTER TWENTY

WHEN THEY returned from lunch, full and happy, Bay took King by the hand. "I have plans for you," he said. "Follow me."

Bay led him to the bedroom and pointed to the bed. "Sit," he said, kicking off his shoes.

King arched that now very familiar eyebrow again, but he did as he was told. "I think I like the 'in control' Bay Whitman," he added.

"This is all about you," Bay said.

"No. Wait," King said. "I thought last night was about me?"

"It was supposed to be," Bay explained. "But it didn't turn out that way. Our libidos sort of got in the way."

"Come on, Bay—"

Bay stepped up and laid his finger over King's lips. "Shh. Just relax and let me do this, please."

Bay had it all planned out. He was definitely inexperienced, but he'd watched a lot of gay porn over the last month, learned a lot, and he was going to put all that knowledge to good use. He'd made a stop on the way home to get the necessary supplies.

King smiled. "Well. Since you asked nicely. But I really don't want you making a habit out of this."

"Okay, then," Bay said. "This will be the last time."

King looked disappointed. "You certainly don't have to go that far," he teased. "Maybe just now and then."

"Shh." Bay pulled King's T-shirt out of his jeans. King raised his arms and the shirt went up over his head and landed on the floor at Bay's feet. Bay smoothed King's hair, brushed it out of his eyes, kissed the top of King's head, and gently pushed at his chest. "Now lie back and relax."

King complied.

Bay, still standing over King, unbuckled King's belt, released the fly one button at a time, and opened King's jeans until his black cotton briefs were exposed.

Remembering all the moves he'd seen in King's videos, Bay was intent on duplicating each of them. He could see King was already getting hard, and he was eager to get started.

Placing both hands on the bed on either side of King's thighs to steady himself, Bay slowly leaned down. With King's underwear still in place, Bay ran his tongue over King's length, licking through the thin layer of cotton. Then he gently bit the growing bulge and ran his teeth up and down it. That move drew a gasp out of King, which encouraged Bay to continue.

Bay nibbled there for another few seconds and then slid down to King's feet and knelt. He pulled King's boots off and tossed them to the side. Then he gripped King's jeans and slid them down over his hips, calves, and feet, taking King's socks with them and then added all the items to the growing pile of clothing beside him.

After climbing to his feet, Bay pulled his sweater over his head and saw that King was watching him with an intense expression. Bay wanted to give him a show, so he released his own jeans and shimmied deliberately as he eased them down and then peeled off each of his socks.

"Slide farther up on the bed, please?" Bay asked. King lifted one leg, dug his heel into the mattress, and pushed himself closer to the headboard.

Bay climbed onto the bed and straddled King's growing erection, wondering again what it would feel like to have King inside him.

Interrupting his thoughts, King reached up, cupped Bay's face, and pulled him down. Their lips met in a crushing kiss, and without hesitation, Bay shoved his tongue into King's mouth as he ran his fingers through King's dark blond hair. When Bay pulled back, he raised up to his knees. "Turn over," he said softly.

King turned under him and within seconds was on his stomach, head resting on his folded arms. Bay leaned over and grabbed a bottle out of the bedside table. He flipped the top back, poured some of its contents into his hands, and rubbed them together vigorously. He then laid his hands on King's shoulders and spread the now-warm liquid over King's broad shoulders. He began to massage, squeeze, and knead the tight muscles until King was purring like a kitten. He continued, paying special attention to the back of King's neck as he'd seen one of those masseurs do in a video. When he'd covered every inch of King's shoulders, he slid down and started working on King's lower back.

Bay moved lower yet, hooked a finger into King's underwear, and—with a little help from King, who raised his torso—slid them down and off. Bay squeezed more oil into his hands, warmed it again, and touched King's asscheeks. He rubbed and massaged the round globes, moved lower to the backs of King's thighs, and then ran his hands back up again. He slid his fingers into the crack of King's ass to brush lightly over his opening, coaxing a long moan from King before he moved lower still. He coated King's calves and feet, and squeezed the muscles there.

"Can you turn over for me once more?" Bay asked when he'd covered every inch of King's backside and had thoroughly worked the oil into King's silky skin.

King again turned over, and his sparkling hazel eyes met Bay's with such gratitude, Bay had a hard time looking away. But he again picked up the bottle of oil and flipped the top. King took the container from him and looked at the label. "Massage oil? Have you given a lot of massages?"

"Just this one," Bay said. "I bought the oil and a few other things on my way home this morning. Did I do okay?"

"Like a pro," King said, handing the bottle back to him.

"Like I said, I watched a lot of porn over the last month. And I plan to do everything I saw in those videos."

"Everything?"

"Everything."

King smiled seductively as Bay spread more oil over his chest and rubbed it in. Bay focused on King's nipples, circling them, pinching them, and then rubbing his thumbs over them. Bay finally closed the bottle and laid it on the bedside table. He kissed his way down to King's stomach and then lower, until he was face-to-face with King's impressive length. He brushed his chin against it, hoping his day-old stubble gave King a little added stimulation and pleasure. A twitch and a moan signaled he'd been successful, and he continued his pursuit. Bay lowered his head and took King's balls into his mouth, moved them around like he'd seen, and teased the undersides with his fingers. King was almost squirming now, and Bay was elated that he was doing something right.

Bay pushed King's legs back to expose his opening, then ran his tongue over it lightly. King gripped the sheets, arched his back, and wriggled. "Bayyyy. That feels so good," King whispered.

Driven now by an instinct that outstripped the lessons of the videos, Bay circled King's opening with his tongue and then pushed the tip inside. King tensed, relaxed, and then tensed again with each attempted breach. Bay ran his tongue back up to King's balls and then higher and took King into his mouth. He attempted to swallow King's length all the way down, but gagged at the halfway point and pulled back. Fueled by pure willpower and desire, Bay relaxed his throat and tried again, determined to succeed.

As if he'd been doing this all his life, Bay succeeded in opening his throat, and King slid all the way to the back. With King deeply seated in his throat, Bay's nose nuzzled in King's crotch hair. It was an odd sensation, but not an unpleasant one. King again arched his back and hissed. "Jesus, Bay."

Bay eased back, circled the head with his tongue, and then swallowed King again. This time there was no hesitation, and he moved freely up and down King's shaft, coaxing moans and groans from King. Seconds later, King took Bay's head in his hands. "Bay, stop!"

Bay froze. But when he looked up, King was gazing at him, and Bay loved what he saw.

A thin layer of sweat had developed on King's forehead, and he'd gone from totally in control to wanting, needy, and vulnerable. Bay had never seen an expression even close to this in any of King's videos, which made Bay's heart swell with pride—and skip a few beats in the process. Shy, introverted Bay Whitman had brought gay porn star and escort King Slater to a place no one else had. At least in a very long time.

"You're driving me crazy," King said. "And I'm so close."

King hooked Bay under his arms and pulled him up so they were face-to-face. He held Bay firmly in place with one hand around his back and the other gripped behind Bay's head. This time when their mouths met, their tongues thrashed in hungry, desperate moves filled with craving and necessity. When they came up for air, King hissed, "Underwear off."

Bay pushed his underwear down to his knees, and King finished the job with his toes and flung the garment across the room. In a single move that Bay would have not thought possible, King lifted him and flipped them both so that Bay was now pinned under King.

King grinned in victory and attacked Bay's neck and shoulder—nipping, biting, kissing, and licking. He slid down and took Bay into his mouth. Bay could feel his erection stretching beyond anything he'd ever experienced, and the desire flowing through him made him feel so wanted. So needed.

As King moved in long strokes, picked up speed, and took him deeper, Bay tangled his hands in King's hair, riding the movements as if he were in control of them. King stopped and gripped Bay's legs, pinning them back and exposing his opening. After last night, Bay knew what was coming next, and he almost trembled with anticipation. Bay sighed and shivered when King gave him what he wanted. King's warm tongue teased and tantalized him, pierced him, prodded him, and he wanted more.

"King!"

King looked up.

"I want," Bay pleaded, "to know what it feels like to have you inside me."

The emerald highlights in King's hazel eyes deepened. Another expression Bay was unfamiliar with flashed across King's face. Was it disappointment?

"No," King said. "No condoms."

Bay grinned, relieved. "In the drawer."

King's expression intensified as he opened it and retrieved a bottle of lubricant and a box of condoms.

He poured lube on his finger and coated Bay's hole liberally. When he slipped one finger inside, it felt intrusive and odd, but not uncomfortable. King moved his finger slowly in and out, and within seconds Bay was used to the sensation. Then King did something with his finger, and Bay's cock jumped. All sorts of explosions went off in his head. "Oh shit!" Bay said. "Do that again."

King did as ordered, and Bay lifted off the bed. He reached for his cock, but King pushed his hand away. "Mine," he murmured.

While King moved his finger in and out of Bay, he stroked up and down Bay's length. Bay felt like he was almost levitating over the bed. He'd never experienced anything like this in his life. The only comparison he could muster was his first orgasm when he was thirteen, and that was a distant second to what he was feeling now.

His opening stung and burned for a quick second when King added a second finger. But again within seconds, his body accepted the impalement and rode waves of pleasure.

After a few minutes, Bay was on the verge. "Now, King! I won't last much longer."

King opened the condom and pulled it on, then positioned himself at Bay's opening. Bay felt pressure when King pushed against him and then waited. More pressure and another pause. Bay felt a pinch and then a stabbing pain. He almost came off the bed again when King breached him, and his erection literally deflated. This was not at all what he'd expected.

"Breathe," King whispered. "And push out."

Bay released the breath he was holding and did as King asked. It hurt like a motherfucker, but he wanted this. Needed this bond. For him and for King.

As time passed, the pain subsided until it became a dull ache. King moved and Bay felt pain again, but not as intense. It was more of a stretching sensation this time. When King moved the next time and pushed in farther, the feeling was totally different. It wasn't pain but more like a feeling of being full. When King was seated all the way against him, Bay gripped the backs of King's legs.

King pulled back, and the fullness eased, but when Bay guided him in again, the feeling was less foreign. He guided King in and out, and King allowed him to set the pace. Within minutes Bay was able to meet King's thrusts by pushing against him. Somewhere along the line, the pain had turned to pleasure, and Bay's cock was once again hard. King stroked him as he moved, and every sensation seemed heightened. The sensation of King gliding deep inside him and stroking him in unison had Bay once again soaring.

"You're beautiful," King whispered.

Bay opened his eyes to find King's expression was now akin to what it had been last night. He was elated to know he could take King to such places. A man who had literally pleasured hundreds of men, and Bay was bringing *him* pleasure. King's hand picked up speed, as he drove more quickly into Bay.

"Bay!" King cried. "Oh my God."

King threw his head back and closed his eyes as he pushed into Bay over and over. In turn, Bay's orgasm built from the tip of his toes, crawled up his legs, curled around his spine, and then exploded, the first round of his release hitting him on the chin with more force than Bay thought humanly possible. King was now thrusting frantically, and Bay matched his pace. King lunged forward again, still pumping Bay in rhythm. Bay's second round landed in the middle of his chest, and his third on his stomach. Seconds later, King collapsed on top of him, breathing frantically but kissing Bay's lips, his face, and his neck. He licked Bay's release from his chin and chest and kissed Bay again. Bay tasted himself on King's tongue, and the reminder of the act made his cock jump again.

The wonder of it all was almost too much for Bay to handle. His heart was racing, his head was spinning, and now that the act was over, his ass hurt. He felt overwhelmed, but in an excellent way. King had taken him almost to the edge and then brought him back safely. King shimmied to Bay's side, wrapped his arms around Bay, and faced him.

Their gazes met, and King's scrutiny seemed to search Bay's eyes for something. Bay hoped they conveyed warmth, admiration, compassion, and contentment—the whole complicated mixture of what he was feeling.

King must have read everything Bay intended and more, because he smiled and once again his eyes were back to the normal, sparkling hazel Bay adored. King tightened his hold, and to Bay, it was like coming home. Whatever inhibitions Bay might have had melted away, and for the first time in his life, he felt safe and secure.

CHAPTER TWENTY-ONE

SATURDAY MORNING found King and Bay cuddled up like they'd been every morning for the last week. Bay was fast asleep with his head on King's chest, and King basked in the warmth of the early-morning sun on his face. It was the closeness of these quiet times he was beginning to cherish.

The week had flown by in what seemed like mere hours. King had gone to his addiction meetings each day and met with his sponsor over coffee a couple of times, where he was sure he'd gushed like a teenager with his first crush, but he hadn't been able to help himself.

He and Bay had spent every evening and night together since they'd had dinner, and King was beginning to crave Bay's company. Not in a sexual way, which surprised him, but in a more intimate way. Yeah, the sex was good. Hell, it was great. But it was the times like this—the quiet between the lovemaking—that he began to long for and treasure.

A couple of nights they had even crawled into bed shortly after dinner, cuddled, made out, talked, laughed, and before they knew it, woke the next morning wrapped in each other's arms as they were now. That was what King was beginning to pine for. His logical brain told him it was crazy. A man at his age and in this stage of his life pining for another man. Ridiculous. But the closeness and understanding they were beginning to share was like a drug to King. It both terrified and excited him. But as long as Bay matched his enthusiasm, King wanted to enjoy the ride, however long it lasted.

Throughout the week King had continued to do his shoots, but he was becoming less and less patient with the business in general. The video work had always been his least favorite part of the job, but it was necessary to keep his name and face out there, at least for now. If Bay had a problem with his shoots, he didn't show it, voice it, or even act like it upset him, and King was grateful for that. But he hadn't taken one single escort job and had no desire to. They were both jobs, but while one was a necessity, the other felt wrong right now.

He'd had a personal appearance midweek at a large gay bar in Manhattan and had convinced Bay to join him. But he'd also convinced

Bay to hang back and avoid the cameras while King signed autographs and hung with his fans. He would have been happy to introduce Bay as his boyfriend, but that probably wouldn't be good for Bay. If and when they decided to take their relationship to the next level, or go public with it, Bay owed it to his publisher to not blindside them.

Where Bay was concerned, he had assured King the third book in the trilogy, *Discovery in Paris*, was moving along nicely. Each day he'd been writing and more than making the word quota he'd imposed on himself in an attempt to balance the welcome distraction King presented and the obligations that came with a seminormal life. Now, whether or not his publisher was going to like it was another question altogether, but he was writing it just the same.

The alarm sounded, and King quickly reached over and tapped the Snooze button to allow Bay a few more minutes of peaceful slumber. In all honesty, King knew it was he who wasn't ready to move. But luckily, Bay stirred, then snuggled right back down against King's chest and settled in.

Today was Bay's book signing and press conference at Barnes & Noble. King had heard him on the phone with his assistant, Rachel, his publisher, and the reps from DreamWorks over the course of the week, and it sounded like the Hollywood wheels were well in motion. Bay had seemed a little nervous and hesitant after each call, but King had tried his best to reassure Bay that he deserved this and that he was going to do a great job. But as he'd convinced Bay to do during *his* shoots, King was going to hang back, way back, at the signing. Bay really wanted him there, and he wanted to be supportive, which was the only reason he was going, but the resemblance between him and Jack Robbins was uncanny, and he didn't want to do anything to take away from Bay's success.

The alarm sounded again, bringing King out of his thoughts. Before he could tap the Snooze, Bay leaned over and beat him to it. King kissed the top of Bay's head. "You're awake," he whispered.

"Yeah. I've been awake for a while now, just lying here and listening to your heartbeat."

"Sound okay?" King asked.

"Sounds perfect," Bay said, angling his head up and puckering his lips.

King gave him a nice long good-morning kiss and Bay settled back down and laid his head against King's chest.

"Today's your big day," King said.

"Don't remind me," Bay said, burying his face in King's chest.

"I told you," King reassured him, "you're gonna do great."

"You mean Jack will do great," Bay said. "Today of all days I'll need his persona to get through this."

"I think you're wrong," King whispered. "But you're allowed to do what you need to do to get through it."

Bay sighed. "Thank you."

King kissed the top of Bay's head again. "What's your schedule?"

"I have a meet and greet at ten thirty, lunch with the DreamWorks people at eleven thirty, the press conference at one o'clock, and the book signing immediately following."

"You're gonna be busy as hell."

"I know it," Bay said. "But please tell me you're still coming."

"If you want me there, I'll be there."

"I do," Bay said. "Oh, and I have a car picking us up at nine thirty. I'll drop you by your place, and then you can meet me at Barnes & Noble at one. I told Rachel you were coming but you wanted a very low profile. She will be on the lookout so you don't have to stand in line."

King tightened his grip on Bay. "Thanks." He glanced at the clock. "As much as I'd like to stay like this all day, it's after eight. You better get a move on."

Bay grunted. "Just a few more minutes."

King chuckled and jabbed a finger in Bay's side. "Up and at 'em, mister."

"Nooooo," Bay whined.

King started attacking every spot on Bay's body where he'd discovered Bay was ticklish, and Bay began flopping like a fish out of water.

"You don't play fair," Bay said, gasping for breath.

But in the blink of an eye, Bay kicked the covers off them both and was up on his knees straddling King, giving King a dose of his own medicine. After several minutes of Bay's tickling assault, King had had enough. "Okay! Okay! I give!" he said, panting heavily. "You're stronger than you look."

"And don't you forget it." Bay reached around, took King's morning erection into his hand, and squeezed.

King's cock jumped at the touch, and Bay started moving his hand up and down slowly.

Closing his eyes, King breathed deeply, enjoying the sensation. Then he remembered they didn't have time for this. Bay needed to get dressed. King grabbed Bay's hand, brought it to his lips, and kissed it. He captured Bay's other hand and did the same. "As much as I would love to follow this wherever it's going, you've got to get dressed."

"Party pooper," Bay teased.

"Hey, I'm losing out as well," King replied.

"Fine." Bay gave King a quick kiss, hopped off the bed, and strolled to the bathroom in all his glory. King watched, amazed at how much Bay's confidence had grown since they'd returned from Vegas. He was truly coming into his own, and King was so impressed.

King heard the shower come on, and then Bay stuck his head out of the bathroom, sporting a goofy grin. "Care to join me?"

King smiled and pointed at him. "Good try, but not enough time to do what I'd want to do to you if I did join you."

Bay frowned and flipped King off before he disappeared back into the bathroom.

King got up, made the bed, and dressed in his clothes from the night before. He padded to the kitchen with his shoes in his hand, put on a pot of coffee, and grabbed the newspaper from outside Bay's front door. Minutes later he was on the terrace, sipping hot coffee and scanning the newspaper. He stopped when he saw the center spread: "Bay Whitman signs copies of his latest Jack Robbins novel, *Revenge in Monte Carlo*, at Barnes & Noble. Today at 2:00 p.m."

On the following page, the Entertainment section featured a story about Bay and the press conference, which was expected to involve an announcement of the long-awaited big screen adaptation of the Jack Robbins novels. The writer went on to say his sources had confirmed that *Revenge in Monte Carlo* was the first of a three-book deal signed by Bay to bring the playboy private eye to the movies. He described the character as a cross between James Bond and Jason Bourne, and speculated that the films could be big at the box office.

King put the paper under his arm, poured Bay a cup of coffee, and trotted off to the bedroom. He stopped short when Bay stepped out of the closet looking like the hottest *GQ* model King had ever seen. "Nice!"

Bay held out his arms and turned. "You like?"

Bay was in a three-piece navy blue suit that had a slight sheen to it. His shirt was light blue with a white collar, and his tie was gold with blue diagonal stripes.

"Hell yeah I like," King said, handing the cup of coffee to him. "You look incredible."

"Thanks. Again, all the credit goes to my handlers."

"Speaking of handlers," King said, giving the paper to Bay. "Someone leaked your press conference."

Bay took a sip of his coffee and skimmed the article. "Oh, that. I knew my publicist was going to leak some information yesterday to get some attention in advance. Apparently that's standard procedure."

King shrugged. "Who knew?"

The phone rang, and King sat on the side of the bed and handed it to Bay.

"Hello," Bay said. "Okay. Thank you. We'll be right down." He hung up and kissed King in the process. "Our car is here."

"All I have to do is brush my teeth and put on my shoes," King said. "I'll only be a minute."

When King came out of the bedroom, Bay was standing in front of the mirror, frozen, with his arms by his sides and his eyes closed. "Are you okay?"

Bay opened his eyes and looked at King. "Just summoning some strength and preparing myself for today."

King walked up behind him, slid his arms around Bay's waist, and kissed his neck. "You are going to be fantastic. Just be yourself."

Bay laughed. "Now that would truly be something," he said sarcastically.

King tightened his grip. "It *would* be truly something. And in a good way, I think."

"I seriously doubt that." Bay turned in his arms. "You ready?"

"Yep."

Bay grabbed his leather satchel off the entry table. "Then let's go and get this over with."

As they drove, King noticed Bay was not his usual self. He'd seemed to retreat to someplace other than the here and now, and it had King concerned.

He rested a hand on Bay's thigh, and Bay jumped and then turned to King and offered him a weak smile.

"You okay?" King asked.

Bay nodded. "Just trying to mentally prepare myself."

"Talk to me," King said, taking Bay's hand.

Bay's expression spoke of something akin to embarrassment or maybe even shame, but he didn't speak.

"Please, Bay."

Bay sighed. "You're gonna think this is pathetic."

"I doubt that, but let me be the judge."

"Okay, but don't say I didn't warn you," Bay said. "Normally before I leave my apartment for one of these personal appearances, I have this mantra where I become Jack. I take on his confidence, swagger, and mannerisms. That's why so many people believe Jack was created in my likeness. But today I was having trouble making that transition. I couldn't seem to get into Jack's head."

King thought about what Bay was saying and didn't respond right away.

"See?" Bay said. "I told you it was stupid."

"No, it's not," King said. "A little unnecessary, but not stupid."

"Oh, I think it's necessary."

"Did you ever stop to think that maybe your confidence has been slowly building and you don't have to hide behind Jack anymore?"

Bay laughed.

"Laugh if you like," King said. "But I've been paying attention, and lately when we're in public, I see less and less of Jack and more of who I believe to be you coming through. It's subtle, but it's there."

"King. I can't do this without Jack. Today I've got to interact with a shitload of people. I've got to make small talk, listen to what they have to say, sign my name hundreds of times, and then as if that's not enough, I have to try to charm the DreamWorks executives. I can't do that alone." Bay heaved another sigh. "This is going to be a long day."

"I think you're wrong," King said. "But it's you who has to make that decision."

The car pulled up to the curb in front of King's apartment. The driver got out, and while he was walking around the front of the car, King leaned over and kissed Bay. "You've got this, and I will be there at one o'clock to cheer you on. If you get stuck or need support, just look at me. I'll get you through it."

Bay nodded and smiled. He leaned in, kissed King on the cheek, and withdrew as the door opened.

King got out of the car and leaned his head back in. "Remember what I said."

Bay nodded, and King closed the door.

CHAPTER TWENTY-TWO

KING WASHED his face, changed his clothes, and practically ran the seven blocks to the community center where his sexual addiction meetings took place. When he walked into the recreation room, his normal group was already there and seated in a circle. He'd chosen this particular group because although he *was* a spiritual person, he was not, nor would he ever be, a churchgoer. He didn't believe in organized religion, and this group was more a "higher power" focused group then a "God" focused group. Since God was mentioned in a couple of the twelve steps, this section used the word as an acronym for "Good Orderly Directions" or to mean "Love" for the agnostic.

Panting, he took his seat. "Sorry I'm late."

"No problem," his sponsor, who was the group's step leader, said. "We just sat down."

Most of these fourteen men and women had been a huge part of King's life, his lifeline, so to speak, for over three years, and they were his extended family. Hell, they knew him better than his own family.

The leader opened the meeting. "Hello, my name is Bob, and I'm a recovering sex addict. Welcome to this meeting of Sex Addicts Anonymous."

They all stood, held hands, recited the serenity prayer, and then gave everyone a minute of meditation time to allow those who prayed to do so or those who were still suffering to gain strength and confidence.

When that time ended, they all sat down again.

After someone read the "Who We Are" introduction from the SAA literature, one by one everyone in the circle said their names with either "sex addict" or "recovering sex addict" after it.

The leader then read the step from the 12-Step program pertaining to that particular month. He then spent the next ten minutes sharing his particular take on it, how he had applied it to his recovery, and encouraged them to apply it to their own lives. Each of them then discussed any issues or milestones they'd had since the last meeting. A couple of the members had stumbled, which was normal, and they were not judged in any way but embraced and supported. The only repercussion was a restart of their clock and getting right back on their healthy sexual sobriety plan.

When it was King's turn to talk, he felt more empowered than ever when it came to his recovery, and he wanted to share that with the ones who were not as far along in their own journey.

"For starters," King said, "right now I'm in the best place I've been since my recovery began."

Everyone smiled, clapped, and seemed genuinely happy for him.

King continued, "As you all know, I was scared shitless about taking the next step in my recovery, but we all knew I had to eventually test the waters. You are aware of what I do and how complicated my recovery was, but I had become one with it. After my initial ninety days of abstinence, I was able to differentiate between my work and my recovery, and although my work fulfilled the physical need, I avoided any personal or emotional intimacy. In other words, I only had sex when I was being paid to do so."

King held up a hand. "If we had newcomers here today, I'm sure they would call bullshit, but hey—it worked for me."

Another round of applause.

"Thank you. Thank you," King teased, bowing at the waist while still seated in his chair. "Seriously, I think I have found a person who cares for me, gets me, and accepts my flaws and all that I am. As of late, I find I'm craving intimacy and closeness with him, and believe it or not, it has nothing to do with sex."

King held up his hand again. "Don't get me wrong, the sex is good. Really good. But it's healthy good. More importantly, and this is in part because of you, these meetings, and my sponsor, I can say for the first time in my adult life, I'm really seeking an emotional connection. Sex is not at the top of the list, but is a byproduct of the emotional connection and the intimacy we share."

Everyone stood and applauded again.

King fought the tears stinging the backs of his eyes. He'd waited years to be able to say this, and the day had come. All because of Bay Whitman.

King stood. "The main reason I'm telling you all of this is because if I can do this, come this far, each and every one of you can as well."

The group surrounded King. He felt arms around him, kisses on his cheeks, slaps on his back, and heard so many words of congratulations.

After everyone had spoken and the meeting was coming to an end, the leader stood and read the "Seventh Tradition," which basically describes the way the group supports itself by personal contributions, and then the leader passed a basket.

Everyone stood again while the leader read the closing and the serenity prayer, and then the meeting was adjourned.

When King left he was flying high on life. He decided he liked the feeling and resisted the urge to skip back to his apartment, figuring a muscular six-foot-four-inch man skipping down West Fifty-Sixth Street might look just a tad funny. When he got home, he showered, dressed in his best suit, and called a cab.

The cab was waiting for him when he made his way downstairs. When he got to Barnes & Noble, a line was already stretching down the street and around the corner. He bypassed it and went straight to the head. "I'm a friend of Bay Whitman's, and I was told to ask for his assistant, Rachel, and she would escort me in."

The guard looked around, apparently saw no one in asking distance, and unable to leave his post, told King he would have to wait a minute.

King nodded and in seconds the first person in line held up her copy of Bay's book, looked at the cover, and then back at King. "He's Jack Robbins. Oh my God." She turned to King. "You're Jack Robbins."

The guard looked at the book cover and then at King. "Hey. She's right."

King heard mumbles and soft voices, and people were beginning to point at him. King turned to the guard. "You might want to let me in before the crowd gets all worked up."

"Good idea," the guard said, opening the door and allowing him inside.

Once he was through the doors, he saw a large table. Two people were unpacking cases of *Revenge in Monte Carlo* and stacking them on it front and center. The place seemed to be in complete chaos. Staff members were running around frantically, moving tables, setting up chairs, and arranging a podium on a low black-velvet-skirted stage.

King looked at his watch. It was noon, so he had an hour to kill before the festivities started. He spotted Rachel with three people standing in front of her as she hurriedly thumbed through a three-ring binder. Luckily she didn't look up, and he walked around the perimeter of the store to avoid her and went into the café, where he ordered a cup of coffee and found a quiet corner.

Leaning back in his chair and crossing his leg at the knee, King sipped his coffee and watched the organized chaos unfold before him. He suddenly heard a thunderous noise, almost like the sound of a stampede. He looked through the café doors and saw mounds of people all scrambling for the best seats in the house. The hour had passed in what seemed like minutes since he'd been so captivated by the comings and goings of the preparations.

King made his way out of the café and found a corner where he would be visible to Bay if he looked for him, but enough out of the way as to not garner any more unwanted attention. Minutes later, King smiled when he saw Bay, with three men in dark suits and two conservatively dressed women, enter the store through an unmarked door, with Rachel in the lead. The crowd clapped politely as the men lined up on the small stage.

AS SOON as Bay walked through the door, he slipped his trembling hands in his pockets so as to not reveal his nervousness. He scanned the room and released a deep breath through his plastered-on smile when he saw King standing in the far corner, arms crossed over his chest and smiling at him.

King nodded, and Bay was flooded with relief. So much so, his phony broad smile became a real smile and got bigger. *Thank God he's here!*

No matter how hard Bay had tried, he not been able to do his usual transformation. Jack just wouldn't come to him. All morning he'd struggled through introductions and niceties with the DreamWorks people, and honestly he thought he'd done okay but with nowhere near Jack's usually confident and outgoing persona. He'd made it through all the small talk, and when he finally found some time to himself, King's words rang through his head. *"Did you ever stop to think that maybe your confidence has been slowly building and you don't have to hide behind Jack anymore?"*

Bay heard his name, pushed all the negativity out of his mind, and focused on his publicist standing at the podium. "Ladies and gentlemen, may I introduce the six-time *New York Times* best-selling author, and mastermind behind private eye Jack Robbins? Let's hear it for Mr. Bay Whitman!"

The place erupted with applause.

Bay took a deep breath. *Jack Robbins or no Jack Robbins, here I go.* He walked up to the podium, smiling broadly. He gripped the sides of the wooden structure to hide his shaking hands and looked back at his publicist. "Mastermind? Really, Meg? That sounds so devious." Bay looked around the room and ducked a couple of times. "I'm waiting for a caped crusader to swing in here any minute, scoop me up, and carry me away."

The crowd howled with laughter. Bay spotted King smiling with an "I told you so" expression all over his face. Bay winked. "Seriously. I can't believe all you wonderful people came out to see little ol' me."

The crowd roared again.

"This is going to be a really fun day." Bay gestured to the group of people standing behind him. "I mean, the suits came out and everything. Aren't they pretty?"

The men and women standing behind Bay all bowed at the waist and laughed heartily. "Now listen to me, and don't let anyone tell you otherwise. I promise you, I will stay until every last book is signed and no one is even remotely interested in talking to me, which after meeting me, will probably be less than a minute."

The crowd all laughed but shook their heads.

"So anyway, I'd like to introduce you to my very loyal publisher. They are the people who make all this possible for you and for me. Ladies and gentlemen, put your hands together for Random House's executive vice president of public relations, Mr. Druid S. Gold. Get up here, Dru."

Bay shook Dru's hand and stepped to the side.

As Dru introduced the DreamWorks executives, Bay sighed with relief. He'd made it through that okay. Then he realized he'd not only made it through, he'd done a decent job. He again locked eyes with King. King's smile said it all, and he made a small silent clapping gesture. Bay nodded thanks and wished like hell King were standing beside him. And he should be. After all, he was Jack Robbins.

Then Bay got an idea. A crazy idea. A bizarre idea that might just work if King went along with it.

When Bay was called up to join the Random House and DreamWorks execs, the exec in charge of media relations announced that in the fall of 2018, everyone could expect to see Jack Robbins in action, in living color and on the big screen, in the first of at least three full-length feature films, starting with *Revenge in Monte Carlo*.

The crowd got to their feet and cheered. Flashbulbs went off, and the press started yelling questions at the podium. "Who will play Jack Robbins, and who will be his first leading lady?"

The DreamWorks exec took the first question. "We're only in the preliminary stages of the on-screen adaptation, so no one has been formerly cast in any of the roles as of yet. But—" He paused for effect and held up a finger. "—we're looking at established Hollywood actors as well as newcomers and unknowns. We're gonna find just the right guy. We promise."

A woman in the front row stood and pointed right at King. "I think they already found the right guy."

Bay saw the surprised look on King's face, which quickly turned to embarrassment. The crowd was abuzz. Murmurs of "Jack Robbins" filled the room. "Hey, that is Jack," one guy said. Suddenly everyone in the room, from the execs to the guests had their eyes on King. Bay spotted Rachel making her way to King and kept his fingers crossed. This couldn't have gone any better if he'd worked it all out weeks ago, instead of only minutes ago.

King watched, mostly in horror, as Rachel approached him and took him by the hand. He was so shocked he was zombielike and didn't even try to resist as she led him to the stage. His brain was telling him to *stop*, but his feet kept moving. *No, King. This won't be good for Bay.* When he reached the stage and put one foot up, he came to his senses and tried to back away, but Rachel stood firmly behind him and gave him a nudge. He stepped up to avoid falling on his face, and before he knew it, he was turning around and facing the crowd, who were now on their feet, clapping and chanting, "Jack! Jack! Jack!"

King glanced back at Bay, who was grinning and clapping with all the other guests. His expression changed. He looked as though he was trying to convey something, but King wasn't sure what. Either way, Bay was still clapping, and that eased King's concerns a little. When King scanned the others on the stage, they were all clapping too, but their mouths were hanging open in apparent surprise.

King looked back at the crowd, smiled weakly, and shrugged.

"So who do we have here?" Dru asked King, giving him the once-over.

King was now really at a loss. Did he give his real name and take a chance that someone in the crowd might recognize him? The last thing he wanted to do was embarrass Bay or his publisher, and it certainly wouldn't be good for Bay's movie deal.

He looked back at Bay and gave him a pleading look. *What do I do?*

When Bay stepped up next to him, King breathed a sigh of relief. "Well, Dru," Bay said. "This is King. He's an actor, and I was lucky enough to meet him during my last promotional tour in Las Vegas. It was all a coincidence, but imagine my surprise when *my* Jack Robbins showed up at one of the scheduled book signings."

What the fuck? Some of the truth. Not how we met, but I did surprise Bay and show up at his book signing. What are you thinking, Bay?

Bay nodded at King, and King took it as a *go with me on this*. Then Bay looked to the execs and then to the crowd. "Believe me, I was as shocked as you are. Isn't the resemblance uncanny? The build, the hair, the eyes. He's all Jack."

The crowd went wild again. "You mean he's not the real cover model for the Jack Robbins novels?" one man yelled.

"Unfortunately not," Bay said to the crowd. "Jack Robbins was a character born in my head. Strictly imaginary. And because of that, his image for the covers was computer generated to match my description of him in the book. But if I had known King when the first novel came out, he most definitely would have been."

Apparently wanting to take the heat off King, Bay said, "Can we get another chair at the signing table? Maybe King will humor us and allow you to take some photos with the two of us."

To King, Bay looked like a man on a mission, and King had been totally blindsided. *What do you have up your sleeve, Bay Whitman?*

King noticed the DreamWorks execs huddling together and studying him. It made him uncomfortable, and he was starting to feel like he was on the verge of being exposed. He didn't care for his own sake. He'd fallen into his profession, and he'd fought that demon a long time ago, but he didn't want to hurt Bay in any way. All it took was one person in the crowd to take a picture and do an image-recognition search, and it was all over with. *What now?*

When someone brought a second chair to the signing table, Bay winked at King, and they both sat.

"What is going on?" King asked through clenched teeth, still smiling.

"Just go with me on this. Please?"

King was still nodding as cell-phone and camera flashes went off right and left. "You could have prepared me, or at least warned me before I got here."

"No time," Bay said, turning his head from side to side so everyone could get a picture. "Just came up with this idea a minute ago."

"With what idea?" King asked, moving as Bay did.

"I'm not totally sure yet, but I'll fill you in later," Bay said. "For now just go with the flow."

King sighed. "Whatever you say."

TWO HOURS later, King had smiled, tilted his head for photos, and signed Jack Robbins's name so many times his cheeks, neck, and hand hurt. Bay, oddly enough, seemed to be in his element. He'd made small talk, chitchatted with everyone, personalized every book, and looked like he could have done it for another two hours.

When they had signed the last book and taken the last picture, Rachel took the mic and thanked everyone for coming and then rushed King and Bay off through the door Bay had entered a few hours ago. The Random House and DreamWorks executives were still there, gathered together and talking quietly. The guy named Druid, the one Bay had referred to as Dru, was the first one to approach. "Hi, King. I'm Dru Gold."

King shook his hand. "Pleased to meet you."

"Man. It *is* uncanny," Dru said, looking between Bay and King. "You are the spitting image of Bay's description of Jack. I watched you walk to the stage and couldn't believe my eyes. Did you study the character?"

"Study Jack?" King laughed. "Not only did I not study Jack, I never knew these novels existed until I met Bay in Las Vegas. I'm not a big reader."

Dru was still staring at King. "I can't get over this. This is the most bizarre thing I've ever seen."

"That's how I felt in Vegas," Bay said. "I was dumbfounded."

"As was I after I read the first book," King said.

Another one of the DreamWorks executives walked up and introduced herself. "Hi, King. I'm Sydney Edelstein. Bay said you're an actor? Where can I see your work?"

King's heart dropped to the pit of his stomach. He looked at Bay.

"Syd," Bay took over. "King is a little overwhelmed. As I said, we met in Vegas and became friends. I asked him to be here today for moral support. He had no idea any of this was coming his way."

"I get it," Syd said.

Bay held up a finger, "King's acting work was all in the theater, but I'm sure he can get you access to some of it. We can talk about his later stuff at another time. Do I take it you're interested in talking to him about the role of Jack Robbins?"

"I think so. Yeah," Sydney said. "He's got the build, the overall look and mannerisms of the Jack Robbins in my head, but only you would know for sure."

"He has all of that and more," Bay said. "I was going suggest you talk to him at some point anyway, so I'll get Rachel to set something up."

King couldn't believe his ears. *Bay wants me to play Jack. Is he losing it?*

"Perfect," Sydney said. "I'll look forward to meeting with you, King."

King nodded. "I'll do the same."

King was still reeling when they climbed into the back of the sedan. Bay squeezed his knee. "I'll fill you in as soon as we get to my place."

King nodded but didn't say anything. His head was spinning like a top.

"You did really good today," Bay said. "You signed nearly as many books as I did."

"What? Oh yeah, that was bizarre," King said. "And speaking of doing good, you knocked it out of the park. You were witty and very charming at that podium."

"Thank Jack."

"That wasn't Jack," King said. "I know your Jack Robbins impersonation. Today was all Bay Whitman."

"No."

King nodded. "Yes."

Bay stared out the window, but after a while he looked back at King. "You know, I did feel a little different. I didn't totally get into Jack mode, but I managed okay."

"You did way better than okay," King said. "You were Bay Whitman, and you did great."

"If I did do okay," Bay said, "it's because you were there with me."

BAY UNLOCKED his door and pushed it open for King. He followed King into the living room and dropped onto the couch with a sigh. "Man I'm tired, and my feet hurt. It's been one long day."

"Okay, enough stalling," King said, loosening his tie and releasing his top button. He tapped Bay's legs and motioned for Bay to swing them into his lap. King untied Bay's shoes, took them off, and dropped them to the floor with a thud. "What in the hell just happened?"

Bay wiggled his toes, and King took the hint. He rubbed Bay's feet, but his eyes never left Bay's.

"It wasn't premeditated, if that's what you're thinking," Bay admitted.

"But you told Syd you were going to suggest we talk."

"I made that up," Bay said. "I wanted this to be her idea."

"You wanted *what* to be her idea?" King asked.

"When I was standing up on that stage, watching you in the back of the room looking as handsome as ever," Bay said, smiling, "in my eyes you were Jack Robbins *and* King Slater. That's when the thought hit me. You do have acting experience, and I've been discussing Hollywood actors versus unknown actors with the studio, so why not consider you?"

"Me? Jesus, Bay. You know what I do. All they have to do is google me, and it's all there."

"So?" Bay said. "I'll bet every famous actor did shit to make ends meet. Things they wished they hadn't done."

"But what I do is not something I do just to make ends meet. I make a damn good living at it. And I'm not ashamed of it, Bay."

Bay turned his head and cursed under his breath. "Sorry. That didn't come out right. I know you're not ashamed of what you do, and neither am I. What I meant to say," Bay continued, "is that for many, getting into show business is a long and arduous path. People have to survive while they beat the pavement. And they do a lot of things. Eventually stuff comes out."

King started to speak, but Bay stopped him. "Please let me finish."

King paused.

"But... if we meet with the studio and they like you, we'll tell them everything up front. If they still want you, maybe they can find a way to work this all into the movie launch. I mean, if they leak it themselves, the right way, it could bring a lot of attention to you and the movie."

"Can I speak now?" King asked.

Bay nodded.

"How do you know I even want the role?" King asked.

"I don't," Bay said. "But please cut me a little slack. I just came up with the idea while I was on that stage, and I didn't have time to really think it through. You have acting experience, and you said you really enjoyed the work, so I didn't want to pass up an opportunity if it presented itself. And boy did it ever."

King appeared to be considering Bay's points. "I don't know, Bay," King said. "This is all so bizarre. King Slater on the big screen?"

"Probably not *King* Slater. You'll probably have to use a different name, but it would still be you. And you'll probably be required to give up your current line of work."

King went silent again.

"Look," Bay said, "I know this is a lot to take in, and if you don't want to do it, that's okay with me. It won't change a thing between us, and we'll go on with our lives. We simply tell the studio you're not interested, and we never have to speak of it again. End of story. But please just hear what DreamWorks has to say and then decide."

King sighed, arched that all-too-familiar eyebrow.

"For me?" Bay pleaded.

"Since you went to all this trouble, I guess we can meet with them. And Matthew."

Confused, Bay repeated, "Matthew? Matthew what?"

"Matthew is my given name. Matthew King Slater."

"Ohh. Matt Slater. I like it."

Bay swung his legs to the floor and dove on top of King. He kissed him and then leaned back to look in his eyes. King was smiling, and Bay smiled back and then kissed him again. The next kiss went from gentle to deep, tender to strong, and then it turned needy, all in the span of a few seconds. King did that to him. Made him want. Want King. Want a normal life. Want everything this world had to offer.

Bay stood and pulled King to his feet. He led King to the bedroom, knowing his life was changing at an extremely fast pace. Surprisingly, he embraced it.

CHAPTER TWENTY-THREE

KING NERVOUSLY sat in the inner waiting room at the offices of DreamWorks Pictures with his leg crossed over his knee at the ankle, watching Bay pace. "Bay, please, sit. You're making me dizzy."

"I'm sorry." Bay took a seat next to him. "This is all so exciting."

King looked around and saw no one in sight, so he leaned over and kissed Bay on the cheek. "I know, but pacing is not going to change the outcome."

The secretary appeared out of nowhere. "Mr. Lowenstein will see you now."

King and Bay stood and followed the attractive blonde.

"Bayyy!" David Lowenstein said, meeting him in the middle of his massive office. "It's great to see you again."

"You too," Bay said, shaking his hand. "And this is King Slater."

David eyed King up and down, his hand on his hip. "King Slater? King Slater? Where do I know that name from?"

David looked like he was racking his brain while he ogled King, but obviously gave up. "Nice," he said as they shook hands. "I've heard a lot about you from my team."

Short attention span, King thought.

The office door closed behind them, and King glanced around and then did a double take when he saw Rob Offernan, one of Hollywood's legendary producer/directors, standing there.

"Hey, Bay," Offernan said. "How's it going?"

"Going well, Rob. And you?"

"Can't complain."

He couldn't believe Bay knew these people and talked to them like they were best friends. No signs of Jack Robbins, only Bay.

"Rob, meet King Slater."

"Hi, King. We've heard nothing but good things about you."

"That's flattering, but—"

"Oh, just take the compliment," Rob said, taking a seat and gesturing for everyone else to join him.

David sat on the edge of his desk. "So, you want the role of Jack Robbins, huh?"

"To be honest, I'm not sure," King said. "Don't get me wrong, I'm very intrigued, but everyone owes it to Bay and to Jack to get this right, and I haven't really acted since college."

"He's way too modest," Bay interrupted. "I've seen him act, and he's great. Not to mention he's the spitting image of Jack Robbins."

King felt David and Rob's eyes on him, and it made him terribly nervous.

"He is that," David said, offering a crooked grin. "Easy on the eyes too."

Rob nodded. "I agree. Well, you know. Not the eyes part. Although you are. Oh never mind."

Bay tossed a CD on David's desk. "Here's some of his theater work. Take a look, and I'm sure you'll be impressed."

Much to King's amazement, David pressed a button, the lights dimmed, window blinds lowered, and a velvet curtain opened behind his desk, revealing a fairly large movie screen. David fiddled with something else, and seconds later King's face appeared on-screen. It was his senior year in college, and he was playing the leading role of Magnus Pym in NYU's production of *A Perfect Spy* by John le Carré.

The play cut back and forth between the present-day manhunt for Pym, an undercover spy on the run, and Pym's first-person reminiscences of his life in and out of hiding.

In the play, King had massive amounts of dialog to memorize, and no one with whom to interact but the audience as he relived his life out loud while writing his memoirs.

"You can turn it off," Rob said after only fifteen minutes. "I think I've seen enough."

"I told you Bay and Jack deserve better." King stood. "I'm sorry we wasted your time, gentlemen."

"Nonsense," Rob said. "Sit."

King stopped and sat.

"I liked it," Rob said. "Despite what some think, that's not easy to do."

"I agree," David said.

King couldn't believe his ears.

"I told you he was good," Bay said.

"Let's order a screen test," David insisted.

King swallowed back a nervous laugh at that request. All they needed to do was go to *Pornhub* and they could see all the screen tests they wanted, but luckily he'd kept his cool.

Bay stood. "Guys. Before we go any further, there are some things you should know."

"Like what?" Rob asked.

He we go. The beginning of the end.

Bay and King had already discussed their approach. Bay thought David was going to be an easier sell because he was gay. David had no idea *Bay* was gay, but all that was all about to change. In Bay's analogy, they'd decided to lay all the cards out on the table and let the chips fall where they may. Except for the sex addiction. That was a private matter and totally anonymous. The only people who knew about that were King's sponsor and his support group, and they were all sworn to a code of ethics. He trusted each and every one of them with his life. But if it came out, they would deal with it later.

"Well," Bay said, "for starters King and I—" He looked back and forth between David and Rob and then at King. "—are a couple."

David's eyes widened, but Rob didn't seem at all fazed by the admission.

"And?" Rob said.

"We met in Vegas. And to tell you the truth, it's a very funny story." Bay laughed. "I won him in a poker game."

"Won him?" David asked. He looked at King and whistled. "I'd like to know where I can get in on a poker game like that."

Bay filled both men in on how he and King had met, the fact that he was a gay paid escort, and what had transpired between them since.

"That," Rob said, "sheds a whole new light on all of this. It could present a problem down the road."

"There's more," Bay said.

"I'm also a gay porn star," King admitted.

David slammed his hand on his desk. "That's where I know you from. You're *the* King Slater. I knew I recognized that name. I've seen a lot of your later work," he said with a touch of sarcasm as he batted his eyelashes.

"Wait, what?" Rob said. "A hooker and a porn star?"

"I'm afraid so," King said, standing again. "I really appreciate your time, and I totally get it. No hard feelings."

"If I have to tell you to sit one more time," Rob said, "I'm outta here."
King sat down again.

"Now look," Rob said, "this is highly unusual, but not unheard of. A lot of young actors take roles when they're trying to break into the business. And no press is bad press and so forth and so on. You know the drill. But this pushes even the limits of that a bit." He looked at David, who was still ogling King. "It's pretty obvious *you* like him."

"Yeah, I like him," David said. "But I don't sleep with another man's boyfriend."

Rob rolled his eyes. "I don't mean like that, dammit."

"And yes," David said, "I think we should schedule the screen test and talk to PR. If they can come up with a way to spin this, it might just work in our favor."

Bay smiled, and King could see the relief on his face. "That's great," he said. "Look, guys, it's not a secret that I want him to get this role, and not because we're dating, but because I think he would be perfect for it. In my mind, he is Jack Robbins. That's what so bizarre about this whole damn thing."

Rob looked at King. "The big question is—if we can work this out, do you want the role?"

King met Bay's eyes and held his gaze. He could almost see the pleading there. "If you all think I can handle the job, I'll give it a shot."

"We still need to do the screen test and work out the logistics with PR," Rob said. "But if all that goes well, we'll consider you for the role."

"That's all I can ask," King said.

"I don't think you'll be sorry," Bay said.

Everyone stood but King. They all offered him a funny look. "I wasn't sure if I should get up again."

"I like a man who can take directions," Rob said.

"Me too," David agreed with a wink.

A WEEK later King and Bay were in the same office waiting to see David again. All David's secretary said when she'd called was to be there at ten this morning.

Over the course of the week, Bay had been on pins and needles. He'd come out to his publisher, which was surprisingly not at all difficult, and told them about the meeting they'd had with David and Rob. But apparently word had traveled fast, and the public relations departments of DreamWorks and Random House had been in close contact already, putting their heads together to see if they could make this all work out.

Bay had also accompanied King to his screen test and was not at all surprised that King looked incredible on the big screen. He *was* Jack Robbins, inside and out, and the screen test only confirmed Bay's convictions.

They were waiting for no more than three minutes when the secretary appeared and escorted them into the office.

"Make yourselves comfortable, gentlemen," David said, pointing to the couch. He again perched on the corner of his desk. "So I'm sure you're anxious to know why you're here."

"To say the least," Bay said.

"In short, after much deliberation, a shitload of meetings, and, to be honest, a lot of pot," David said, "we think we have a plan in place where we can control the information and leak it accordingly."

"What exactly are you saying?" Bay asked.

"We're saying we'd like to offer Mr. Matthew Slater the role of Jack Robbins."

Bay jumped to his feet and looked at King, who had an expression of disbelief written all over his face. Then King jumped up as well, took Bay into his arms, and swung him around in circles.

David smiled. "I take it you're pleased."

"Hell yeah, we're pleased," King said. "And I promise I'll give this everything I have."

"I know you will, or I'll personally take it out on your hide," David said.

"Over my dead body," Bay teased.

"Welcome to DreamWorks Pictures."

EPILOGUE

KING STARED at his trembling hands in the mirror as he attempted to tie the knot in his bow tie. The long-awaited premier of *Revenge in Monte Carlo* was finally here, and King was as nervous as he'd ever been. He smiled, sighed, and relaxed a little when Bay stepped up behind him, wrapped his arms around King's waist, and squeezed.

"Relax, baby. You're gonna be the most handsome man at the premier. Now turn around and let me help you."

King turned in place and Bay swatted his hands away. Bay smiled broadly as he effortlessly tied the silk tie.

It had been a little over two years since that first meeting with DreamWorks. To their credit, with all the facts on the table, they had been able to navigate the waters and make the premiere a success.

King still had no idea how much pressure Bay had put on them to make it all happen, but when asked, Bay denied any behind the scenes involvement. King didn't entirely believe that, but it didn't really matter. The only thing he could do to repay Bay was to bring Jack to life in the best way possible. And he hoped he'd done that.

After their first year together and with the relationship getting stronger each passing day, they had, with the help of Bay's publicist, come out to the world. There had been the usual negativity from the right-wing conservatives, but overall no one really cared. It was 2017, after all.

With King's help and support, Bay had been working hard on his public life, and he never ceased to stop surprising King with the strides he was making. With each passing day, King saw more and more of the Bay Whitman in public that he saw behind closed doors. Bay was becoming the strong and confident man he was always meant to be. It had taken some counseling to recognize and accept where all the insecurities had come from and how they had stifled him, but he was well on his way.

King had long ago left the porn and escorting businesses behind and started going by his given name, Matthew Slater, and he had worked exceptionally hard to channel his inner Jack Robbins. In all honesty, he hadn't found it that hard to do. It really was as though the character was written in his image, so playing himself had proved to be fairly easy.

After little negotiation, King had signed a three-movie deal with DreamWorks, and they were already in preproduction and about to start filming *Assassination in Argentina*, the second in the trilogy, and on the heels of that release, *Discovery in Paris*.

Personally they were rock-solid, but professionally, it hadn't exactly been all fun and games.

A couple of days before the scheduled leak by the studio's marketing and public relations team about the porn aspect of King's life, one of his ex-costars did an interview with TMZ and broke the story for them. And man did the press have a big ol' time with the news. King's handsome face, as well as his naked body—private parts blurred of course—had graced the cover of every tabloid magazine and newspaper for at least two weeks.

During contract negotiations, King had suggested his addiction as a way to help explain the porn and how King dealt with it, and the studio had agreed. In King's mind, his addiction had been in the shadows long enough. It was time to shed light on a type of addiction many people neither understood nor took seriously. He took it as an opportunity to help not just himself but the many other sufferers. It gave him a platform on which to stand, and who doesn't pull for the underdog?

So right after the news broke, they all jumped into action, and it only took a tense few days to get ahead of the story. King started doing the talk-show rounds, gave interviews to all the entertainment news periodicals, and had most interviewers sympathizing with him within minutes. Of course the right-wing conservatives didn't go away, but that would never change and no one expected it to.

In the end, the whole experience reminded King of the Rob Lowe sex-tapes scandal. It stayed around for a couple of weeks, but as soon as the next big story broke, he was old news. And luckily a particular movie mogul, who got busted for sexual harassment, flooded the news, totally taking the heat off him. It couldn't have been planned better.

Bay's phone alerted them to a text message. Bay rose on his tiptoes, kissed King on the cheek, and fished it out. "Limo is here."

Butterflies danced in King's stomach, but he did his best to ignore them as Bay lifted his coat over his shoulders. "Tonight is going to be a great night. I love you."

"I love you too," King replied. "And thank you for loving me."

BAY AND King walked hand in hand down the red carpet, both decked out in midnight-blue Versace tuxedos, stopping to pose every few feet. When someone screamed King's name, he tugged on Bay's hand, and they turned and smiled into the almost-blinding flashes of light as the cameras went off from every direction.

King squeezed Bay's hand. "Here goes nothing."

Bay leaned over and whispered in King's ear. "Fingers crossed. If this goes well, it will certainly help pave the way for *Discovery in Paris*."

The second movie was in preproduction, but it was with the planned third movie where things got interesting. For the first time in history, a leading man, in this case Jack Robbins, was going to have another leading man. Bay had convinced DreamWorks that because of the changing tides regarding the acceptance of the LGBTQ community, it was time to make a statement.

When Bay first approached the studio, they were skeptical. They didn't think it was right that Jack would suddenly go from straight to gay, and neither did Bay and King. They all agreed that plot line would only fuel the propaganda that homosexuality was a choice. But since these were new books in the series written especially for DreamWorks, Bay had an idea he thought would work.

In the third book, Jack, Bay proposed, would go undercover to infiltrate the inner circle of a well-known Parisian husband-and-wife team who were being paid handsomely by ISIS to help facilitate a terrorist attack on the Eifel Tower on New Year's Eve.

After almost a year, Jack finally works his way into the inner circle but is still not getting any vital intelligence. When the handsome, charming Parisian man eventually makes sexual advances toward him, Jack sees it as the only way to get the information he needs and reluctantly becomes the man's paramour. In a matter of weeks, Jack becomes a trusted confidant, gets the intelligence, and the Parisian couple is arrested. Plot spoiled.

The best part of Bay's idea was that when all was said and done, Jack would decide, surprisingly, that he enjoyed playing the part and would begin to embrace his bisexuality. Home run!

Finally, the gamut of press and fans having been run, Bay and King took their seats, front row center. The theater darkened, and King took

Bay's hand. He leaned over and whispered in Bay's ear. "No matter how things go tonight, we both have winning hands already."

Bay was happy. King was happy. And more importantly, they were whole and happy together. Everything had fallen into place for them, and King would be forever grateful for one man's loss at a poker table that had taken Bay Whitman from a Jack to a King.

SCOTTY CADE left corporate America and twenty-five years of marketing and public relations in 2004 to buy an inn and restaurant on the island of Martha's Vineyard with Kell, his husband of over twenty years.

He started writing stories as soon as he could read, but only in the last eight years for publication. When not at the inn, you can find him on the bow of his boat writing romance novels with his Shetland sheepdog, Mavis, at his side. Being from the South and a lover of commitment and fidelity, all of his characters find their way to long, healthy relationships, however long it takes them to get there. He believes that, in the end, the boy should always get the boy.

Scotty and Kell are avid boaters and spend the summers on Martha's Vineyard and winters in Greenville, South Carolina.

Website: www.scottycade.com
Facebook: www.facebook.com/scotty.cade
Twitter: @ScottyCade
Email: scotty@scottycade.com

Two cadets from very different worlds.
One forbidden love.

KNOBS

SCOTTY CADE

Angus Conrad (Gus) McRae is a privileged Charlestonian following family tradition and attending the Citadel, harboring big dreams of a military career. With the infamous Hell Week behind him, he quickly realizes being a Knob (a freshman cadet) is just as tough—especially for a man like Gus who must keep his sexuality a secret. Then a sudden dorm reassignment lands him with a roommate in the form of one of the football team's top players—working-class jock Stewart Adam (Sam) Morley—and life gets increasingly complicated.

Gus can't imagine a man like Sam as gay, yet there's something between them—exchanged glances, the occasional innuendo. Sexual tensions rise, leaving them more than friends but less than lovers. Gus and Sam know there's too much to lose and they must keep their attraction hidden. If they fail, they risk destroying their hopes and dreams for a prosperous future in a military world that's not yet ready to accommodate masculine gay men.

www.dreamspinnerpress.com

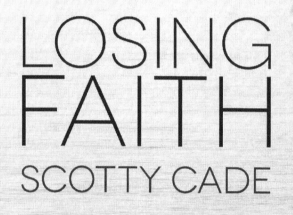

Praying for answers, longing for love.

LOSING FAITH

SCOTTY CADE

HOLY
BIBLE

Father Cullen Kiley, a gay Episcopal priest on hiatus from the church, decides to take his boat, *T-Time*, from Provincetown, Massachusetts, to Southport, North Carolina, a place that holds an abundance of bittersweet memories for him. While on a run his first day in Southport, Cullen comes upon a man sitting on a park bench staring out over the Cape Fear River with his Bible in hand. The man's body language reeks of defeat and desperation, and unable to ignore his compassion for his fellow man, Cullen stops to offer a helping hand.

Southport Baptist Church's Associate Pastor, Abel Weston, has a hard time managing his demons. When they get too overwhelming, he retreats to Southport's Historic Riverwalk with his Bible in hand and stares out over the water, praying for help and guidance that never seem to come. But Abel soon discovers that help and guidance come in many forms.

An unexpected friendship develops between the two men, and as Cullen helps Abel begin to confront his doubts and fears, he comes face-to-face with his own reality, threatening both their futures.

www.dreamspinnerpress.com

ONLY FOREVER

SCOTTY CADE

A love stronger than time.

Master Captain Theodore Gourdin has always loved the ocean. But his devotion to maritime life left little possibility for a long-term relationship. After two failed marriages, Theo gave up on finding the person who completed him and decided the sea was his soul mate. When offered the opportunity to captain the newly launched megayacht *Eternity*, Theo jumped at the chance. With *Eternity's* maiden voyage looming, Theo focused all his energies on hiring his crew and readying his ship. The last thing he expected was to finally lose his heart in the process.

After twelve years at sea, First Officer Heath Rawlins was restless and in need of a change. A gay seaman's life could be a lonely one, but to Heath the positives far outweighed the negatives. With excellent recommendations and an impressive résumé, he was quickly offered a position on the private megayacht *Eternity*. Heath's heart skipped several beats when he finally met the ship's captain. He was handsome and charming. And… familiar? Had they met somewhere before? Highly unlikely. But as smitten as Heath was with the gorgeous captain, everything inside him screamed, *Abandon ship! Rough seas ahead!*

www.dreamspinnerpress.com

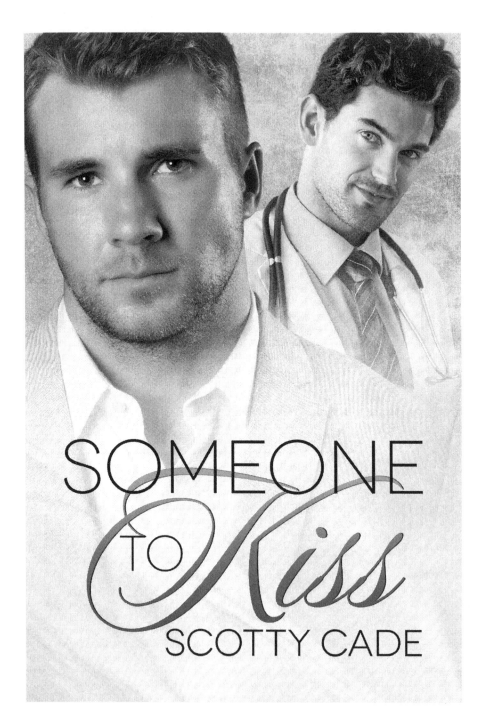

SOMEONE
TO *Kiss*
SCOTTY CADE

Dane McCormick's job negotiating leases and building out furnished office suites takes him all over the country. He stays until the job is done—and then he moves on. As satisfying as the job is, it leaves him no place to call home and no chance to build a personal life. After arriving in Greenville, South Carolina , for a job, a severe stomach virus knocks Dane for a loop. He finds a local urgent care clinic... and a tall, dark, and handsome doctor who goes well above and beyond his duties to treat Dane. The doctor's bedside manner makes Dane forget all about his stomach flu.

Carter Baldridge has dedicated his life to caring for others. Since graduating from medical school, he has spent all his time and energy building his urgent care business, But the morning he steps into his examining room and sees Dane McCormick on the table, he realizes it might be time to devote some attention to a part of life he has neglected. The spark is there, but so is a major obstacle in the form of Dane's peripatetic lifestyle and a bad experience in Carter's past. Both have to decide if the risk is worth the reward.

www.dreamspinnerpress.com